REVENGE

Filip Forsberg

ISBN 978-91-985195-8-7

REVENGE

Contents

1

When the gunshot's muffled sound reached him, he was already dead. The man's head snapped back, and he toppled softly onto the snow-covered ground. Quick steps approached, then dragged away the lifeless body. Swiftly, purposefully, a shadow slid past the spot where the guard had stood moments before when he'd been alive; the shadow studied the next obstacle.

Xi Liu stared at the heavy steel door in front of him, memorizing the details. He hadn't had much time to plan the Novus attack, but given the resources available, he was sure the team would succeed.

Behind him, the muted roar of two hulking, dark vehicles grew stronger. Twelve seconds later, they sped past the entrance to the house the guard had been patrolling. The whirling snow whipped up by the cars drifted lazily around him. His black body armor and combat helmet—dark visor pulled shut—glittered.

Xi ignored the cold as it wrapped itself around his body. Two men, also wearing dark body armor, jumped out of the front car as it pulled to a stop. They ran past Xi and kneeled in front of the locked metal door. They performed their work silently and expertly, and when they were done; they quickly withdrew.

Another seven men stepped out of the vehicles and formed an attack formation behind Xi. He gave the sign, and five subdued explosions echoed through the darkness of the freezing Friday morning.

He loved this part of a job. The controlled chaos, the brutal violence. He signaled once more, and the men rushed past the broken, smoking door. A flight of stairs stood behind the door, bathed in red from the flashing warning lights. Sirens howled throughout the space, but Xi didn't care. It didn't matter; they had the element of surprise on their side.

Surefooted, he took the stairs two steps at a time, swinging deftly around the corner as he reached the second floor. A huge, bearded man stormed through the doorway in front of him, but the brute didn't have time to say a word before Xi's front man put a round in his skull. The man fell backward into the room he'd just exited, and voices screamed hysterically.

Xi smiled behind his dark visor and signaled for the others to push forward.

*

He froze when an explosion caused the entire building to shake. Plaster fell from the ceiling in chunks, and Felix Xavier jumped up. He rushed to the door, tore it open, and looked out into the hall. His corner office was the one furthest from the door that led to the stairwell. Flashing red lights and smoke rose from the stairs. This was clearly not a drill.

The dozens of men and women who populated this floor of the office landscape all stared at this mouth of a volcano that was the exit doorway. Everyone, that was, except Leo, who took three giant steps to meet the threat. Leo would do that—of *course* Leo would, the bastard. Always striving to do what needed to be done, even when it meant making a jackass move like this. The others looked at one another with barely concealed terror. Two seconds later, Leo's body came flying back through the air, thudding hard against the hallway wall. He slumped over onto the floor, blood trickling from a gash in his temple. He was dead.

"Take shelter, now!" Felix shouted. But all the workers were screaming, and no one heard him. It was too late, anyway. Before anyone had time to react, the shadowy figures of doom arrived, spreading death and annihilation as they advanced with their weapons. Felix threw himself back into his office and slammed the door. He rushed over to the desk and retrieved his mobile phone.

His fingers were trembling so terribly that he had to press his thumb down with his left palm so the phone could read his fingerprint. The roar outside his door was closer now. A sudden gunshot smashed the window in his office door, and thousands of glass shards rained down onto the carpet. The jagged hole exposed the red, flashing chaos outside.

"Hugo! Can you hear me?" Felix stared wildly at the phone. Nothing. He called out for his brother again. "Hugo!"

"Felix?" came the voice at last. "What's happening?"

"We're under attack! Call the police! They're killing everyone!"

A dark, heavy shape loomed in the smoking doorway, and Felix froze as the black visor turned in his direction and locked onto him. Felix raised his arms and dropped the phone.

"Please. I'm unarmed. Please. I have a wife and children."

The dark figure raised his weapon and released a long burst of bullets, never hearing the voice that continued screaming from the phone on the floor long after Felix had fallen.

2

The light turned red, and he ran across the street into the park. The thin, crunchy layer of snow on the ground creaked under each footstep as Hugo Xavier continued along the edge of the pond. A flock of birds ascended as one from the ice cap and headed south.

Hugo's hot breath rose in white puffs as he sprinted the last stretch around the pond and continued down toward the Margaret Pavilion. At this hour, the park was more or less abandoned; the sounds of the city were far away. An ambulance howled somewhere in the distance. He raced up the wide stairs toward the amphitheater, slipping and nearly falling. His leg muscles burned with lactic acid when he finally reached the top. He raised his arms in silent triumph.

He was alone—or that's what he'd thought. Hugo turned his head slightly, listening. No, he wasn't alone. His well-developed sense of danger had saved his life more than once, and now the alarm was going off. He looked around, studying his surroundings. A dark hedge to the left. Trees lining a steep hill to the right. His eyes were drawn to the left once more. Rotting, brown-black leaves hung down and obscured the view.

There was an opening in the hedge. Hugo moved toward it, his senses on full alert. Snow swirled through the opening, but he ignored it and continued through. Then he saw her.

A woman's big, frightened eyes stared at him. A man wearing a dirty, tattered cap stood behind her, holding her in a tight grip with a hand over her mouth. Another man stood next to him, staring hatefully at Hugo, a knife in his hand. He sneered, showing off his crooked, yellow teeth, and croaked, "Walk away."

Stepping closer, Hugo pointed at the knife. "Be careful not to hurt yourself," he said.

A hiss came from the other thug: "Cut him!"

The woman's eyes widened like watery globes. Hugo looked from her to the two men, then back again. The most pressing thing was to disarm the guy with the knife. After that, Hugo could help the woman escape the other one's grip. He flexed his fingers inside his thin mittens to force blood into them.

"I'm only going to say this once. Drop the knife and walk away." He paused. "Just go."

The first man stuttered, "C . . . cut him!"

The yellow-teeth man glanced anxiously at his friend and then back at the stranger who had arrived from nowhere. His gaze flickered. It had been going so well. They could've easily robbed the woman and maybe had some fun with her. But then this idiot had come in and ruined things.

The man, gangly and scruffy, took a step forward and waved the knife in front of him menacingly.

"You damn— I'll—" Before he could say anything else, Hugo slid toward him like mercury and grabbed his wrist with an iron grip. He pulled it down swiftly and then yanked upward. The man gasped as white-hot pain radiated up his arm. The knife dropped from his fingers, but before it could land in the snow, Hugo caught it with his left hand and thrust it upward through the man's bicep.

The man screamed, fell to his knees, and gawked at the blade stuck deep in his flesh. With that one taken care of, Hugo turned to the other man.

"Let her go. Now."

The man stared at his injured friend who was now sitting paralyzed in a red-spotted snowdrift. Everything had gone downhill so fast. He didn't know what to do. Should he release her? Her hair smelled so good, like it was freshly washed, and he desperately wanted to keep that scent. The intruder in front of him stared calmly and steadily at him, and a shiver rolled down his spine.

The man faltered, and his grip over the woman's mouth loosened for a fraction of a second. That was all it took. The woman bit into his fingers. Blood spurted, and Hugo saw his opening. He exploded forward, pushed the woman aside, and shoved a powerful fist into the jaw of her assailant. The target fell like timber.

The woman collapsed onto her knees, sobbing and shaking. She wiped her bloody mouth on the back of her arm. She spat, and reddish mucus stained the snowdrift. Hugo helped her up, then pulled off his beanie and wiped her face.

"Easy, now. Are you hurt?"

The woman shook her head, and her dark, curly hair danced where it peeked out from beneath her thick white hat. Hugo studied her. She looked to be around forty, maybe Spanish. Her eyes were clear; she didn't seem to be in shock.

"No, I think I'm okay."

Hugo nodded toward the two men. "You know these guys?"

She glared at them. "No."

Hugo took the woman's hands, held them in his, and breathed warm air onto them.

"Want to call the police?" he asked.

She stared at them, shrugging.

The man with the knife in his arm stammered, "We just wanted your money, nothing else. If you let us go, we swear we'll never do this again."

The woman walked over and slapped him in the face. "Bastards!" A long stream of angry words, all in Spanish, flew from her mouth.

Hugo grasped her shoulders. "Either we call the police or we let them go and make sure you get to the hospital. It's a good idea for a doctor to make sure you're okay." He looked at the unconscious man and said, "That one's jaw is broken, so he'll be sucking soup for weeks."

The woman turned to Hugo. In her eyes, he saw that the clarity of a few moments ago was dwindling. Her pupils were dilated, her skin pale and grayish.

"Miguela," she said hoarsely. "My name is Miguela."

"Nice to meet you, Miguela. My name is Hugo."

"Hugo." She took a shuddering breath, shook her head, and cleared her throat. "Thank you for helping me, but I'm fine now. I don't need to see a doctor."

Before Hugo could answer, his cell phone rang from his armband. He pulled it out. The screen displayed the name *Felix*.

"Hi, brother."

*

The smattering of automatic weapon fire made him jerk, instinctively pulling away from the phone. Miguela stared at him with wide eyes; she'd also heard the sound.

"What was that?" she gasped.

Hugo ignored the question. "Felix!" he shouted. "Can you hear me?"

"Hugo!" Felix sounded a million kilometers away.

"Felix? What's happening?"

"We're under attack! Call the police! They're killing everyone!"

Hugo's focus instantly zeroed into a fine pinpoint of ambition: his brother's life. His eyebrows pushed toward each other in the middle, and he said firmly, "Who's shooting, Felix?"

He got no answer. Hugo pressed the phone harder against his ear and heard his brother's distant voice.

"I'm unarmed. Please. I have a wife and children."

A thick snowflake landed on Hugo's cheek in the same second he heard what sounded like a huge zipper being pulled closed. His focus shattered, and his blood froze to ice.

"No! Felix!" He listened hard for his brother's voice but heard nothing. For a split-second, a wave of doubt rolled through his body. Everything around him slowed down. Heavy snowflakes descended, becoming one with the white quilt that covered the ground. He turned to Miguela, but before he could say anything, she nodded and handed him back his cap.

"Go, I'll do it myself. Thanks for everything."

He took the hat, and without answering, he started running. His legs were machines pumping rhythmically, tirelessly, and he sprinted back the same way he had come, toward the apartment at Magistrate Park.

He dialed the emergency number as he ran. A woman answered after two rings.

"SOS Alarm, what's your emergency?"

Through his ragged breath, Hugo said, "I was talking on the phone to my brother when I heard an automatic weapon being fired. He works down in the industrial harbor. It sounded like they were under attack."

"Automatic weapons you said?"

Hugo gave the address of the Novus building and explained who he was while he continued running toward the red light at Carl Gustavs Road. Car horns blared, and two vehicles thundered angrily past him, but he ignored them. A lady stared wide-eyed and pulled her twitching, barking dog closer to her as he rushed past.

"Send any backup you have! Now!" Hugo shouted. He didn't wait for a reply, jamming the phone into his pocket and feeling for his car keys. He sprinted past his apartment, where he knew Lita was waiting for him. He couldn't call now— there was no time. It would simply have to wait. She'd only be stressed if she heard him in this state and found out what had happened. At six months pregnant, it wasn't a good time for surprises.

Hugo ran straight to the car and yanked open the door. He started the engine, revved it once, and raced out onto Foereningsgatan so fast the snow sprayed behind him. He reached under the seat, finding the cool surface of his SIG Sauer handgun.

As Hugo approached an intersection, a taxi swiped across the lanes in front of him, and he slammed on the brakes, barely missing the cab's rear bumper. A stream of obscenities fell absently out of Hugo's mouth. When the lights at the Triangle turned green, he stepped on the accelerator. But it was Friday morning, and traffic was picking up. He pressed down hard on the horn to get the cars and pedestrians to make a hole as he hurtled through town, his aim set firmly on his brother.

3

It was so strange. Oddly, at first, he didn't feel any pain. Felix didn't know how long he'd been unconscious, but his hands came away slick and sticky after he touched his midsection.

And then it came. Oh God, the pain came and came and came. Like a burning, runaway train, it ran over him, thundering over his body. Adrenaline flowed through him like a waterfall, and he nearly fainted as he struggled to pull himself into a half-seated position.

He peered out the doorway. The smoke from the red-flashing corridor was lighter now, and he saw two dark figures moving about in it. They were talking to each other, but Felix couldn't make out what they said. His cell phone sat on the floor a few feet away from where he sat. He reached for it, but his sticky fingers struggled to grasp the smooth surface.

At last, the fingernails of his middle and ring finger found purchase on the edge of the phone where it met the case. He pulled it toward him and scrolled down his contact list until he found what he was looking for. It rang twice before a woman answered.

"Felix. Is that you?"

He tried to say something but only managed whispering, creaking sounds. The woman spoke again.

"Felix? Can you hear me? Are you hurt?"

With effort, he cleared his throat. "Yes, it's me. Shot . . . shot . . . in the stomach."

"Oh my God. Okay. Stay where you are and keep hidden. We've already called the police. They're on their way."

A wave of relief rolled through him. "Okay, Madeleine. I'm not going anywhere. Where are you?"

"In the panic room. There's five of us here— Freya, Mikko, Sussie, me, and Sebastian." She paused, then repeated, "Stay where you are."

The room spun around Hugo, and the fire continued to burn in his stomach.

"I will."

"We can see them on the cameras. They're standing outside the panic room trying to get in."

Felix heard someone near Madeleine shout. Then Madeleine moaned.

"Are you hurt too?" he asked.

"Maybe a concussion. Nothing serious."

Felix knew it was worse than she was letting on, but before he could say anything else, their conversation was interrupted by more shouts. Moments later, the building was rocked by another explosion. Ceiling tiles began to crash to the floor, and dust clouds drifted in through the red-flashing doorway. The explosion caused Felix to drop the phone, and chaos rushed around him, pulling him down into the darkness again.

*

The room shook so hard that she fell. Madeleine screamed as she collapsed and felt her left ankle snap.

Sussie rushed to her. "Madeleine!"

Madeleine knew right away that her ankle was broken, and overwhelming powerlessness cascaded through her, but she reminded herself that help was on the way. "How long until the police get here?" she asked.

Sussie looked up at the battery-powered digital clock on the wall and replied, "They should be here any minute."

Along one side of the panic room, four vaulted screens showed the devastation outside their small, isolated world. Lifeless bodies were strewn about as if a giant had stormed through and left destruction behind. Thick clouds drifted past, giving the dark figures outside a surreal appearance. A man with a dark visor walked up to the thick door of the panic room and put his hand against it.

Madeleine swallowed; the thug on the monitor was less than two feet away from her body. This creature from hell that had torn her world apart. This had been her responsibility; Novus was *her place*, and this was her fault. Sebastian had pointed out the security flaws in their building many times, but Madeleine had kept postponing the needed investment.

Sebastian sat in the corner, staring silently at her. She ignored him. This was not the time to point fingers. Right now, it was about getting through this misery with anyone who had survived.

The man on the screen pulled up his visor, and his dark eyes peered straight at her, sparkling in the flashing lights. He pulled his finger across his throat with a sinister smirk. In the distance, Madeleine heard the faint sound of sirens and smiled, exposing bloody teeth.

*

The first thing the guard saw as he swung around the corner was the thin line of smoke drifting from the building. He narrowed his eyes. Was it on fire? It didn't appear to be—the smoke wasn't thick enough. He drove closer in his white Securitas car, then froze when he saw the two dark Jeeps parked in front of the thick, cracked metal door. He reached for his radio, but at the same time, a dark figure stepped out from behind one of the Jeeps and lifted something out in front of him. Too late, the security guard realized what that thing was, and the last thing he saw in his life was his windshield shattering as high-speed ammunition penetrated it.

The figure studied his work for a couple of seconds, then resumed his position behind the car. He spoke into his radio. "Central, we have a visitor. Looks like a security car. The threat has been neutralized."

The voice that answered through the radio's speaker carried a distinct Chinese accent. "Roger that. We're almost finished here, thirty seconds."

"Roger."

The dark figure nodded to his companion, who was hidden behind the adjacent car.

"It's time."

They got into the Jeeps and drove them into position in front of the building's exit doors. But just as they did, a blue-and-red flashing light approached. The figure froze. A police car rounded the same corner as the guard car had done five minutes earlier, but this time, the car stopped further away. The dark figure stared at the stationary, flashing police car. It was scarcely thirty meters from the Jeeps. A woman's authoritative voice echoed from the police car's loudspeaker.

"Get out of the vehicles and raise your hands above your heads!"

It had started to snow again. The figure hesitated, then opened the door and stepped out, careful to hold his hands high enough that they were visible.

"Don't shoot!" he called back. "I'm unarmed." The passenger door of the police car opened, and a male police officer pointed his weapon at the dark figure. The voice of the cop who was still in the car thundered again.

"Get on your knees! Put your hands on your head!" To the other Jeep, the officer shouted through the loudspeaker, "You too—out of the vehicle!"

The dark figure did as he was told, kneeling on the coarse asphalt and interlacing his fingers behind the crown of his head. The officer ducking behind the passenger door stood and moved carefully toward him. But he hadn't gone a few steps when the second man stepped out of the other Jeep, aimed, and opened fire. The police officer threw himself back behind the door, but two of the shots sunk themselves into his legs.

The kneeling man scrambled onto his feet and rushed back to his Jeep.

"Now!" he cried into his radio. "The police are here!"

The Asian accent replied, "We're coming."

The female officer stepped out of the driver's side of the police car and aimed her sidearm in the direction of the men.

"Drop your weapons!"

A split-second later, six armed men came streaming through the distorted metal door and opened fire on the police. High-velocity rounds hit the police car with a thunderous rumble, easily tearing it to pieces.

*

Snow shot into the air like rockets as Hugo revved the engine and skidded across the road. The car hit a snowdrift, and he felt the car slide toward the sidewalk. He jerked the steering wheel and the car straightened, narrowly missing a head-on collision with a pickup truck. The truck's driver laid on the horn, still honking long after he passed.

His destination wasn't far away now, but Hugo still pressed his foot even harder against the accelerator. The French Peugeot bellowed like a living, growling animal and hurled itself forward. Hugo dialed the emergency number again.

"SOS Alarm, what's your emergency?"

"Yes, I called earlier—I'm on my way to my brother's office. Have you sent help?"

"What?"

Hugo groaned. He knew he shouldn't have hung up when he'd called earlier.

"Listen, I called five minutes ago. My brother works at Novus, down in the industrial harbor in Malmö. I was talking to him on the phone when the place was attacked. Have you sent help?"

The woman hesitated. "Hold, please."

Another truck appeared from nowhere, and Hugo yanked the steering wheel for king and country. The woman came back.

"A patrol car was nearby and was sent to check it out. They should already be there."

"Only *a* patrol car? You need to send more!"

"Listen, sir, I don't know who you think you are, but it's standard procedure to send a patrol car first before we send the cavalry."

Hugo lost what was left of his patience when he saw the faint red-and-blue flashing lights two streets away. A thin pillar of smoke rose into the sky along the side of the building.

"Do it now! Send everything you have!"

The woman hesitated, then stammered, "Okay, I understand. I'll . . . I'll send out another couple of patrols."

He took a deep breath before ending the call. "Thanks." He tossed the cell phone down onto the passenger seat and exhaled. The snowstorm had increased in strength, and thick, greasy snowflakes swirled in front of his windshield as he turned toward the Novus headquarters parking lot.

Novus wasn't a well-known name in the security world, but they had in a relatively short time managed to establish themselves as a serious player in the industry. The company had been founded and was managed by Madeleine Singh, and she had created a security consulting firm that served companies and well-funded individuals. *Total discretion for the customer*—that was Novus' motto.

Hugo glanced around the corner. Two police officers were squatting behind a police car, and four black-clad, hulking men stood in a crescent-moon formation. Without warning, the men fired their automatic weapons at the police car, which was reduced in seconds to a twisted metal lump.

The men stopped shooting for a moment when they saw a silver vehicle come sliding around the police car, but to their surprise, it neither stopped nor escaped the scene; instead, it increased speed in the men's direction. One of them shouted a warning, but it was too late.

The silver sedan skidded around the cop car so tightly that the rear bumper scraped the front of it, but then the car continued forward, sliding sideways, its tires screaming, and cut down two of the men.

"Shoot! Shoot him!" Xi yelled.

The remaining dark men opened fire on their new targets, but the silver car's driver knew what he was doing. He skidded hard against a snowdrift, causing the snow to fly. Xi and another goon barely had time to throw themselves back and take cover. Xi hurried to his feet just as the car's tires got stuck in the snowdrift, and he gave a joyful cry.

"Now, men! He's stuck! Shoot him!" Xi and the others who remained started shooting again, and the normally quiet parking lot of Novus' offices was once more transformed into a hurricane of flashing lights, screaming men, and blazing automatic weapons. Xi watched as the silver sedan turned into scrap metal in front of his eyes. He signaled for the shooting to stop, and motioned for one of the men to check on whether the driver was dead.

The man stepped forward, ripped open the door, and gave a surprised howl.

"There's no one here!"

Xi gritted his teeth. Somehow, the driver must have gotten out when the vehicle circled past the police car. That was the only possibility. How had he not seen it?

His thoughts were interrupted by gunshots. The goon who had opened the car door to check on the driver stumbled back and fell to the ground hard.

*

Hugo had no real plan as he turned the corner and caught sight of the police car. Despite his speed, he made brief eye contact with one of the cops kneeling behind the car. A fraction of a second later, he yanked hard on the steering wheel and slid past both squatting policemen, using his vehicle as a weapon against the dark figures who stood lined up in a semicircle.

He managed to smash into two of them, sending them flying. When Hugo saw the wall of a snowdrift on his right, he acted on sheer instinct. He threw open the door and curled himself into a ball, rolling out and thumping into the thick, soft snow. Muffled shouting reached his ears a couple of seconds later, and a jolt of satisfaction passed through him as he realized his improvised plan had succeeded. He crawled backward away from the car and the approaching men. The cold air and the snow made the hair on his skin stand on end, but he didn't even notice it.

Hugo watched as one of them approached the car and flung the door open.

"There's no one here!"

Hugo raised his weapon and aimed. He squeezed the trigger, the gun coughed, and his target topped backward. The rest of the goons shouted and opened fire in any and every direction, without any clue as to where the threat was coming from. Hugo flattened himself on the ground and could only hope that more police officers were on the way.

A faraway voice yelled, "There are more of them. We have to move!"

Hugo peeked out over the snowdrift and saw one of the dark figures skulking toward the police car. The man raised his weapon.

"Whoever you are, come out now—or we'll shoot these cops!"

Hugo knew the guy wasn't lying; he could see it in his eyes. He pursed his lips. These assholes had him after all. He rolled over and stood to his feet.

"Hey!" he called out. "I'm here!"

Xi raised his visor. The heavy snowfall mostly obscured his face, but the long scar running from his forehead, around his eye, and down his cheek was still clear. He pointed to the fallen men.

"Most impressive."

"Thanks."

"Are you a cop?"

"No."

"Military?"

"Ex."

Xi shrugged. One of his men came up beside him and whispered close to his ear, motioning toward the fallen men.

"We have to go," Xi said to Hugo. "Again, very impressive. But . . . you will pay for that."

Hugo heard the faint sound of sirens growing louder. There was more than one—more than a few. People must have heard the shooting and called the police. Xi and his men climbed quickly into their two waiting Jeeps, and as they burned rubber out of the parking lot, Hugo saw a small, dark object sailing toward them through the heavy snowfall.

"Grenade!"

The two cops, who had only just gotten up on their unsteady feet, now threw themselves down again. The ground shook as the explosion thundered and shattered their world.

4

The heavy snow dampened most of the force of
the explosion. Hugo pulled himself up and rushed
over to the policemen, helping them up again. One
of the cops had a long gash on his cheek, and blood
trickled in a steady stream down his throat. The
other officer seemed to be in shock but was
otherwise unscathed. Hugo studied the wound on
the first officer's face.

"It doesn't look like it's that deep. If you're
lucky, you'll only have a hairline scar later. Just
enough to show off at the bar."

The policeman blinked uncertainly at the
unexpected comment, then made a strange,
chirping sound. At first, Hugo was concerned that
the officer was suffering delirium from blood loss
or was having a stroke. He understood a moment
later that what he was hearing was laughter—or an
attempt at it, anyway.

"Whoever you are, thank you," the officer said.
"You got there at just the right time. A few seconds
more, and they would have shot us to pieces."

Hugo shook his head. "Don't worry about it.
Stay here—help is on the way." The sound of sirens
drawing closer confirmed his words, and he
nodded his head in their direction.

The policeman shot his hand out and took a
surprisingly powerful grip on Hugo's arm.

"But who are you? Why are you here?"

Hugo shrugged and pointed to a row of broken windows that lined the building above them. "My brother works in there."

"But you can't go in. You can't. You have to wait for help. There may be more in there—"

Hugo shook his head. "No, they're gone. Stay here and wait for reinforcements. I'm going in."

The officer continued to protest, but Hugo ignored him. He ran toward the broken door and disappeared up the stairs.

*

Hugo rushed up the staircase and almost stumbled over the dead body lying inside the doorway at the top. He stopped short, surveying his surroundings. It looked like a pack of rabid hyenas had torn through the room, and the smell of gunpowder, blood, and death made his stomach turn. Two women whimpered somewhere, but Hugo couldn't see them. He stepped over the dead man and nearly slipped in a pool of blood that was steadily growing in diameter.

"Felix! Do you hear me, Felix?"

No answer. There was a movement to his right, and he shifted his gaze in its direction. In an office across the hall, a bloody arm extended from below a desk.

A woman whimpered, "Please help me."

Hugo rushed over to the woman and pulled away the debris that had fallen against her desk. It had served to hide her during the attack but had also trapped her in a dark, grim sort of cell. After Hugo had freed her from the rubble, he righted an overturned desk chair for her to sit in. Her face was distorted with terror, and her left arm hung limp; Hugo could see it was broken.

"Here, sit down and rest. Help is on the way."

"Thanks," she mumbled. She slid her hand over her dusty face and pushed the white hair out from in front of her eyes. A flash of recognition crossed Hugo's face as he realized he had met this woman before. Yes, they had met a few weeks ago, when he'd come to pick up his brother.

"Jenny? It's me, Hugo."

Jenny blinked.

"Oh, sure, now I recognize you. You're Felix's brother, right?"

Hugo nodded and scanned the room. "Where is he? Have you seen him?"

She shook her head. "No. It went down so fast. They just came, just, all of a sudden . . . and started shooting. The ceiling fell right where I stood, and that's when I hid."

She fell silent and her face became even paler. She was going into shock, Hugo knew. He pulled off his jacket and wrapped it around her. She smiled weakly.

"Thanks."

Hugo sensed movement behind him and spun around. A woman was rushing toward him at full speed. He raised his hands.

"Stop!"

Madeleine stopped abruptly. "Hugo? What are you doing here?"

"Felix called me. I couldn't tell what was happening because of the gunshots. Where is he?" Hugo again looked around the desolate room. More bodies lay to the right of him, still and silent.

Madeleine pointed to a door further away and said in a small voice, "That's Felix's office."

He was there in seven big steps. He heaved the door open and stepped into a large room dominated by a rich mahogany desk. Hugo froze. Two feet lay motionless next to the desk. Violent nausea began to push its way through Hugo's stomach.

"No, no . . ." He rushed to his brother and dropped to his knees beside him. Felix wasn't moving. There were at least two bullet wounds in his midsection, but the amount of blood wasn't as great as Hugo thought it should have been. Maybe that meant . . .

Felix's left foot twitched.

"Felix! Oh my God. Hold on, help is on the way!"

*

Hugo pulled off his shirt and pressed it gently against his brother's stomach to stop the bleeding. He sat beside him, trying desperately to keep him alive until help arrived. They had always had a special connection, perhaps because they were twins, perhaps not. He didn't think that was all there was to it. It was something else, a bond that could not be broken and which no one could come between.

During their upbringing, their mother had believed that the boys' connection was almost supernatural. As they grew older, they had impressed plenty of girls with their uncanny ability to know what the other was thinking. More than once, a friend or teacher had told one brother to think of something, and the other would seem to have the thought in his mind—in most cases, it had been accurate.

The memories washed over him as he knelt beside Felix's bloody body beside him. He cursed at the damn paramedics for taking so long. Finally, he heard voices outside the room and fast steps.

"Help! In here!" Hugo called out. Two police officers charged into the room with weapons drawn.

"Don't move!"

Hugo ground his teeth.

"My brother's shot—he works here—get help here, now!"

The cops looked at each other, processing the situation. Then a voice blared from the hallway. Another officer, the one Hugo had helped earlier, stepped into the room and between the other two cops.

"He's one of the good guys," he told them. "Get help for his brother—go!"

The two policemen spun and hurried out. The third cop reached Hugo and crouched down beside him.

"All right, help is on the way. Where's he shot?"

"Stomach. Two rounds."

"Make sure to keep pressure on it. I'll make sure the paramedics come in here first."

He disappeared, and Hugo was once more left alone with Felix, who was sliding in and out of consciousness. He felt utterly helpless. He pressed the wounds and stared at his brother's pale face, willing him to keep breathing. Suddenly, Felix twitched and gave a brief cry.

Then there were voices outside the door again. A woman, dressed in green and yellow, entered the room, a large first aid bag slung over her back.

"George! In here!"

Another medic jogged in, and they both rushed over to Felix.

"Where's he shot? Stomach?"

"Yeah. Two rounds. Both right through, two exit holes in the back. He's barely conscious." Hugo's fingers trembled on Felix's chest.

The medic made a quick assessment and said, "You've done well here. Scoot back—we'll take over now. George, prepare the pressure dressings."

Hugo did as he was told and pulled away to give them space to work. A third medic came in pushing a stretcher, and together, the three of them got Felix onto it. Felix moaned and opened his eyes. Ignoring the cracked, dried blood covering his fingers and palms, Hugo took his brother's hand. His fingers felt like he'd just come in from the snow.

"Hey," Hugo said gently. "I'm here."

Felix's voice came in a whisper. "I knew you'd come."

"We need to get him to the ER," said one of the medics. He'll go in for surgery right away, and we'll just cross our fingers. Okay?"

Hugo nodded numbly and the small group disappeared, leaving him alone. Lost in thought, he stared at the window—just *at* it, not through it—as faint voices from the room next door trickled past his ears unheard. He wasn't aware that he was sitting on the floor, shirtless, his own brother's blood smeared across his torso, arms, and face. How long he sat there before he heard the rapping on the door he didn't know.

He looked up. It was Madeleine. Her skin was pale, and she was pushing herself along on a rolling chair with her right foot while her left was supported by the cushion of the chair. Her left ankle was wrapped thickly in gauze. She had a thin red streak down one cheek where a stream of blood had coagulated.

"Felix is in the ambulance," she told him in a monotone. "He's on his way to the hospital now."

"Yes."

Madeleine pushed herself closer and put a hand on his shoulder. "How are you holding up?"

Hugo shrugged. "I'm fine. I just can't believe what happened. To Felix and—and this." He swept his hand around the room.

"I know."

"Who would want to do something like this? Does Novus have any enemies?"

Madeleine's face tensed. "I have a strong suspicion of who it was. In fact, I'm pretty sure I know who was behind it."

"Who?"

"A wry little German bastard named Klaus Horst."

Hugo waited for her to continue. She spat on the floor.

"He contacted us two weeks ago. For a job. We accepted, but he gave me a bad feeling right from the start. We started doing some research, but the more information we got, the more sure I was that he was using us as bait."

*

A young woman entered the room and walked over to Madeleine.

"Hey, how are you?"

Madeleine erupted. "Freya! You're alive!" A big smile spread across her dirty face, and she pulled the woman in for a long hug. When she released her, there were tears in Madeleine's eyes. She glanced at Hugo and said, "Freya, this is Hugo, Felix's brother."

On instinct, Freya stuck out her hand for Hugo to shake, as if it were any other ordinary day at work. Instantly realizing what she was doing, she shook her head sheepishly and began to retract her hand, but Hugo reached out and took it, shaking it gently.

"Nice to meet you," he said with a smile. Freya had blonde hair in a disheveled ponytail. She seemed nervous but unharmed.

"I heard they took him to the hospital; hope he pulls through."

"So do I."

Freya looked down at the floor and the pool of blood Felix had left there. She pursed her lips and turned away. "That was a lot of blood he lost."

"Yeah, it was."

Freya turned to Madeleine. "Everyone in the basement is okay. When the alarm went off, the automatic doors closed, and they're only now opening."

Madeleine slapped her hand on the table edge. "Ah! Who was down there?"

"Three people besides me: Mikko, Sussie, and Tony. The police are debriefing them now."

"Great. Well, that's some good news, at least." A tear slid down Madeleine's cheek, and she hurriedly wiped it away. "Let's gather everyone in the conference room as soon as possible. We should go over everything together."

Hugo stood and wiped his bloody hands on his jogging pants. "Good idea. I want to be there."

Both women looked at him in surprise.

"Why?"

"Because I want to know who did this to my brother. And to you."

Freya saw the anger blazing in Hugo's eyes and felt the suffering he'd gone through. There was an inferno burning inside him It contrasted sharply with the snow that was falling even harder now, visible through the windows behind him.

Freya looked at Madeleine and then said, "Okay, Hugo, come with me and I'll show you the way to the conference room—or what's left of it, anyway. And maybe we can find you a shirt somewhere." To Madeleine, she said, "I don't think the elevators are working, so we'll have to get you down the stairs."

"It's fine—don't worry. I can manage."

Freya raised her eyebrows in a "yeah, right" expression and said, "I don't think so. Come on, Hugo and I will help you. You can just hop all the way down."

It was slow going, with a few breaks needed to ease the burning in Madeleine's hopping leg, but the three of them finally made it to the conference room. Four other people waited there, one of them a police officer. The sharp smell of smoke was less intrusive here.

The cop stood when Freya and Hugo entered the room. To the other three, he said, "Thanks for the information. I'll be right back." Then he exited the conference room, leaving the gathering in silence. Freya helped Madeleine to a chair, and Hugo studied the reasonably harmless collection of people. One of them was a man of about his size. He had a thick but well-trimmed beard—and, Hugo couldn't help but notice, he was wearing a sweater on top of a white dress shirt. The man approached Madeleine and took her hand. She smiled.

"Mikko. I'm so glad you're okay."

Mikko answered in a weak, Finnish accent, "It was pure luck, nothing else."

Hugo smiled and offered his hand to Mikko. "Hey, I'm Hugo."

Mikko returned the smile, shook Hugo's hand, and looked the other man up and down. "You okay there, Hugo? You look like you've been in a brawl."

Hugo looked down at his bare torso and the blood dried on his arms, hands, and chest. "Uh, yeah—it was pretty rough up there. Hey, any way I could borrow that sweater for a little while?"

Mikko's mouth fell open, and his eyes flitted to Madeleine's and back to Hugo again. "I . . . sure, yes, of course." He pulled the sweater over his head and handed it to the blood-smeared stranger.

"I appreciate it, friend," Hugo said. "I'll be sure to have it cleaned and get it back to you pronto."

Another woman and a man walked up to Madeleine and embraced her.

"Sussie, Tony," Madeleine said. "Are you guys all right?"

They both nodded shakily.

"Good." Madeleine gestured toward the oval table. "Let's all sit," she said. Dust and dirt were strewn across the table, and on the far end lay a part of the collapsed ceiling. Hugo pulled up a chair and sat down beside Freya. Everyone's eyes were fixed on Madeleine. She cleared her throat and steeled herself. She was on the edge of exhaustion, but she had to hold it together a little longer, just until she'd gotten this discussion over with.

"We're down for the count, no doubt about it," she said, looking steadily into each person's eyes in turn. "We've lost more than half of our team. Tom, Lena, and Ilsen are dead."

At this, Sussie gave a little cry. Mikko gasped audibly, and the others stared at Madeleine, frozen in place.

Madeleine continued, "Emma, Jens, Felix, and Caesar are injured—they're at the hospital now." Bitterness flooded every word that left her mouth. Novus was her creation; it was she who had hired every single one of the names she'd just mentioned. Hugo could almost physically feel her red-hot wrath; he recognized it to be the same as his own.

"For the time being," she went on, "the police are going to put a lid on as much of this as possible. The press is already outside trying to find out what happened."

Hugo pounded the table with a fist.

*

"What *happened*?" he shouted. "You were almost eradicated, that's what happened! And I want to know why! My brother is fighting for his life!"

Madeleine glared at him, and her voice came out icy. "Yes, thank you, I know very well what happened here. Your brother is still alive, though. That's more than we can say about some of our colleagues. This company is my creation, and I'm responsible for every single person here. We will do everything we can to make sure whoever did this is held accountable."

Hugo fell silent and his shoulders sank. "You're right. Sorry—I didn't mean to attack."

Madeleine took a deep breath and said, "It's okay, I understand you're upset. We all are. But we have to regroup now if we're going to have any chance of overcoming this."

There was a knock, and the group turned around as one to see a female police officer standing inside the doorway.

"Hi, am I interrupting?"

Madeleine shook her head. "No, come in."

"Thanks. I just want to have a few words with you if that's okay."

Madeleine stood, got her leg into position on her chair, and she and the officer went to the far corner of the conference room. Hugo couldn't hear what they said, but as he watched, the officer produced photographs that they studied together. After a few minutes, the cop left the room without another word, and Madeleine rolled her chair back to the table and sat down.

"What was that about?" Freya asked.

"The people who attacked us were recorded when they left."

Everyone stood up at one time and began shouting in astonishment.

Mikko said, "What? How? They destroyed the cameras here!"

"It was two blocks away," Madeleine answered. "There are two cameras at the train station."

"Of course. So they have pictures of them?" said Sussie.

Madeleine nodded. Hugo was torn. He should go to the hospital and be with his brother. And he should also call Lita—he had completely forgotten about her in all the commotion. He pulled out his phone. There were seven missed calls. He laid it face-down on the table.

"So, do we know who it was? Was that what the officer told you?"

"Not with a hundred percent certainty, but it looks like it might be someone we know."

Sussie broke in. "Who?"

"Klaus Horst."

Mikko pounded the table so hard the dust swirled. "That bastard! Was he the one who attacked us?"

Madeleine raised her hands. "Calm down, please. He wasn't in the pictures the officer showed me. But Xi Liu was, and since Xi works for Klaus, we can be almost certain he's the one who arranged this."

"Time out," Hugo said. "Who are we talking about? Someone you know?"

"Klaus Horst hired us two weeks ago to perform a mission."

Hugo scrunched up his eyes. "'Perform a mission'? What kind of mission?"

Sussie shrugged and looked over at Madeleine. "Now might not be the best time to go through this, you think?"

Madeleine hesitated. She had an instinct, a feeling about Hugo. He was Felix's twin, and Felix was one of Novus' best employees. Maybe—maybe—his twin brother was as capable as he was. She had heard rumors; this brother of Felix had been a Swedish special forces soldier—later an officer—and had also joined the special protection group. It was all in his file. The rumor also whispered about his legendary tolerance for pain. Assuming it was all true, if anyone was competent enough to shoulder his brother's role, it was Hugo.

Madeleine turned her attention completely to Hugo. "Klaus wanted us to retrieve a Russian scientist and his discovery and hand them over to him."

"You're talking about kidnapping?"

"That's not what's important here. Call it what you want. That was the mission, and we started doing some preliminary investigations. But after our initial analysis, we decided the assignment wasn't for us. So I contacted Klaus to let him know we were rejecting the op. That was two days ago."

Hugo drew a line in the dust on the table as he pondered. "Let me guess. As a thank-you for that, he arranged for this attack. To teach you a lesson?"

"That's the hunch. A man by the name of Xi Liu was with Klaus the two times I met with him. And Xi was one of the people in the pictures the cop showed me."

A memory of Xi's dark eyes flickered in Hugo's brain. "So, what made you give up your assignment?" he asked.

Sussie was about to protest again, but Madeleine silenced her with a glance.

"Sussie managed to hack one of the Russian scientist's servers and found some interesting information. It seems he'd invented a way to gain control over a human being."

"What do you mean 'gain control'?"

"He was creating a specially developed drug and injection that could get nearly total control over a person."

Hugo shook his head. "I still don't get it. It sounds like science fiction. So that's what made you pull out?"

Sussie broke in, "No. When I was on the server, I found evidence that it had already been hacked. The tracks led to a server in Paris."

"Okay, and?"

Madeleine got up and walked around the table. "Every time I talked to Klaus, there was a warning bell that rang in my head. Add that to the fact that the Russian had already been hacked . . . it all smelled funny. So to play it safe, I canceled the mission."

"Well, that was a mistake," Hugo said dryly.

"Apparently."

5

He trembled. But he also knew it was only the adrenaline that was beginning to vanish from his body. The snow swirled as the car slipped under a red light.

"Take it easy! The last thing we need now is to get the cops' attention. Slow down and follow the plan."

Obediently, the driver eased his foot off the accelerator.

Xi Liu pulled off his helmet and scratched his scar. He pointed. "Take a right here. Make sure you take us through town without any problems."

They continued through the city center, and by this time, the traffic had died down. It was still early morning and lunch traffic had not started yet. Xi took a few deep breaths and thought through what had happened. It had been a success; they had performed their mission with minimal damage, and considering how little time they'd been given for planning, he was very pleased.

The only problem was the late arrival. But it didn't matter; whoever he'd been, there wasn't anything he could do now. He pulled his mobile phone from his inside breast pocket and scrolled down the contact list. He tapped a name to dial, and a surprisingly bright male voice answered.

"Yes?"

"It's done. Mission accomplished."

The man on the other end laughed. "Excellent! Very good job, Xi. Any problems?"

Xi recapped the mission in as much detail as he could and was careful not to omit anything. He had no doubt it would be noticed if he tried to do so.

"Fantastic job, Xi," came the response when he'd said everything. "I knew there was a small risk that the person you described would find his way there, but I didn't really think it would happen. The odds were minimal."

Xi frowned. "You mean you knew about the guy who showed up at the end?"

"Well, I don't want to say I *knew* it—it was more of a very remote risk. Which turned out to be true."

A wave of unrest slid through Xi, and he scratched his head with scorn as he thought back on the moment the stranger had arrived just in time to rescue the police. There was something about his face. It was familiar; he had seen it before.

"The man who came," Xi said. "He was the brother of one of the people we shot in the office, right?"

The man chuckled. "You're right, Xi. That's him. It's his twin brother, as a matter of fact. His name is Hugo Xavier, and he is a special person."

"Special in what way?"

"Hugo has a résumé that would make a secret agent jealous. He's currently unemployed, but he's done hunter training, he was a professional soldier with a handful of different stations around the world, and he spent even more time in the US working with a Navy SEAL team."

Xi ground his teeth. "This would have been good information to have had before the hit, wouldn't you say?"

"Come now, Xi. You shouldn't be bitter that you don't know everything. That's why we each have a role to play. You know more than your soldiers, and I know more than you. And above me, there's someone who knows even more. Those are the rules of the game. You know that."

Xi watched the thousands of thick snowflakes whirl by, passing the city library and approaching the tall, blue Kronprinsen. "Yeah," he replied. "I guess so."

"Good. Make sure to get to the meeting place and change transport vehicles, and then go to Kastrup for further transport."

"Roger that."

*

Not all that glimmers is gold—but almost. Klaus Horst did not wait for a reply from Xi but ended the call. He put his cell phone—complete with its ornate gold-and-diamond encrusted case—back in his pocket. Time was not on his side, but he had made an excellent attempt at salvaging the situation.

Klaus was a man driven by ambition, always had been. Ever since early childhood, he'd had a violent desire to gain power no matter the cost. It wasn't how you came into power that was important to Klaus; it was the fact that you acquired it that sanctified all means.

And that desire had taken him far—all the way here, as an assistant to one of the board members of QuantumCorp. He shrugged. The assistant title didn't sound all that sexy, but he knew his role meant far more power than any ordinary man could ever dream. And when his gaze glided over his surroundings, the feeling was confirmed. He walked slowly through his huge apartment on Rue des Saint-Peres, one of the most exclusive parts of Paris. He passed through a hallway lined with exquisite Chinese vases dating from the Ming Dynasty. Every single one of them was worth more than two million dollars.

The hallway ended at a massive, wooden door. He knocked.

A voice answered, "Come in."

Klaus pushed the door open and entered the room. The smoke of incense lay heavy in the air, and he held his breath as he approached the large figure sitting on the dark wooden floor in the lotus position. Klaus stood and waited. The cross-legged figure began to move and rose effortlessly, despite her overweight frame.

Heidi Leibowitz pulled her precious kimono more tightly around her. Her wrinkled face was furrowed, but her eyes were clear.

"How did it go?"

"It went well," Klaus replied with a wide smile. "Xi says the mission has been completed. All their targets were eliminated, and they sustained just a few minor injuries themselves."

"Excellent. Excellent." Heidi went to a side table and poured a glass of chilled Svalbarði water—only the best was good enough. "Do they know we were the ones who arranged the hit?"

"No, I don't think so."

"So the next part of the operation can continue?"

"It can. Xi and his men are in the process of changing transport. When they're done with that, they will head to Kastrup for the next part. It shouldn't take more than two hours before they call in another update."

"Good, Klaus."

Klaus stretched to his full length. This was what he had been born to do. He had found his place as the executive hand of one of the most powerful people in Europe. There was nothing he couldn't do.

He noticed he was hard.

*

The two dark vehicles stopped abruptly. Without a word, people began streaming out. Strong arms carried equipment from the Jeeps to three smaller cars, heaving it into the trunks. Two men took containers of gasoline and soaked both Jeeps. Xi gave a sign, and one of the men lit a match and tossed.

Roaring flames engulfed the Jeeps in a red fireball. The men stepped back as the inferno grew and the heat scorched their faces, but the heavy snowfall soon dampened the raging flames. Xi signaled again, and the men quietly split into three groups, each standing by one of the vehicles. Xi walked over to his captain. The young French soldier was a specimen of excellent, cold efficiency.

"All right, Sebastian?"

"All right, Xi."

"Next stop, Kastrup. We go nice and easy. Straight up the freeway and over the bridge. Okay?"

The atmosphere in the group was top-notch; it was always like this after a successful mission, when the adrenaline was still pumping and everyone was excited. They all jumped into the cars and drove off, leaving the burning Jeeps behind. It took ten minutes before an elderly woman, out walking her dog, noticed the burning car and called the police.

By the time the fire trucks arrived, Xi and his men had long since fled the scene.

*

It is said that those who dare win.

Klaus cleared his throat. "There's some new information about the Russian researcher, as well."

Heidi set down her glass.

"About Markov?"

"Yes. Our hackers have been working around the clock to get into his computers. They got through one of the firewalls, but it seems there are subsystems hidden behind additional firewalls."

"Can't our guys get through them?"

Klaus shrugged, and a rush of anxiety surged through him. He cleared his throat again. "Well, if they had more time, they would undoubtedly be able to do it. They're running out of time now, though, so it's doubtful that they'll make it."

Heidi allowed her eyes to fall closed. That's how it was in her world—there were always a lot of decisions to make based on incomplete information. But she hadn't come this far by hesitating. Her motto had always been to hit first and hard and ask any questions when the dust settled.

"Have them continue," she said finally, her eyelids fluttering open. "They may get lucky and manage to get through. And if not, then Xi will still be there soon to take care of the rest."

"True. So true."

Heidi stretched. "Leave me now. I'm going to change. Meet me in my office in ten minutes."

"Absolutely."

She raised an eyebrow and Klaus felt his cheeks blush. "Sorry. Of course, madame."

He turned on his heel and headed hurriedly to the library; when he got there, a big screen on the wall showed a female news anchor at a desk. Klaus increased the volume.

"And now, over to José Sánchez in Chile."

The scene changed to a male reporter standing next to a middle-aged farmer. The reporter looked into the camera and then over to the farmer.

"Rachel, I'm standing here with Darío, a farmer here in Chile, five hours after a second major earthquake rocked the country. Dario, what happened to your flock?"

A grimace darkened Darío's furry face.

"The earthquake came without warning. It was . . . insane." His voice broke, and he coughed lightly. Then he continued, "The ground opened and swallowed half my herd of animals. Instantly. They just disappeared." Darío fell silent, noticeably shaken. José put his hand on the farmer's shoulder and turned to the camera.

"And this is just another story on top of the hundreds of similar ones happening over and over in South America. As for a cause, everything points to the intense mining efforts of QuantumCorp. And it appears that the occurrence of these earthquakes is only increasing. Rachel?"

Klaus swore. The damned peasants, unable to even keep their animals in order. *And they have the nerve to blame* us *for their incompetence!* He thought. He cursed again, turned off the TV, and threw the remote across the room.

7

The police poured into the office. In the blizzard that raged outside, some thirty reporters stood behind the barrier that surrounded the building. Hugo had never seen anything like it. He looked down at the crowd, and as he appeared in the window, a chorus of voices shouted up to him.

"What happened?"

"How are you? Did anyone die?"

He flinched and stepped back, and Madeleine rolled up to him. Her gaze flickered, but there was still a fire in them.

"How does it look out there?"

"Like a pure zoo."

Madeleine smiled. "You're like your brother."

Hugo swallowed hard to push away the nausea. He hoped to God that Felix would pull through his surgery; he didn't know what he'd do if his brother died.

"Thanks. He's a good asset to the company, I hope."

"You know he is—he's one of the best. He's the leader of one of the two action teams we have. The other team is out of action now—one death and two seriously injured."

"And Felix's team?"

"You've met them. Freya, Sussie, and Mikko."

Hugo stared at the swirling snowflakes. The flashing lights of the police cars made the entire scene seem even more surreal.

"And what happens now?" he asked.

"Well, there will certainly be an investigation into what happened. We'll be talking with the police, and I imagine they'll use a lot of their resources to solve it."

"Solve it?" Hugo frowned. "But you already know who it is."

"Yes, *I* know, but it hasn't been proven yet. Even with the picture we've got of Xi Liu, it's too early to make a one hundred percent absolute statement that he's the one who was behind the attack."

Hugo turned from the window suddenly and began pacing the room like a trapped bull. Anger surged through him; he could barely hold back the white-hot rage that was struggling to explode from within.

"But you just talked about this Klaus Horst and Xi Liu, about their motives, why you were sure they did it," he said, using all his effort not to shout. "You said they came from QuantumCorp. What kind of company is that, anyway?"

"It's a large, international security company. They're locked in a tough fight with Techyx, a security field competitor. Techyx has a big press conference planned for tomorrow morning in

London with a top team of their environmental scientists."

Hugo stopped pacing and turned to Madeleine. "You know who makes the decisions at QuantumCorp?"

She tilted her head at him curiously. "Sure. Their board does. Twelve people—youngish, spoiled, too powerful for their own good. I know them—well, I know *of* them. Every man and woman on that board is incredibly driven and will do everything possible to promote their own advancement. Their ambition is money and power. One of the members of the board has a guardian, Klaus Horst, who's a real cold fish, and he's the one who I think was behind the attack." She paused, seeing that Hugo wanted to interrupt. She held up an index finger—*wait, there's more*—and went on. "A group of Techyx's top researchers, who are also the best environmental researchers in the world, are going up against QuantumCorp in a bunch of scientific trials, which means QuantumCorp is at risk of losing billions. They needed a way to get Techyx's research panel discredited, so Klaus took matters into his own hands. He contacted a rogue Russian scientist who had made, shall we say, questionable discoveries in the field of chemistry, and hired him to program someone to murder the researchers during the press conference."

Hugo stared at Madeleine.

"What a mess. That's crazy."

Madeleine didn't answer. She felt that there was a possibility she could get Hugo to take on Felix's responsibilities; after all, he looked and acted just like him. Admittedly, it was a gamble, but still. She couldn't let the opportunity slip by. The company had received a severe blow and was down for the count.

But Madeleine also knew it was under those circumstances—hurt, bloody, and down for the count—that the true master was most dangerous.

There was a knock on the door, and they spun around.

*

A man stood in the doorway. He was tall and wore a dark suit. He brushed away the accumulated snowflakes from his shoulders and opened his arms.

"Madeleine, I'm so sorry about what happened here." He looked at her wrapped ankle as she stood to greet him, and he winced. "What happened to your leg there? You okay?" He walked over to her, and she hugged him.

"Henrik. I'm so glad you're here."

"I came as soon as I heard."

"I'm okay," she said, nodding toward her ankle. "Broke or sprained it, but it's nothing that won't heal. At least I'm alive."

"How many did you lose?"

Madeleine grabbed the report she had received from the police half an hour earlier and handed it to him. Henrik scratched his forehead as he read.

"Good Lord, Madeleine, this is awful," he said, giving it back to her. "Listen, we're ready with any and all resources you may need. Just ask, and we will fix it."

Hugo, who was standing silently at the window, cleared his throat; the other inhabitants of the room spun around at the sound.

"Oh, sorry, Hugo. This is Henrik Albertsson, our contact with the Swedish Military Forces. Henrik, this is Hugo. His brother Felix works here."

Hugo reached out his hand. "Nice to meet you."

"Likewise, Hugo. I hope your brother is one of the survivors?"

"Thanks, he is, but he's injured. He actually called me as the attack was happening. I dropped everything and drove here. When I got here, I found him unconscious on the floor. He's in the hospital now."

Henrik put his hand on Hugo's shoulder and looked at him with clear, slate-gray eyes. "I'm so sorry."

Madeleine said, "I just filled Hugo in about QuantumCorp and Klaus Horst."

"Ah. Yes, I heard that Xi Liu was caught on camera when the attackers were leaving. And where you find Xi, you can be sure that Klaus is close by."

"Here, please sit," Madeleine said, pointing to a chair. Henrik pulled off his heavy coat, hung it on the back of the chair, and sat. Madeleine sat opposite him; Hugo stood beside them. Henrik drummed his fingers on the table.

"So now what?"

"Well, like I just told Hugo, there's going to be an investigation, and I assume that the police will launch a big investigation. It's not often that something like this happens in Malmö."

Henrik's eyes flashed. "Let me interrupt you right there, Madeleine. You've had an awful time, to be sure. But we still need you—maybe more now than ever before."

Hugo could tell that Henrik was serious. He knew the type all too well—military types with only one goal before their eyes: the mission. The mission was everything, all the time, no matter the cost.

Henrik continued, "When we contacted you to investigate Markov Tupolev, we did that with a definitive goal of acquiring his discovery. And if it wasn't possible, get Markov himself."

Hugo turned sharply toward Henrik. Investigate Markov? Hadn't Madeleine said it was Klaus Horst who had contacted Novus to kidnap Markov?

He remained silent. Madeleine's face was like a stone mask.

"True," she said. "But at the moment, Novus isn't able to perform any part of that assignment, no matter how much the Swedish Armed Forces need it done."

Henrik held up a hand. "You misunderstand me, Madeleine. It isn't me or even the Swedish Armed Forces that need you to continue. Markov's discovery is too dangerous to fall into the wrong hands. That's why you've got to continue with the mission I gave you. Obtain Markov's discovery or Markov himself."

As the seconds passed, Madeleine's face became redder and redder. Finally, she hissed, "We don't have an intervention team that can do this anymore. The staff we had are either dead or injured in the hospital."

Hugo looked through the window at the crowd below again. A thin layer of snow had settled on everyone's hats and coats as they hopped in place to keep warm. He knew what he needed to do. It was his brother who was lying in the hospital, badly injured. He thought of Lita but just as quickly pushed her away from her thoughts. He had to call her later, but now was not the time to hesitate.

"I'll do it."

Madeleine and Henrik both looked at him with genuine curiosity.

"What do you mean?" Madeleine asked.

"Just what I said. I'll take Felix's place as team leader, and we'll carry out the assignment. With a bit of luck, we'll get hold of both Klaus and Xi."

Madeleine could hardly believe her luck. Her plan had succeeded. "Why are you doing this?"

Hugo stared out the window and the howling storm outside.

"Revenge."

*

The decision was made. Hugo took a deep breath and rolled his shoulders.

Madeleine stood and touched his arm. "Are you sure about this?"

"Yes, I am."

Henrik cleared his throat, all business and all about the mission. "Okay, in that case, we have no time to lose. The press conference is tomorrow morning in London. Can you get to St. Petersburg and secure Markov before then?"

"I'll do my best."

Madeleine picked up her iPad from the table and told the men, "This is the latest information we have about Markov. He also has an assistant in

Finland who is a key player, too. Go ahead and read through all of this now."

Hugo took the tablet and started reading. While he did, Henrik pulled Madeleine aside.

"Are you sure about this, Madeleine? You're taking a huge risk here."

"I know. But it's better than nothing, right?"

Henrik nodded gravely and said, "Yes, much better."

"So I'll call the other team members and go through the situation with them."

A few minutes later, everyone was sitting quietly around the table. Madeleine made her review short and to the point, and when she was done, Mikko was the first to speak.

"And you think this is the best solution?"

"I don't know if it's the best, but it's a solution. And at the moment, it's the only one we have."

Mikko huddled with Sussie and Freya, who sat on either side of him. They deliberated for a few minutes and then turned to Madeleine.

"Okay. Given the situation, we agree it's the best option."

8

The plate broke into a thousand pieces as it smashed into the kitchen cabinet. Hugo held up his hands.

"Calm down!"

Another plate came flying, and the broken pieces rained down into the sink. Lita Marquez's eyes flared with rage.

"Who do you think you are? You think you can just leave me alone now? Now, when I could give birth at any time? Are you stupid or what?"

Hugo gritted his teeth. He didn't have time for this. The others were waiting in the car, and Xi was surely on his way to Russia by now in search of Markov.

Hugo took a slow breath, unclenched the muscles in his shoulders, and said as calmly as he could, "I know it sounds insane, but I have to do this. Felix is in the hospital hovering between life and death, and the ones who are responsible for it murdered at least four other people. They'll get away if no one does something."

"But why does that person have to be you? It makes no sense at all. Isn't this why we have the police?"

"It would take days for the police to get anywhere with their investigation—that's always how it is. If a crime isn't resolved within twenty-four hours, the chance of it ever being resolved goes down by a lot. And this hit was made by some seriously professional criminals."

Lita's olive complexion glittered as faint sun rays broke through the waning snowfall outside. She was unbelievably beautiful, with high cheekbones and dark hair that rocked forward and back when she walked. She and Hugo had met just a little less than two years ago, and their relationship was a stormy one.

She could be difficult when things didn't go her way, but then again, he wasn't all that easy to live with himself. She'd been a defining point in his life, though, especially after he'd been discharged from the military three months ago because of his diagnosis (a mild form of hereditary sensory and autonomic neuropathy type V pain syndrome). It was a complicated expression of a genetic defect that made him insensitive to pain. The symptoms had come snuck up at first, but Hugo had known for a long time that something was wrong.

Lita stood in the doorway and leaned against the door frame. "But Hugo, what about the baby? How can you leave me now?"

He knew she was going to cave. When he got his mind set on something, then he did it, no matter the cost. Lita didn't like it, but she accepted it. He went up to her and held her face gently in his hands.

"You know that you and the baby are the most important thing to me. You mean everything. But my brother means a lot to me, too. Someone has put him in the hospital—he might die—and I will move heaven and earth to avenge him. Felix has a competent team, and I can jump in and try to complete the mission Felix had planned."

Lita sobbed. "It's not fair."

He hugged her. She smelled so good, like jasmine and summer.

"No. It's not," he said. "But if all goes well, then I'll be back in two days."

"Do you promise?"

"Word of honor."

They headed to the living room and sat down on the sofa. They didn't say anything but just sat together in silence. It ripped his heart, but he had to do this.

When a few minutes had passed, he whispered, "I will be back. Count on it."

He took his gear and left the apartment. When he closed the front door, he could hear her crying from within.

9

Fine, icy snowflakes whirled past the windows as the car passed the booms and continued up the bridge. The dark sky loomed heavy over Copenhagen, and Hugo tried to relax in the passenger seat. Sussie was driving; Mikko and Freya sat in the back seat.

"Are you sure about this?" Sussie studied him. Now was not time to show weakness.

Looking straight ahead through the windshield, Hugo answered simply, "Yes. I'm sure."

Mikko chuckled behind him. "He's as crazy as Felix. If not more."

Hugo smiled. Mikko and he had met only once before, but the fact that he knew and loved his brother made Mikko feel like a close friend anyway. The big Finn patted his shoulder.

"Right, Hugo? Aren't you a little crazy like your brother?"

"Yeah, I guess I am."

Sussie used her voice to wake up her cell phone, which was docked on the dashboard, and called Madeleine's number. It barely had a chance to ring before she picked up.

"Madeleine? We're on the bridge now," Sussie informed her. "We'll be at Kastrup in ten minutes."

Hugo let his mind wander as they approached the high bridge. A gust of wind caused the van to wobble, but Sussie handled the disturbance with expert skill.

"Sussie," Hugo asked, "what kind of information do we have about Xi?"

Sussie was not only the most adept driver of the group but also their information and communication expert. She pulled an iPad from the door pocket and handed it to Hugo.

"Check it out. Unlock code is one-two-zero-three-eight-four. There's a folder called Xi Liu. The guy's a mercenary, born in the nineties. Grew up in Singapore and later lived in northern Africa. He's worked for a lot of shady types over the years— we've run into him twice during assignments in the last two years. He's an expert in martial arts, has a reputation for being a real sadist type. He's not the top mercenary around, but he's definitely a rising star."

Hugo found the dossier and read through it. At the end were pictures of Xi. He was short, thin but fit-looking. His dark hair fell just over his eyes, and in some of the photos, he wore a thin goatee. A scar ran along his forehead and down his left cheek. Whatever had injured him had barely missed his eye.

They followed the exit from the freeway and continued down into the underground parking

REVENGE

garage of the Copenhagen Airport. Once there, they unloaded their gear, and Mikko tossed a backpack to Hugo. Hugo caught it and swung it over his shoulder, then noticed that Sussie and Freya were staring at him. He nodded congenially. It was okay; he understood that they were wondering how anyone could leave a pregnant wife at home to set off on a mission to avenge his brother.

"I know. You think I'm crazy."

Sussie shook her head. "No, not at all. I'm just trying to take it all in. I'm still disoriented from the attack, so I can only imagine how you must feel."

Hugo shoved his hands into his jeans pockets to keep the others from seeing how badly they were trembling. The truth was that he was still running on adrenaline, though it was finally beginning to slow down.

"Well, I can't just go home," he said. "If the people who did this to my brother risk were to get away with it, I couldn't live with myself."

Freya hoisted a backpack half her size and swung it onto her back. "And what about your wife?" she asked.

"Girlfriend," he corrected her.

"Girlfriend, then. Isn't she pregnant?"

"Yes, she is. She's due any day now, actually."

Before anyone could say another word, Mikko burst out in shrieking laughter. Tears ran down his face and his howls echoed through the parking garage. After all the stress and death, there was something liberating about laughing. The others watched him in various levels of amusement. When a few minutes had passed and Mikko had collected himself, he wiped his eyes.

"You're a really tough bastard," he said to Hugo.

Hugo winked. "Got that right." He threw a glance at Sussie and Freya. He sensed that they still hadn't fully accepted him. If this mission was going to work, he'd need to convince them that he was serious.

"Listen. I get that it's hard to understand why I'm doing this, but I need you to trust me. Felix has told me about assignments he's done, so I know more about his work than you think. And with my background, jumping in to take his place and finish his work is something I can do."

With all eyes on him, Hugo took the opportunity to explain to the group what he'd done before and what his life had been like. He talked until he'd told them everything.

*

It was too late to turn around now. Hugo threw two heavy bags of equipment through the door of the plane. Madeleine had called in some favors at a major transport company and arranged for one of

73

their planes heading for St. Petersburg to allow the Novus team to tag along.

The cave-like cargo compartment was packed with boxes as far as the eye could see. At the end, two rows of seats fit snugly between the load area and the cockpit. The group brought their gear on board and sat, Mikko and Sussie in the second row behind Hugo and Freya.

Mikko patted Hugo on the shoulder. "What do you think? Getting used to things yet?"

"I'm impressed. Madeleine has good contacts."

"She really does." Mikko paused and said, "But I guess you've seen the inside of a transport plane before."

"A few of them, actually."

Freya crossed her arms in frustration.

"What is it?" Hugo asked.

She turned to him in a huff. "You told us the things you've done, but we still don't *know* you as a person." She looked around at the others. "We're just supposed to accept that we've got to carry out a mission with this guy who's basically wandered in from the street?"

Sussie leaned forward toward Freya's seat. "Freya, that's enough. Madeleine vouches for him—that should be enough. It is for me, at least. If she says he's capable, I trust her judgment. And at Felix's."

74

"It's easy for you to say that when neither of them is here."

Hugo turned to Freya and looked her in the eyes. "Listen, I understand how you feel. Considering everything that happened this morning, none of us expected to be here. But now we are, and we need our vengeance. You have your reasons, and I have mine. I promise you that you won't be disappointed. I have experience from my military missions—I've done this kind of work for years. I know it's hard to accept, but you've got to trust me for this to work. Can you do that?"

Freya opened her mouth as she stared at Hugo. His gaze did not fade away, and finally, she shrugged.

"Okay, I guess I don't have any choice. We're here together on our way to Russia, so we have to do this as a team." She put her face in her hands and rubbed her temples for a few seconds, then took a deep breath and looked at Hugo. "Did you say you worked on classified missions?"

"Both classified and unclassified," Hugo answered. "I didn't do classified so much in the beginning, but as the years went by, more and more assignments were abroad. Most of them are still classified, so, unfortunately, there's not much I can tell you about them."

"Why did you quit?"

The question was so abrupt that Hugo froze in his seat for a moment. He recovered quickly and sighed. "It's hard to explain."

Freya wasn't giving up. "I want to know you better, so try."

"All right." Hugo pressed his lips together, then said, "I . . . have a condition, a special sort of disease. It's called CIP—congenital insensitivity to pain. It comes from a mutated gene. I was honorably discharged once they discovered I had it."

Freya narrowed her eyes. "I've never heard of anything like that. You're saying you're invincible?"

Hugo chuckled. "No, I bleed just as easily as you do. It's more that I don't feel pain the same ways other people do."

Freya raised her eyebrows skeptically and opened her mouth to ask another question, but Mikko cut her off.

"So, now that we know Hugo a little better, maybe we ought to go through the mission?" He glanced from face to face hopefully.

The pilot's voice echoed from the speakers just then, "Hey, Novus team, please go ahead and strap in. We'll be descending soon."

After they buckled their seat belts, Sussie pulled out a stack of tablets and gave one to each team member.

"These tablets each have a copy of the dossier we compiled about Markov Tupolev, the Russian scientist. He's just over fifty years old, and he lives and works outside St. Petersburg. For a long time, he worked in the Russian Armed Forces developing various drugs and chemical-technical products. Five years ago, he moved to the private sector, where he's developed some synthetic products that have made him rich."

Hugo pulled up a picture of Tupolev on his iPad. The scientist was short, round, and had one of the most obnoxious comb-overs that Hugo had ever seen.

"Jeez. He looks like a mad scientist."

"Don't let the look fool you," Sussie said. "He may look like a slob, but he's one of the best researchers Russia has. He's top-tier."

"Where is he exactly?" Hugo asked.

Freya indicated for him to swipe to the next page of the report. "Look," she said. "He's two kilometers outside St. Petersburg, staying in a villa that's guarded by a team of some twenty top-trained men."

Hugo's heart rate started to speed up. "Twenty?"

Mikko thumped Hugo's shoulder lightly. "Any regrets yet?"

Hugo hardened his gaze and replied, "No."

Freya continued, "Good. This is going to be difficult. When we did the initial analysis for the mission, we hacked their databases."

"So we have access to all their information?" Hugo asked.

"Not all, but a lot. At least, we think so. And the information we found was interesting, to say the least. All Tupolev's guards are ex-military—special forces—so they're all top-trained."

"What about the villa itself?"

"It's pretty big and is surrounded by land— mostly wooded, which can help us get close undetected. The house itself has four floors—two above ground, two below. Tupolev does his work in the basement, so we have to find a way to get down there. The guards are stationed on the above-ground floors and outside the villa."

A blast of turbulence rocked the airplane, and everyone instinctively grabbed hold of their armrests until it was over.

Hugo nodded. "Okay, let's read through the report, and then we'll go over how to proceed." The team sank into silence as each person opened his or her copy of the document and began to read.

*

Xi Liu could hardly believe his luck. He scrolled down on the screen.

The cooperation between Markov Tupolev and Aino Salo appears to have been of utmost importance. Salo is a prominent researcher who was involved in several heavy collaborations throughout her career.

She has served as Tupolev's right hand over the past six months and possesses a deep knowledge of how the treatment works. Her lab is on the outskirts of Helsinki. According to the latest information, it is likely that a copy of the treatment is in Salo's lab. As previously mentioned, the treatment consists of two parts; the first is an injection of a quazepam copolymer (quazepam and another unidentified benzodiazepine drug), into the patient's bloodstream. This serves to prepare the patient and make him or her receptive. The second step is an injection of autonomous nanobots, which travel to selected areas of the brain and adhere there. For the treatment to work, the nanobots must be injected no more than three hours after the injection of the quazepam copolymer.

Xi slammed the computer so hard that both it and the folding table it sat on shook precariously. Miguel, seated behind him, leaned forward.

"Is everything okay?"

"No."

"What's up?"

Xi's brain was racing as he tried to figure out what to do with the information he'd just read. He would look incompetent if he were to call and tell Klaus that the treatment he was after might be hidden by a researcher in Finland. And he couldn't appear incompetent now. He clenched his fist.

"It seems there's a surprise factor in this assignment that I wasn't aware of."

"And how does it affect us?" Miguel asked is his ever-cool Spanish-accented voice.

"Good question," said Xi. "It isn't clear yet how it affects us or even if it will. But there's a possibility it could change everything."

He was silent as the plane began to roll toward the runway, and he looked out the window. The plane rocked as it turned onto the runway; once there, the pilot gave full throttle and started accelerating. The trees outside moved past faster and faster, and as they eased into the air, Xi knew he had to call Klaus. It couldn't be avoided.

Five minutes later, when the plane reached its marching height, he unbuckled his seat belt, stood, and walked to the back. The flight attendant was working with items in a cupboard when Xi pulled the curtain aside. She spun around.

"Sir, you can't be here now."

Xi held up his phone and waved it awkwardly. He beamed. "Important call—I have to speak with my manager."

The flight attendant did not look impressed. "Sorry, but it doesn't matter. I must ask you to go back to your seat."

Xi sighed. He had hoped he'd be able to avoid confrontation today. He took a step toward her and pulled the curtain closed behind him, leaving them alone together in the small space.

She shifted uneasily. "What are you doing?"

Xi took another step toward her and locked his gaze on her. "You seem like a nice person," he said. "I am too—most of the time. But right now, it's like this: I have to call my employer at once. I would be so grateful if I could get just five minutes to myself here to do it. Would that be something you could consider?"

The woman took a step back and bumped into the drawers protruding behind her. "Yes, yes, I guess I could do that. Sure."

She hurried past Xi and vanished through the curtain. Xi cursed that they had been told to travel commercially. It had been a terrible idea, but Klaus was obsessed with the idea that the mission be completed unnoticed. Xi took a deep breath when he heard Klaus answer the phone panting.

"Yes?"

"It's me."

"Yes?" Klaus repeated impatiently.

"There's some information in the dossier that we were not aware of."

"What kind of information?"

Xi told him what he'd learned about Aino Salo. When he finished, he heard a rumbling sound on the phone. He looked at it, surprised, to see if something was wrong with the phone itself, but he soon realized that the sound must have come from Klaus. Then, without warning, the call was terminated.

10

Finally, it was over. Klaus Horst wiped the sweat from his forehead as he rolled down next to Heidi on the king-size bed. His muscles ached. He wasn't a fan of having sex with his boss, but he had to do it. Heidi had insatiable needs, and as he was her closest assistant, it had fallen to him to satisfy them—maybe not *all* of her needs, but a great deal of them.

He swallowed hard and pushed away the fatigue in his aching muscles. Heidi put her hand on his arm and squeezed.

"That was wonderful. You're so talented."

"Glad you liked it."

No doubt about it—he abhorred having sex with her. She was not only grossly overweight, but there was something innately repulsive about her, something that deprived him of every ounce of his willpower to even be able to perform. It couldn't happen without a few Viagra tablets each time. He cringed. Was it worth it for the advancement? He shook his head to clear it.

"You seem tense," Heidi observed.

Heidi rolled over to him and laid her heavy body on top of his. She had to weigh at least twice as much as Klaus; it felt like he was being suffocated. He put his arm around her.

"No, I'm fine. It's just that there were a lot of details with Xi's mission."

"But everything went well?"

"Sure, but there are still some loose ends to tie up."

Heidi tittered and kissed him hard. "I think you're just saying that because you don't want to have any more sex with me."

He tensed and shook his head quickly. "No, how could you even think that?"

She didn't answer but just looked at him. He sighed inwardly and kissed her passionately. He knew exactly what she wanted.

*

Half an hour later, Klaus gently got up from the bed and pulled on a robe. Heidi snorted heavily, and he shivered. He looked at the clock—half-past twelve. He collected his clothes and left the room hastily. He had to get hold of Xi now, right away. There was no time to lose, and there was too much at stake. Klaus had put everything on the line by planning and executing the hit against Novus. The decision hadn't been sanctioned by the others on the board, but so far, Heidi had been behind him. He had known, of course, that she would back him on it. She was as greedy as he was, if not more so. That was the trait that had taken her to the top. Klaus had seen the possibilities and had therefore struggled to get to the position of Heidi's assistant.

His phone vibrated.

"Yes?"

"It's Xi."

"Xi. What have you found?"

"Miguel and I have gone through most of what got from Novus."

"And?" Klaus had to fight to keep his voice even.

"It looks like Markov's Finland assistant is a woman named Aino Salo, and she's key in the development of the treatment."

Klaus frowned. He'd heard Salo's name before but had thought she was just one of Markov's regular assistants. "Is she more important than his other colleagues?" he asked Xi.

"Very. The documents we took say that she's been invaluable in Markov's success. And it looks like he's given her both the antidote and the scanner used to find out if a person has been treated. I'm thinking he wanted to make sure everything was out of his hands if he were to be attacked."

Klaus murmured, "Why are we only finding out about this now?"

"I cannot answer that."

Klaus clasped his hands together as he thought. "Okay. Then we must adapt. After you get to

Markov, you have to go to Helsinki and pick up this research partner of his, along with the antidote and scanner. I want everything. Is that clear?"

"Roger."

A drop of sweat ran down Klaus' forehead. He wiped it away. "Good. Call me when you've landed and are heading out to Markov's place."

"Okay."

Klaus ended the call and looked out through the large windows and traffic below. Thick snowflakes drifted lazily to the ground, and the cars left thin tire tracks on the roads. He ran his fingers through his hair; he needed to think. There was so much at stake. He would get to the top at QuantumCorp no matter the cost—it had been his goal for so many years that this singular ambition had become part of his very soul. All the sacrifices, all the preparations he has taken, they had led him to this moment. That was the point.

He was jolted from his thoughts when he heard his name.

"Klaus?"

He turned and saw Heidi standing in the doorway.

"What are you doing?"

He shrugged. "I had to make an important call."

She smiled and beckoned with her finger for him to come closer. "We're not done yet," she told him in a dreadful singsong voice.

Klaus smiled stiffly and walked toward her obediently.

*

Markov Tupolev sat heavily in the low, padded chair. The bowl he held in his hand slipped out of his fingers a moment too soon, slamming down onto the antique wood and spilling steaming onion soup onto the surface of the table.

"Damn!" he shouted as he grabbed a napkin to sop up the mess. When that one was saturated, he reached for another one to finish the job. Without looking up, he muttered, "Well, what do you think?"

The man already sitting at the table lifted two dark, bushy eyebrows. His face was weather-worn and frayed.

"What do I think about what?"

Markov belted out a laugh so loud that it echoed around the small dining room. "About what? You're funny, Abram. So funny, 'about what.' About patient twelve, of course."

Abram gave an uncommitted tilt of the head. "He looks promising, I'll give you that," he said, his voice crackly from decades of cigarettes. "He's survived *and* absorbed both injections. I look forward to seeing how he responds to the test this afternoon."

Markov took a spoonful of what was left of the onion soup in his bowl as he listened. He replied, "As do I. Two hours left until we start the test. Is everything ready?"

Abram picked up the tablet that sat in the chair next to his and pulled up the notes on patient twelve. "All preparatory tests and checks are clear. He received the injections two hours ago, and according to the most recent tests, all his levels are within acceptable limits."

Markov grinned like a kid on Christmas morning, revealing well-cared-for teeth except for one on the bottom that was chipped and discolored. "Good! Do one more check thirty minutes before start time. We have to be sure to get the results we want."

Abram put the iPad back down, drank the last of the red compote in his glass, and chewed the small, red berries left over at the bottom before replying, "Of course."

A drop of sweat ran down Markov's back, and he suppressed a shiver. He had been fighting for a long time to get here. The sacrifices he'd made along the way were great, but now he would reap success. When he presented his discoveries to the leaders in Moscow, he would be recognized as a hero.

Admittedly, they had funded his research for years, but over the past year, he had seen a marked decrease in the amount he received. It didn't make things any easier, but his luck would turn up. He just had to keep at it. If there was anything his father had taught him, it was to never give up. Markov opened eyes he hadn't realized he'd closed.

He looked at Abram and said, "Be sure to check the patient again and complete the lab for the experiment. We're starting in one hour."

Abram nodded, then got up and took his dishes to the kitchen. Markov, left alone in the dining room, went over all the details one more time. Nothing must go wrong, not now that he was so close.

He finished his onion soup and cleared his place. Markov found himself alone in the kitchen, as well, and stared out the window over the sink. Something felt off, uneasy—probably just nerves, he figured. He turned his head at the sound of voices approaching. A moment later, two men in thick jackets came through the kitchen doorway. They fell silent when they saw Markov.

"Sorry, Dr. Tupolev."

Markov nodded briefly and gestured. "It's fine, Ilya. I'm heading down to the lab. You and Leonid can have some of this soup—it'll warm you up. The chef prepared too much food again." He pointed to the huge pot on the stove.

Ilya smiled. "Thank you, Doctor. That's very kind of you."

Markov returned the smile. "I'm the one who should thank you. You're taking such good care of our little operation here."

Both men tried to hide their surprise at the unexpectedly friendly response. They pulled off their jackets and residual snowflakes sprinkled down to the floor.

Markov motioned to the men. "Come."

It was good to surprise the employees occasionally, he thought, and he was a master at it. Long ago, he'd learned how to manipulate his environment to get the best possible results. Ilya and Leonid each took a bowl, filled it with hot soup, and sat down at the dining room table.

Markov chuckled and said, "Enjoy, my lords. I'm heading down to the lab—my team and I will be busy for the next few hours, so make sure no one bothers us. Understood?"

"Of course, Doctor," Ilya replied.

Markov stepped to the dining room table and patted Ilya on the shoulder, then went into the hallway and threw a look in the large, gold-edged mirror. His reflection was not as slender as he remembered himself being in the days of his youth. His stomach buckled under the white lab coat, and sweaty strands of hair lay combed over the glossy dome of his head. A surge of disappointment rushed through him, but he shook it off. Now wasn't the time to focus on the negative. Now was the time to win.

He stomped the floor, stretched, and approached the heavy metal door under the stairs. It had no doorknob or keyhole but was simply an imposing, but plain, slab of thick steel. A scanner was embedded in the wall beside it, and Markov placed his palm against the smooth glass. A lime-green line of light slid from top to bottom, and as the door opened, he was met by a familiar odor.

Markov stepped through the opening and followed the stairs down until he came to another door that had no knob. This one slid up as he approached, exposing a chamber that was oblong and quite deep. Four people were feverishly at work, but they looked up as Markov entered the room.

"How does it look?" he asked them.

Everyone answered in a chorus, "Everything looks good."

Markov's mouth tensed into a humorless smile. "Good. Keep on getting things ready. We will start," he glanced at the clock on the wall, "in ninety-two minutes."

The workers returned to what they were doing. Behind Markov, the door slid up again and Abram entered the room.

"Do you have five minutes?" he rasped.

"Yes, what is it?"

"There's something you need to see."

Markov followed Abram into a smaller, nearby room with white walls, bare except for a man lying motionless on a stretcher. Abram approached him and raised his right arm.

"Here, you see?"

Markov came closer and saw what Abram was referring to. A thin, spiderweb-like pattern stretched down the forearm to the hand. Markov leaned in to inspect it more closely, then lifted his eyes to Abram.

"When did this show up?"

Abram shrugged. "It wasn't there when I checked him last, and that was just an hour ago."

Markov studied the unusual pattern, tracing it with his index finger. The lines looked like they'd been drawn with thousands of little red dots.

"It has to be a reaction to the nanobot injection," Abram said. "We didn't see anything on him after he got the quazepam."

Markov nodded, standing. "I agree. Be sure to check and see if it spreads even more." He put his hand on the sleeping man's chest. "If we're lucky, it's just a minor reaction. His pulse is strong."

The last part he said quietly to himself. There was so much at stake—what they'd achieved in his underground lab was nothing short of revolutionary. With this series of injections, one could compel a person to obey almost any command. For so many years, this kind of breakthrough had been the holy grail for the counter-espionage world: to be able to control any human being. And that was exactly what Markov had succeeded in doing with two injections, one consisting of nanobots that infiltrated the brain, and one that enabled the administrant to take control.

Markov stomped the floor with excitement and spun around. "Go through everything once more, Abram. Make sure we're ready."

11

"How are you feeling?"

Hugo turned around and looked at Sussie, sitting behind him.

"Okay," he said. "Just thinking."

"Anything you want to share?"

Hugo studied her. Sussie was quite short, with dark hair and eyes. She had a bounce in her step that made her look like she was hopping when she walked. He'd already taken a liking to her.

"Yeah, just thinking about Felix and when we were growing up. We've always been close, ever since we were little. Some twins have that kind of bond, you know—something deeper. I could always sense when Felix was hurt."

Sussie frowned and held onto her armrests as the plane descended through one last bit of turbulence.

"Really?"

"Yeah. And that ability seemed to grow stronger as we got older. It wasn't always good, of course." He chuckled.

"What do you mean?"

"I'm sure you know how it can be between brothers—everything becomes a competition. Even the smallest thing, like getting our dirty clothes from our rooms down to the laundry room in the basement. We almost drove our parents ballistic."

Sussie laughed. "I can image you two pushing your parents to the limit."

Hugo laughed too, then fell silent again. He knew that Felix was hovering between life and death. He could feel that deep, aching pain far down inside. It was deeper this time, more serious than he had ever felt, and he instinctively understood that Felix stood at the brink of death.

Sussie picked up on Hugo's mood and laid her hand on his arm.

"He'll do well. He's strong. If anyone's going to make it, it's him."

Hugo swallowed and looked gratefully at her. "Thanks."

*

One hundred and seven kilometers to the east of the aircraft lay Pulkovo Airport outside St. Petersburg. A cell phone rang, and a rough, calloused hand pulled it out of a jacket pocket.

"Yes?"

"It's Xi Liu."

Silence. Then, finally, "Yes?"

"Am I talking to Vlado?"

"Yes."

"Excellent. I'm in an airplane heading for St. Petersburg and land in half an hour."

"Yes?"

"Another airplane will be landing just before us. It's carrying a small group of people that I need you to stop. I pay well."

Vlado grinned. "Who gave you this number?"

"Janus. I need a triggerman and you're the closest available." Xi paused. "We pay in dollars."

"Okay, I understand. No problem. Send over the information about which flight and who the people are we're supposed to stop. We'll take care of the rest."

"I hope I wasn't misinformed about your effectiveness," said Xi. "After the job is completed, you'll receive a standard payment of one million dollars."

Vlado had heard enough. "It will be fine. Send the information and I'll take care of the rest." He ended the call and then dialed another number.

A hoarse, male voice answered. "Marat here."

"Hey. Get hold of Makar—we have a job to do."

Two minutes later, Vlado was approaching a closed door in a dusty office corridor. The whole department was under repair at the moment, which gave Vlado an excellent cover as a contractor. Few people—living ones, that was— knew he was one of the most effective assassins in the country. In recent years, he'd been responsible for the deaths of seven people.

He opened the door and headed to a row of metal cabinets. He spun the combination on the lock and opened it. The air in the cupboard smelled heavily of oil, grease, and dirt. Vlado grabbed two AK-74 rifles and placed them in a black cloth bag. In his line of work, you had to be prepared. He would make the attack look like a mafia-type hit that had gone awry. He'd used that tactic before and it had always worked.

His phone vibrated when he received the text messages about the job. Vlado pushed aside a pair of dirty overalls hanging in the closet, exposing another rifle, the newer AN-94. The slender assault weapon made his fingers twitch. He put it in his bag, closed it, and secured the metal cabinet. After this job, he would have to take a long vacation— maybe a year or two, until it all settled down. He'd felt a little worn down by the last one anyway, so it would be good to get some environmental change. He changed into some clean overalls, picked up his bag, and disappeared from the room.

*

The landing was hard, and the plane swerved right as the pilot stepped on the brake. The aircraft rolled and someone shouted, "Hold on!"

Hugo, deep in thought, barely noticed the commotion. He needed to call Lita, or at least text her. She must be sick with worry, he thought.

Mikko bumped his shoulder. "We're here, buddy."

Hugo shook his head to clear it. The four teammates took their bags from the luggage compartment above them, and when the attendant opened the door, they made their way to the stairs. Nearly half a dozen planes were parked around them, and the ground was covered with a thin layer of snow. Fat snowflakes swirled around Hugo's face, and he shivered as a blast of cold air hit him in the face like a tight fist. His breath left his nose in small clouds as he began to descend.

An old, bulky truck swung around a plane parked fifty yards away and headed in their direction. Hugo assumed it was the supply truck at first, but when the heat of the first rounds hissed by them, it was clear that the rest of this day was not going to go as expected. Instinct took over and he pushed Mikko forward.

"Down! Now!"

Mikko threw the bags over the edge of the stairs and they vanished into the darkness. Then he jumped down the remaining stairs, landing in a snowdrift. Hugo prepared to jump after him; Sussie was next in line.

"There's another one!" she shouted, pointing from the top of the stairs.

Another old beast of a truck was heading toward them fast. Its tall, thin tires cut deep grooves in the snow-covered ground. A man hung out of the passenger window holding an automatic rifle. He raised the weapon and fired a long burst, and ten rounds struck the side of the aircraft, busting three of its windows. The harsh, stinging sound reverberated loudly through the air, but Hugo knew the attackers had planned well for this. They were far from the main terminals, and in this weather, the snow would dampen the sound of gunfire. It would probably take a few minutes before the control tower understood what was happening.

Hugo threw himself over the edge of the stairway, thanking his lucky stars when he landed in a snowdrift. He rolled, got to his knees, and saw Mikko. He had gone around the stairs and now squatted behind them.

Mikko pointed at him. "Do you have any weapons?"

Hugo pulled his Glock from his belt holster, and in the crook of his palm, the dark weapon became a part of him. He looked at Mikko, who nodded gravely. Both of the trucks pulled to a squealing stop ten feet from the foot of the airstairs. Hugo could only hope that Sussie and Freya had gotten back on the plane, into relative safety.

Two men jumped out of the first truck, wearing bandannas over their faces. One of them lifted a machine gun and began throwing lead. Hundreds of bullets flew around and over Mikko and Hugo; all they could do was scramble on hands and knees and hide. After an eternity of gunfire, it finally stopped and a third man jumped out of the other truck.

He put his hands to his mouth and shouted, "Get out here! Come out now and the women will live!"

Right, Hugo thought. He knew the truth when it came to guys like these—when he and Mikko were dead, Sussie and Freya would be killed too, or worse. Hugo signaled to Mikko to get ready.

He whispered, "Aim for the guy with the automatic."

Mikko nodded, and both he and Hugo took aim and squeezed the triggers. The thick snowfall distorted the sound of the gunshots, and it looked at first like the attackers didn't even realize they were being fired upon.

Then one man was hit in the shoulder. He spun around and fell to his knees, screaming. "Vlado! I'm hit!"

Vlado rushed over to the fallen man. "Come on, Marat, you're okay," he said as he pulled him up to standing. Then he shouted, "Makar, shoot them!"

Makar raised his weapon, walked toward the stairs, and started shooting. Hugo and Mikko threw themselves back behind cover as hundreds of bullets hit the surrounding steel, ripping open gaping holes in the stairs that protected them. The man was now just five meters away. Hugo looked around feverishly for a way out but saw nothing.

If he or Mikko were to move a muscle, they'd be rewarded with a bullet in the head.

*

Vlado slipped on a patch of black ice, causing Marat to fall to his knees, screaming.

Vlado swore. "Good God, Marat. Get up and shut your mouth. You're all right!"

Marat staggered to his feet. Vlado grabbed hold of him.

"Focus. You were just grazed. You'll live."

Marat's face turned ashen, his mouth like a thin line. "Okay. I'll take them," he said. "Where's my weapon?"

Vlado picked up the rifle from the snowy asphalt and handed it to Marat.

"Step to the side and flank them," Vlado instructed. "They're under the stairs; Makar has them trapped. I'll go this way, to the other side."

Marat spat out blood and bared his red teeth. He grumbled, "Let's take those bastards."

Faraway sirens sounded through the gloomy evening, and Vlado turned toward the sound. "Goddammit," he muttered to himself. Then he shouted, "We don't have much time, men!"

He'd screwed up—or, actually, Marat had screwed up first. He'd opened fire too soon. Vlado had planned for them to start shooting once all the targets were on the ground, but Marat had been overzealous. Vlado shook his head; his warm vacation seemed eons away.

But he couldn't give up now. If his client found out that he had given up, his own life would be over. So he motioned for Marat to go left as he went right.

"Makar."

Makar stopped shooting, and a huge cloud of smoke rolled past him. The air was streaked with gunpowder.

"What?"

"We're coming up behind you. Hold them in front of you and we'll flank them."

Makar opened fire again, and the heavy noise of the machine gun shook the surrounding air. Vlado followed suit, raising his weapon and letting off blasts from his semiautomatic. He grinned—the targets were pinned down, unable to go anywhere, like rats in a cage. Bullets continued to grind everything they touched into shards.

Someone screamed, and for a fraction of a second, Vlado believed it was over. Then something flickered past his eyebrows. A shadow slid forward into the plane's doorway—and the shadow was carrying something big. A deep rumble shook the airstairs as whoever owned the shadow began shooting. Heavy rounds sent up small clouds of snow as they made contact with the ground, and Makar threw himself to the side. He barely missed a shot to the head, but once on the ground, got a bullet to his foot and screamed.

He froze as the realization hit him—their weapons were completely overwhelmed by this new one. He turned and looked at the woman at the top of the stairs who had the barrel of an AK-12 pointed right at him.

Makar blinked, rolled quickly to his left, aimed his weapon at her, and fired.

*

Hugo saw one of the men fall when someone above him started shooting. With snow tearing at his face and the icy cold stiffening his fingers, he knew that if he and Mikko had any kind of chance, now would be the time to act.

One of the other men rushed forward, opened fire, then threw himself back into shelter again.

Hugo cursed. This wasn't working. They had to do something. He checked his gun—he had two rounds left.

"Mikko!"

Mikko wriggled from his curled-up position under the stairs. His face was ravaged and thin, and a trickle of blood ran along his cheek.

"How many rounds do you have left?"

"Four."

"Open fire on my signal. We have to counter-attack. If we stay here, we die."

Mikko didn't answer, but Hugo saw the gleam in his eyes. He nodded.

"Now!"

They began to shoot, and the men standing in front of the stairs threw themselves down in cover. There would only be a matter of seconds before this window was gone, Hugo knew. He sprang to his feet and rushed forward; behind him, Mikko shouted something he couldn't understand. His whole being was focused on getting to the target as quickly as possible. His legs hammered like pistons.

He slipped on black ice as he passed the stairs but grabbed the handrail and managed to keep going. He passed one of the attackers, who was lying in a large pool of blood. One of the other men stood next to him, and the third one was over beside the nearest truck. Hugo reached his hand into the front of his jacket and took hold of the rubber grip on one of the knives strapped to his chest.

In a single, sweeping motion, he pulled it out and threw it in the direction of the truck. The blade flashed in the air and then found its mark, sinking into the flesh of an exposed neck. A bubbly, bloody grimace crossed his face before he fell backward to the ground.

The other man cried out, "No!"

Still running like an express train, Hugo automatically reached in for another knife handle. Adrenaline surged through him, and he perceived everything in sharp focus. His mind was like a high-definition video recorder, taking in everything around and within him—the crackling snow, the icy wind, the heat inside his body. With a cat-like leap, he crashed into the survivor, and they tumbled together on the snow-covered ground.

The goon grinned sadistically. "You bastard. I'll kill you!"

Hugo scrambled to his feet and noted the ground as he moved a few steps away. "You've been trying to do that for the last three minutes," he said in a low voice. "Now it's my turn."

During the scuffle, his opponent's weapon had gone flying, and now he searched the ground frantically for it. There—three meters away, too far to reach. He turned toward Hugo and pulled out his own blade—a broad, brutal military knife. He took a few steps toward Hugo, but Hugo moved softly backward. Hugo had been in knife fights before; he knew the chances of survival increased greatly if you didn't rush into anything. It was rare for a knife fight to last more than a few minutes, so it was all about avoiding mistakes.

"What's your name?" Hugo demanded. "Why do you want to kill us?"

The man chuckled, his cheeks rosy from the cold and giving him a strange resemblance to a murderous Santa Claus. "It doesn't matter, does it?" he snarled.

"Well, yeah—it does for me. This is the third time I've been to Russia, and it's the third time someone has tried to kill me here."

"So, 'welcome back' is appropriate then, I guess."

"Thanks. But the other times, I knew the name of the people who wanted me dead. I don't know now."

The man pulled back his lips in a shark-like smile. "My name is Vlado."

"Nice to meet you, Vlado. My name is Hugo."

They started to circle each other, looking for openings, some weaknesses to exploit. Vlado made a couple of moves, but Hugo waved them off easily. Hugo took a step forward but slipped on a dark patch of ice. Vlado saw his chance. He thrust his knife forward.

Hugo slid aside deftly, having fooled the thug. When Vlado's arm came within reach, he shoved his knife into it. He'd severed an artery, and blood gushed from the wound in a torrent. Vlado shouted in panic and dropped to his knees. The knife in his hand clattered to the ground, and Hugo kicked it away.

"Give up. I don't want to kill you."

Vlado grumbled something Hugo couldn't hear. A fraction of a second later, jolly old Saint Nick lunged forward—but Hugo anticipated the move. He slammed Vlado in the head with his fist, and the thug fell unconscious the ground.

*

Mikko approached Hugo. Vlado lay there in front of them, dead.

"Why were they trying to kill us?" Mikko asked, his subdued voice betraying his weariness.

Hugo shrugged. "I wasn't able to get an answer out of him on that. They look like hired killers to me, guns for hire. Brutal types."

"But who knows we're here?"

"Obviously, someone who has the money and power to hire a team of killers in a matter of hours."

Freya and Sussie appeared in the aircraft doorway and came down to them. Sussie was pale, but Freya's eyes were on fire. Hugo had seen that look before; some people were energized by using weapons.

Sussie pulled a cell phone out of her jacket pocket. "Hello?"

She was silent for a few seconds and then answered in Russian—a language Hugo didn't know. She ended the call and explained to the group, "That was our ride—he's on his way. He'll be here in a minute."

Mikko tilted his head. The sound of sirens came closer. "Sounds like the police are on their way too."

Freya hugged the weapon she was holding to her chest. "Okay," she said. "Let's collect our stuff so we're ready to leave as soon as our ride gets here."

Mikko nodded. "Agreed."

They worked quickly, lugging their gear off the plane. The airplane was full of bullet holes—Hugo suspected this would be a major scandal in tomorrow's newspaper. He could see tomorrow's headlines: *Shots Fired at International Airport.*

A minute later, a white van peeled in front of the plane. A young man jumped out and rushed around the front.

"Sussie?"

Hugo pointed at her, and she jogged up to the driver. After they'd exchanged a few words, he nodded and Sussie spun around.

"All right, move it! Let's get going!"

The group grabbed their equipment and loaded it into the van. As they pulled the side door closed, they could see flashing blue lights approaching. The white van roared, leaving the chaos behind.

12

Dr. Markov Tupolev's heart pounded as he opened the door and went into the other room. The woman who was strapped to the cot did not move. Her face was pale and sweaty, yet still beautiful. Markov felt a surge of excitement as he walked closer to her. He put his hand on her shoulder and squeezed, and she jerked in her sleep anxiously.

"Anna? Are you awake?"

Anna opened an eye and tried to raise her arm, but it only lifted halfway before the handcuffs halted her movement.

"Anna, it's me. Markov. Do you recognize me?"

Anna stared at him, eyes narrowed, and moistened her cracked lips. "Yes, I think so."

"Good, Anna, very good."

"Where am I?"

Markov did not respond but turned around and walked to the far wall, where a set of four monitors was lined up on a long desk. He studied the various graphs that displayed Anna's vitals. Everything looked okay—blood pressure was perhaps a tad low, but that wouldn't affect the experiment. He walked over to Anna again. She was more awake now, staring at him.

"Where am I? Why am I here?"

Markov's voice was smooth. "But Anna, don't you remember what happened? You fell. You hit your head."

Anna blinked, trying to remember. "Fell? Where did I fall?"

"Out there. On the stairs. You fell and hit your head. You were unconscious for quite a while. You don't remember anything?"

She shook her head and mumbled, "No. I don't remember that at all."

"Well, it doesn't matter now. Just lie here and rest a bit longer, and everything will be fine."

Anna raised her other arm, but it too got stuck halfway. She jerked it, and the handcuffs rattled against the metal frame of the bed. Panic crept into her voice.

"Why am I strapped in? Let me go—now!"

Markov shivered with pleasure. "Not yet, Anna. Not yet. You were a little violent before. Now, don't let that upset you—that kind of thing can happen when a person experiences head trauma. The restraints are for your security as much as mine. When you're better, we'll remove them. I promise."

Anna continued to twitch. Markov went to the table, picked up a flat, square object, and went back to her.

"Here. This will help you relax."

"I don't want anything. Let me go."

Markov opened the packaging of a small patch, and before Anna could say anything, he stuck it on her shoulder. The effect was immediate. Her eyelids became heavy, and he studied her while his special quazepam copolymer disbursed into Anna's bloodstream.

"That's good, Anna. Very good."

There was a knock at the door. He whirled around.

"Yes?"

Abram's muted voice replied, "It's Ilya, the guard. He says you need to come up."

"I don't have time right now."

"He says it's important. It's something about the computer program that handles rooftop security."

Markov gave an exasperated sigh. "Christ. Okay. Tell him I'll be there in a minute."

He laid a hand on Anna's right breast and squeezed. "I'll be right back." Then he disappeared from the room.

*

Markov shoved the door open. Ilya flinched but quickly regained his composure.

"I'm sorry to have to interfere with your work."

Markov's good mood had evaporated. "Yes, why are you bothering me? What's so important?"

Ilya flexed his jaw. "Look at this," he said. He approached one of the big screens hanging on the wall, and Markov followed.

"What?"

"Here. Look. There's a hole along one edge of the fence." Ilya pointed to the thin, red line that marked the border of the villa's property.

"Go on."

"We don't know where it came from, but it wasn't there earlier today. It just showed up. We're thinking someone might have tried to break in."

Ilya fell silent. Markov glared at him.

"Are you serious? You called me down here for that?"

Ilya's face flushed. "I'm sorry if I went too far, sir, but I'd rather be safe than risk a break-in."

Markov hissed, "You idiot! I have more important things to do than this. Just fix the damn hole!"

Ilya cringed. 'Yes, of course, Doctor." He hurried to the door and opened it. As Markov stormed past him, Ilya put a hand on his shoulder. Markov shrugged it off and kept going. He disappeared down the hall, heading back down to the basement.

*

Goddamn idiot, Markov thought as he sank into the chair in front of his desk. He didn't have time for this kind of incompetence. Not now. There was too much at stake.

"Abram," he called to his assistant across the room. "Is everything ready?"

Abram scanned the monitors, his thick mop of dark, coarse hair sitting like a helmet on top of his head.

"Yes," he answered after a few minutes had passed. "Everything looks good. Green across the board."

"Excellent. Continue with the next phase."

Abram activated the controls next to the screens, and two metal arms descended from the ceiling above Anna in the next room. Markov rose and stood by the long, high window in the wall that separated his office from the experiment room. Anna didn't move as the metal arms neared her body, but the moment one of them touched her, she jerked.

Markov breathed faster. This was only the third time he'd conducted a complete experiment, an experiment that went all the way, regardless of the outcome. It was both illegal and unethical to test on humans like this. If he were caught, it would be a devastating scandal. But he was lucky—he had contacts in the military who not only protected him, but supported him, and generously at that.

With all that support, though, there followed some expectations, and that's what had pushed him to accelerate the process as much as possible. If this had simply been a normal medical experiment, he wouldn't dare be taking the risks he was now. But this was different. Now, he had to push for results—both for the sake of himself and his patients.

Anna winced as she dreamed, and Markov smiled. It was an advantage to be in his position, to be able to enjoy the participants in his experiments.

Abram joined him at the window. "Phase two completed. Should I wake her up?"

"Yes," Markov said breathlessly.

Abram touched a control next to the screens at his station, and a faintly green substance was injected into Anna's arm. After a few seconds, her eyes flickered open. The next part of the experiment would be the truly interesting one, Markov knew. That's where he and his team had made their fantastic breakthrough. This is where they could access and control the human mind. Well, maybe not totally, but almost. Via a custom-built transmitter that controlled the nanorobots, the individual would follow any instructions you gave.

This dream of countless spy organizations and intelligence agencies was now a reality in Markov's hands. Back in the sixties, the CIA had carried out some controversial experiments under the code name "MK Ultra." The KGB had also worked for many years to develop this type of technology to create the perfect spy. Both the Americans and the Russians had failed—but Markov had not. He had pulled it off.

Anna opened her eyes and noticed again that she was strapped down. "Let me go," she said to the empty room in an even, but indignant, voice.

Markov tapped the glass, and she turned her head and looked at him.

He smiled, tilted his head, and replied sweetly, "Not yet, my dear."

*

The temperature outside dropped rapidly as the Novus team left St. Petersburg and continued out into the countryside. The roads became trickier to navigate, but on the plus side, the amount of traffic had dwindled.

Their driver rolled over a beach-ball-sized pothole in the road, and the sudden jolt made everyone in the van moan.

Sussie hissed at the driver, "*Остерегайтесь этого!*" (Watch out!)

The man mumbled something unintelligible in response and slowed down. Hugo, seated in the van's center row, opened one of the backpacks, removed two knives, and checked their condition. He examined them both from various angles and carefully touched the blades. When he was satisfied, he nodded to himself and replaced them.

Mikko was sitting two seats to his left, next to the window. "Those your knives?"

"Yep."

Mikko turned to look out the window at the swiftly growing darkness that increasingly engulfed the snow-clad surroundings. "I had a friend who was a knife specialist," he said. "There was nothing the man couldn't do with a knife."

"Was?"

"He was killed. Three years ago." Mikko paused and said, "There's always someone better."

Hugo scratched his scruffy chin. "I'm sorry," he said.

Mikko frowned and slapped his knees. "It doesn't matter now. We have other things to tend to."

Behind Mikko, Freya kicked the back of the seat. "You better believe it," she said. "I've gone through our equipment."

Hugo turned and looked at her. She sat in the back row with four of the team's heavy bags surrounding her. Two huge machine guns were lying across her knees, making her look strangely like a child. Her blonde hair stuck out from

117

underneath a beanie. Freya met Hugo's gaze and winked.

"Everything looks okay. What we've got is in good condition."

"Good. How much do we have?"

"We have these two," she patted the two M249 belt-fed light machine guns, "plus two Steyr AUGs, two Glock 19s, and a shit-ton of ammunition."

The van hit another hole in the road, and Sussie lambasted the driver. Hugo didn't understand what she was saying as she railed on him on and on, but given the driver's body language, she was probably cussing him up and down. Sussie was petite, but not dainty; she compensated for her small frame with a violent, volatile temper.

Hugo leaned over to her. "Hey, I never said thank you."

Sussie laughed and replied, "Don't mention it. You don't have to thank me."

"Yes, I do. If you hadn't arrived at just the right time, Mikko and I would've been dead."

She shrugged but didn't answer.

"So, thank you."

"You're welcome," Sussie said with another shrug.

Mikko rolled his shoulders and stretched. "We're almost halfway to the villa. We need to go through the last details."

During their flight, the team had established a relatively simple plan of attack. Two of them would conduct a diversionary attack on the eastern side of the area that, with any luck, would pull away most of the guards. They assumed Markov would remain where he was; the other two team members would go in under the cover of darkness and grab him. It was the best plan they could come up with on the short flight, and Hugo gave them a fifty percent chance of survival.

"You're right," he said to Mikko. "Let's do it."

Sussie handed him an iPad and he activated it. A greenish map slid forward on the screen, surrounded by a black, uneven line. Sussie handed out tablets to the rest of the team.

"Novus just sent us their most recent satellite images. Madeleine had to twist a few arms over at the Department of Defense to get them."

On the map, there were half a dozen dark red dots—some stationary, others creeping along slowly, a couple on their own, the rest in pairs— that surrounded a dark square in the center.

"Those dots are the guards. There are six of them that we know of, and we have to assume they're all armed. Two cars and three vans are parked to the northeast of the house. Markov is in the basement with all his security. The two floors above grade serve as his lab."

Hugo slid his fingers over the map, zoomed in, and tapped on two dark circles that sat between the house and the cars.

"And this is where we'll detonate?"

"Yes. Because of Markov's research, they had to install gas and pressure vessels for oxygen."

Mikko chuckled. "That's going to be a fabulous bang."

Sussie bared her teeth and chuckled dryly. "Hell yeah, it will. But that'll be the easy part. When it goes off, we're betting that most of the guards will run. Mikko and I will stay in the van with Zeb." She nodded toward the driver, who turned his head at the mention of his name.

She continued, "As the guards get closer, we'll take off. We'll go fast enough to get away, but slowly enough that they're sure to see us escape. Then it's up to you."

Freya nodded. "Right. That's when we'll go to work."

A tinge of excitement glimmered at the base of Hugo's skull—that familiar feeling of elation before a dangerous assignment. It had been six months since he'd last felt it, and now it was flowing through him again, clearing away everything that didn't matter. All he could see now was the raw focus on the mission that thundered inside him. He turned and locked eyes with Freya.

"We go in quick and quiet, okay? We're both professionals—I saw your capabilities back at the airport."

"Yes, we are." Freya lifted her chin a little and looked ahead stoically. "Indeed. We get this done quickly and efficiently."

Hugo gazed out into the gloomy afternoon and wondered what fate had in store for them.

13

Zeb slowed down too late. When they hit the soft snowdrift, everyone inside the van flew forward into the brusque arms of their seat belts. There was a collective grunt.

Before Sussie could bark at him, Zeb started talking. Although Hugo didn't understand Russian, he got the gist through Zeb's body language: *sorry, sorry*. Sussie looked like she was going to hit him. Hugo put a hand on her shoulder.

"Come on," he said. "We have work to do."

With a last glare at Zeb, Sussie gathered her things that had slid onto the floor, pulled open the side door, and hustled out. Hugo and the others followed. They were less than four hundred meters from the electric fence that surrounded the villa.

The van had been alone on the deserted stretch of the gravel roadway it had followed for the last ten minutes. They hadn't seen a single oncoming car, and Hugo was sure they could avoid detection here. The soft snow made everything around them subdued and dreamlike.

Mikko wrapped his arms around his body. When he spoke, large clouds erupted from his mouth. "Jeez, it's almost as cold here as it is in my hometown in Finland."

Hugo turned to Sussie. "What do you need?"

Sussie pointed at two of the big, dark bags in the van and said, "That one, and that one too."

Hugo and Mikko each took a bag and dragged them out into the snow. Hugo opened his, pulled out an iPad, and gave it to Sussie.

"Thanks."

Mikko and Hugo worked fast, putting the different components together under Sussie's direction. After three minutes, it was done. Sussie took a step back and nodded contently.

"There you go, looks good. Now I'll just need to run a couple of diagnostic programs so we know everything's okay before we start."

While Sussie was working on that, Hugo took out a pair of powerful zoom binoculars and went up to the tree line. There, he surveyed their target and saw a couple of dark figures moving along the fence. Despite the cold, Hugo felt warm inside. He'd done this many times before. With all the missions he'd performed, all the people he had liquidated during the secret assignments, he'd become something of a legend in military intelligence circles.

But this mission was different. The other times, he'd been sanctioned for use of deadly force, and that was a clearance he didn't have now. Madeleine had been quite explicit on that point— no lethal violence, except in self-defense.

He lowered the binoculars and made his way back down to the others.

"We do our utmost to avoid killing anyone," he reiterated to the team. "It may make things a little more difficult, but that's the way it has to be on this mission."

Mikko pulled a weapon from his pack, checked it, and secured it in its holster. "That's nothing new for us," he replied. "We're used to working that way."

Before Hugo could answer, Sussie gave a thumbs-up.

"Okay, we're ready. Everything's working the way it should."

"Good. Let's go through the plan one more time," Hugo said.

Soon, Hugo and Freya grabbed their backpacks and weapons and headed into the dark forest toward the goal. The deep snow made the walking take longer than they'd planned, and now it was getting dark; without a word, they each activated the night-vision settings on their helmets.

Hugo checked his watch. It was twelve minutes until Sussie would be activating the next step in their quickly progressing plan. Freya motioned for them to stop, and he froze. Hugo held his breath and listened intently, but heard nothing.

Freya pointed to the right, and Hugo stared hard into the greenish darkness. Ah, there! A shadow moved. He raised his weapon with his right hand and held the binoculars to his eyes with his left.

A bear. Hugo cursed under his breath and lowered his weapon. The bear, thirty meters from where they stood, didn't seem to have discovered them—Hugo hoped so, anyway. He and Freya watched as it milled about and scratched the ground with its huge paws. The minutes crept along as the bear continued foraging, but eventually it tired of the spot and trudged on. Hugo exhaled heavily, his breath pounding the cold air like a sledgehammer.

Freya motioned to continue on. They walked for a few more minutes until they arrived at the fence. A cracked, worn metal sign was tied there, its bilingual message weather-beaten but still legible: *электрический забор. Electric Fence.*

Hugo dropped to his knees and looked through his binoculars. A lone guard was coming around the corner of the house thirty feet away. The smooth quilt of snow stretched to the edge of the cleared path that circled the house. A wider road extended away from the house toward the parked cars. Two large floodlights blared from one side of the house, but the others were dark.

Freya squatted beside Hugo and whispered, "How does it look?"

"Just as we thought. It's not abandoned, but there's not much activity, either. One of the guards just turned the corner."

Freya pulled a thin microphone down from inside her helmet. "Come in, Talisman," she murmured. "This is Hammer. Come in."

"Talisman here. Go for Hammer."

"We're in position. Surroundings look clear. Ready for step two."

"Roger, Hammer. Step two commences in sixty seconds."

Hugo raised the binoculars again and surveyed the surroundings. Everything was calm—maybe a little too calm, he thought. During his years as a special forces soldier, Hugo had acquired a highly developed sense of danger, and even though it wasn't on full alarm right now, something still felt strange.

He lowered the binoculars and was about to turn to Freya when a hazy, rumbling figure began to race toward them. Hugo turned toward the movement and saw the bear, and instinct took over. The massive animal pulsed through the spraying snow, the snarling growing louder the closer it got. It was twenty meters away now and fast approaching. Freya staggered to her feet and stared, mesmerized, at the beast. It was close enough now that they could see its silver teeth.

Hugo raised his rifle and reluctantly took aim and shot a short, muffled burst. The powerful rounds hit their target, but the bear didn't stop. Then, a second later, blood spurted from its nose. The bear staggered but continued forward. Freya threw herself aside and almost disappeared as she sank into a snowdrift. Two more shots slowed the animal down even more, but still it continued. Finally, Hugo had to leap out of the way, too.

The bear stumbled forward and collapsed against the electric fence. Its heavy body cracked the bottom strands, and four of the previously darkened floodlights around the house turned on, bathing the area in light.

*

Ilya had just closed the door, taken a glass of vodka from Leonid and downed it when the alarm went off. The blaring sound cut through the room, and all the men recoiled. Everyone's eyes turned toward the wall of video monitors. Leonid pointed.

"Look!"

On one of the screens, a section of the fence was visible and a dark shadow lay still in the middle of it. Ilya rushed over to Andrei, the tech sitting in front of the monitors.

"Can you zoom in?"

Andrei adjusted the camera and zoomed in on the dark shadow. Ilya leaned forward, squinting.

"What is that?" he asked.

Andrei zoomed to the right and pulled back. He narrowed his eyes and looked up at Ilya. "It looks like a bear."

"A bear? Why would a bear throw himself against the fence?"

"No idea," Andrei said. "Maybe something in the woods scared him, so he panicked and rushed into the fence and died."

Ilya frowned. He'd never heard of something like that happening before. Sure, half a dozen small animals—foxes, things like that—had met their creator when they'd come upon the fence, but never a bear. The blaring of the alarm continued; Ilya couldn't think with all the damn noise.

"Turn the alarm off! And send out some men to cut power to the fence so we can see what this thing looks like." He turned to Leonid and said, "Go down to Markov and tell him what happened. He doesn't need to do anything, but we should probably keep him informed."

Leonid hesitated. "Uh, do I really need to? Honestly, the boss gives me shivers. Especially down there in the basement."

Ilya frowned at Leonid and glared. "Are you kidding me? What, do you think he's going to eat you? Don't be stupid—toughen up and just do it."

Leonid pursed his lips, then spun around and walked away.

Ilya sighed, turned to Andrei, and asked, "Is the power off?"

Andrei stood, and went to the breakers on the wall, and snapped down a switch. "Is now."

"Good." Ilya pointed to two of the other men in the room. "Niktin, Orlov, take a quad drag away that bear, or whatever it is. Make sure that as little damage as possible is done to the fence. We'll fix it tomorrow, first thing. Okay?"

The rough-headed Niktin nodded and slapped Orlov, stern-faced and dull, on the arm.

"Roger. Come on, Orlov. Let's go pull a bear."

The two men trudged from the room, leaving Ilya and Andrei alone.

"Keep track of when those two idiots pull the bear away," Ilya instructed. "Given how clumsy they are, they might tear half the fence off with it."

Andrei chuckled, then dropped his smile as he saw the dark shape of the Novus team approach the fence.

*

When the floodlights came on, Hugo and Freya threw themselves to the ground. They high-crawled through the soft snow, Hugo barely noticing the cold through his pumping adrenaline.

He pulled down the microphone on his helmet. "Talisman, this is Hammer. Come in."

"Talisman here. Go for Hammer."

As Hugo opened his mouth to speak, he heard an engine start up.

"Cancel, stand by," he murmured into the mic.

"Roger."

He gestured to Freya to keep going, and they crawled along the track the bear had left as it had stormed toward them.

"Go, go," he hissed. The sound of the engine was getting closer. Hugo peered over a snowdrift at the light dancing over the whitewashed surroundings. He didn't think they had left any trace behind them, and if they were lucky, the guards would think it was only the bear's trail that they saw.

A four-wheeler swung around the corner of the house and headed toward the fence. It rumbled off the roadway and continued toward the motionless bear. Surprised voices rolled over the snow; Hugo was able to make out a few of the words.

"*Там!*" (There!)

Two men jumped off the ATV and approached the downed bear. One of them stood to the side and held a rifle while the other kicked at the motionless animal anxiously. When it didn't move, the men calmed down and started to talk to each other.

The cold began to creep into Hugo's legs, and he gently turned his head toward Freya. She was lying three meters away with her eyes fixed on the men. She gently pulled up her weapon, but Hugo shook his head.

"No. Wait."

Freya's eyes glittered, and for a moment Hugo thought she hadn't heard him. But after a couple of seconds, she lowered the weapon. They watched as the men attached a thick rope around the bear's humongous corpse. Then one of them jumped up on the four-wheeler and gunned the engine. The little vehicle struggled and the tires spun, but eventually, they found purchase and the massive animal began to slide away from the fence.

The men howled with delight, and a wave of relief rolled over Hugo.

*

No fear.

Leonid took a deep breath and knocked on the door. The sound was louder than he had intended it to be.

A dull voice answered from behind the door, "Yes?"

"Yes, Doctor, it's Leonid. I need to inform you of something. Can you please open the door?"

"Not now, we're busy."

Leonid hesitated. Most of all, he just wanted to leave—but if he did, Ilya would think he was a coward, and he couldn't stand that thought. He clenched his jaw.

"This is something you need to know, sir. Ilya sent me."

A few seconds later, the lock clicked, and a startled Markov stood inside the door. His sweaty hair was glued to his head as if it had been painted there.

"What do you want now? Can't you see we're busy?"

Leonid bowed involuntarily. "I apologize once again, Doctor, but a bear has run into the fence and died."

Markov stared blankly at Leonid and shook his head. "What do you mean?"

Leonid repeated himself, and Markov raised his hands.

"Stop. Why are you telling me this? Is this something that affects me?"

Leonid's courage sank like a stone as he feverishly sought answers. He cursed Ilya again for having sent him down here.

"I—no . . . no. It was just that Ilya wanted you to be informed in case you heard something strange." Leonid regretted what he'd said the same second it came out of his mouth. Markov's face turned bright red, and he raised his finger.

"This is incredible. I'm in the middle of a very important experiment, and you interrupt it to inform me that I should not be disturbed by a strange sound because a bear has attacked our fence. Do I have it right?"

Leonid swallowed, and his dry throat clicked. "Yes, sir," he managed.

"Out!" Markov shouted in his face. "Get out!" He slammed the door, and Leonid stumbled backward. He staggered up from the basement in a daze, fighting away idiotic tears.

*

The cold was making his legs throb. After five minutes, Hugo gave Freya a signal to continue.

"How are you feeling?" he asked her.

Freya licked her lips and said, "I'll manage."

Hugo swept over the area with the binoculars; everything was again quiet and calm. Where the bear has been, there was now a big hole in the fence. He smiled—how lucky for them.

"Talisman, this is Hammer. Come in."

"Talisman here. Go for Hammer."

"We're moving ahead. We'll try to get closer. Three minutes."

"Roger. Three minutes."

Hugo counted. It was something you learned when you went on secret assignments—a few

133

seconds could often be the difference between life and death. He motioned to Freya to follow and set off running. He and Freya pounded through the snow along the same track until they reached the hole. Figured the guards must have turned off the electricity running to it, they passed through.

Ninety seconds.

Voices carried in the wind from a distance but did not seem to be getting any closer. Hugo and Freya made their way to the wall of the house and pressed themselves against it. Thick snowdrifts extended from the corner outward. The road where the ATV had driven continued around the corner, and guard-shaped shadows crept across the ground. Hugo stared at them but exhaled as they got smaller and finally disappeared.

Sixty seconds.

He snuck up to the corner of the house and peeked cautiously around it. A lone guard stood smoking fifteen meters away. Billows of smoke swirled around him.

Hugo sensed Freya behind him and whispered, "A guard."

A few seconds later, the cigarette landed with a hiss on the ground. The guard stomped it and disappeared into the house. Once the massive wooden door had closed behind him, Hugo turned around.

"Hide."

They sank into the big snowdrifts that surrounded the house.

Ten seconds.

"Now!"

He and Freya covered their heads with their arms. Two seconds later, a deafening noise resounded through the night air.

*

The rumble echoed through the walls of the basement. Markov Tupolev froze when all the equipment in the room shook. He pulled the mask from his face and let it hang around his neck.

"What's happening?" he asked, eyes wide with uncertainty.

Abram adjusted his monitors. He rubbed his face and said, "Earthquake?"

Markov waited while the rumbling subsided. After ten seconds, everything was calm again.

"No, not an earthquake," Markov said.

Abram jerked his head from screen to screen. "Then what is it?" he asked.

Markov murmured, "It has to be something to do with the morons with the bear. They must have done something."

Abram hesitated. "Well, then . . . shall we proceed?"

Markov pulled his mask up again and turned to face the woman on the gurney. "Yes. Of course we should. When this is done, I'll talk to them."

*

The shock wave tore through the snow. Hugo knew that any second, someone would throw open the main door and come storming out. He took a deep breath. Just as he'd expected, as he exhaled, the massive door was flung open and men rushed out, yelling and screaming and looking for the source of the explosion. A fireball rose in the east, and the men pointed.

"Look at that! What is that?"

Some of the men raised their weapons.

"We're under attack!"

A man dressed in a dark uniform rushed out onto the porch. "Kolja, Niktin, Leonid. Check out what happened. We'll contact the others and get them out here."

The three men rushed off toward the still-rising fireball. When everyone had gone, Hugo and Freya crawled out of the snowdrift.

"Ready?" Hugo asked.

Freya nodded. They slunk to the door and dropped to their knees. Hugo could hear voices behind it. He held his breath—they had the element of surprise on their side, and they needed to make the most of it. The explosion would give them five minutes, maybe ten before the guards came back.

Hugo and Freya stormed into the room with weapons raised. Two men watching a wall of monitors—one seated, one standing—spun around and stared at them in amazement.

"Hands up!" Hugo shouted at them. He pointed to the seated man. "Stand up!"

Both men did as they were told.

"Check them for weapons."

Freya searched them and discovered a gun on one of them. Hugo gestured to the men to go to the other wall.

"Get down on your knees and put your hands on your head."

The men went to the wall, sat down, and reluctantly interlaced their hands on their heads. While Freya guarded them, Hugo went to the screens and scanned the displays. Most of them showed various areas outside the house. On a couple of them, Hugo could see the men who had left the house now approaching the destroyed gas tank fifty meters away. So far, the plan had worked well. Simplicity was always preferred. A couple of the monitors on the bottom rows showed a white, tiled room. Hugo sat down in the chair and drew closer.

"What do we have here?"

As he leaned in, one of the men on the ground moved suddenly as if to make a break for it.

Freya hissed at him, "Try it and I'll send you to your creator. Understood?"

Hugo wasn't sure this person actually did understand what Freya was saying, but her body language was clear enough; the guy slunk back down, glowering.

Hugo looked at the men and tapped the screen. "This is the basement, right?"

Neither of them answered, so Hugo repeated the question. Still no answer. He stood and approached the one he figured was the leader.

"What's your name?"

The man didn't move a muscle but merely glared at him. Hugo ran a hand through his hair; he was losing patience. They didn't have time for this. It had already been two full minutes since he and Freya had entered the room. It wouldn't be long before the other men came back. He detached one of his knives from his chest harness, and the glossy polished blade gleamed. Both men's eyes followed the knife in Hugo's hands.

"This is the last time I'm going to ask. What's your name?"

The man yelled, "*Blyad*!"

Hugo could only imagine what that word meant. Without giving any warning, he took three quick steps and grabbed the insolent man's ear. All it took was one hard twist to produce howling screams. Hugo lifted the knife and held the blade against the sensitive hunk of cartilage and flesh between his fingers.

"Ilya! My name is Ilya!"

Hugo eased the pressure on the ear but didn't let go. "Well, look at that. So nice of you to share."

After a few seconds, he released his grip with a shove. Sobbing, the young guard reached for his ear.

"You bastard, you tore it off!"

Hugo rolled his eyes. "No, it's still there. But that's the least of your problems now." Pointing at the monitors, he said, "Those are the lower levels, right? The basement?"

Ilya nodded shakily.

"How do we get there?"

After a nervous glance at his wide-eyed compatriot, Ilya answered, "Down the stairs and through the first door. You need an access card."

"Okay. Where's the access card?"

Ilya fumbled through his jacket pocket and pulled out a yellow card. "Here. Hold it up to the scanner and the door will open. The doctors are there."

"Four minutes," Freya spoke up.

"Good," said Hugo. He took the card from Ilya's hand and nodded his head in the direction of the captives. "See to them."

Freya retrieved a small plastic spray bottle from her pack and walked over to the kneeling men.

"What is that?" Ilya asked anxiously.

The other guard held his hands up in front of him. "No, please—we are sorry," he said dopily.

Freya lifted the bottle and pulled the trigger twice. Almost instantly, as if she'd hit them with white spray paint, all the color drained from the guards' faces. Their eyes rolled back into their sockets, and they collapsed.

Hugo placed his fingers on their jugulars. "Pulses are strong," he said. "Well done."

"Easy as taking a cookie from a kid," Freya replied.

"What?"

Freya didn't respond but headed to the door that led to the basement. "Coming?" She stepped through, followed by Hugo, and they vanished into the darkness.

*

Surprises always come when you least expect them. Xi Liu sat in the cabin of a massive military helicopter and yawned. He rubbed his eyes; when he opened them again, something out the window caught his glance. A red ball of fire was climbing into the sky on the horizon.

"What the—" Xi narrowed his eyes.

"What is it?" Sebastian, who was sitting opposite him, turned toward the window. "Holy shit. Looks like it's coming from the direction we're headed."

Xi stared at the fireball, bewitched, as it rose high above the treetops in slow motion.

Planning out this day had been a relatively simple task. Even without much time for planning, their preparations were sound. Now, this wrench—whatever it was, exactly—was messing with the agenda. Xi rubbed his hands together uneasily. The stranger he'd met in Malmö had gotten him off balance—not many people had that effect on him—and Xi had a sneaking suspicion that this man was behind the fiery explosion in the distance.

He shook his head to clear his mind, then patted the pilot on the shoulder and pointed. "That's where we're going. Put us down as fast as possible!"

14

Hugo and Freya reached the heavy metal door at the bottom of the stairs, and there was the scanner, installed on the wall next to it. Hugo held Ilya's yellow access card up to it, and the door clicked.

He lifted his eyebrows at Freya. "Ready?"

"Ready." She cocked her Desert Eagle handgun and gave a curt nod.

Hugo pushed the door open. Behind it stretched a corridor dressed in old, white tiles. A simple fluorescent bulb in the ceiling spread a sterile glow through the hallway. Another door stood further down, and they snuck up to it and took their positions. With his ear against the door, Hugo could hear weak voices but nothing that indicated their presence had been detected.

He motioned for Freya, readied his weapon, and grabbed the handle. Throwing open the door, they rushed in.

They found themselves in a room that extended deeply to the right; along one wall were two rank chairs that held two men in white coats. The next wall contained a picture window that separated the room from another, smaller one behind it, which housed a simple gurney. A woman was lying unconscious on top. Another person in a white coat—this one also wearing a medical-grade face mask and surgical gloves—stood next to her.

Then, two things happened at the same time: a piercing scream issued from the woman's lungs, and the men in the lab coats stood up brusquely.

"Hey! Who are you?" the younger, more built one shouted.

Hugo lifted his rifle and aimed it at the man's chest. Next to him, Freya trained her gun on the older man, who raised his scrawny arms over his head on instinct.

"Quiet," Hugo said.

There was a blink, then a shifty glance. Hugo shook his head.

"Don't do it. It's not worth it."

Neither of the lab techs said a word. The older one—probably in his sixties—still stood there with his hands stretched so far upward that it looked like he was trying to touch the ceiling. In the other room, the doctor went about his business. He hadn't noticed them yet.

Hugo pointed to the chairs. "Sit back down. Both of you."

The older tech plopped quickly down in his seat and hesitantly lowered his arms. The other took his time, gradually working his way down to the chair.

Hugo grabbed his radio. "Hammer here. Come in, Talisman."

"Talisman."

"Goal in sight. Three minutes."

"Roger."

The second he'd made the call, Hugo knew it was a mistake. The young tech, having not yet sat down and still in a crouch, sprang forward like a raging bull. He threw himself toward Freya.

"Doctor!" he shouted. "Look out! They're coming!"

Everything that happened next was a whirlwind. Out of the corner of his eye, Hugo saw the scientist in the other room spin around. The two locked eyes. Freya took a step aside, raised her weapon, and pistol-whipped the young man in the head. He collapsed onto the floor like a sack of potatoes.

In the other chair, the other man sat whimpering. Hugo raised his weapon again and walked to the window in the wall. The scientist faced him head-on, glowering, as Hugo tapped the glass with the end of his rifle barrel.

"Dr. Markov," he called out, motioning backward with his head. "Let's go. We're going to take a little trip."

Markov pulled his mask down so it hung around his neck.

"Who the hell are you?"

Hugo looked past the doctor at the woman on the gurney, then returned his gaze to Markov. "What are you doing there? You're hurting that woman."

Markov shook his head disdainfully. "You know nothing about what we do here! This is the future!"

"I don't know anything about that," Hugo said with a shrug. "But I do know you're coming with us."

"Never! You can't get in here. The door is locked, and I have the only key."

Hugo threw a look over his shoulder at Freya. "Will you take care of that problem, please?" he asked her.

Markov's face drained of color when Freya raised the Desert Eagle and shot the deadbolt completely off the door. His screams mixed with the violent thunder of the blast, and he threw himself down on the ground as the two black-clad figures stormed into the room and grabbed hold of him.

*

They worked fast. Hugo grabbed a pair of strong cable ties from his pack and tied Markov's hands behind his back. The Russian said nothing as they lugged him from the room, but when he stumbled and banged into the door frame, he let out a moan and dropped to his knees.

Hugo yanked him up again. "Get up! We don't have time for this."

Freya approached the woman on the gurney. Her sheet-white face was sweaty and ravaged, and she had urinated on herself. Freya flinched slightly at the sharp odor, but then came closer and stroked the hair from the traumatized woman's forehead.

"Hey, can you hear me?"

She was answered with a weak moan; the woman's eyelids fluttered but did not open. Behind Freya, Hugo held Markov in a firm grip.

"What have you done to her?" he growled.

"Nothing you could understand."

"Sure about that? Could it have something to do with control, maybe? Injections? Drugs?"

Markov closed his eyes and sighed deeply. "How do you know any of that? This is secret research."

Gently, Freya pulled one of the woman's eyelids open; even with the overhead light shining down, her pupils were enlarged.

"She's definitely drugged."

Markov swallowed hard but said nothing.

Freya turned toward him and asked, "She's drugged, isn't she?"

No answer. Hugo took a step forward and swung, hitting Markov square on the mouth. The scientist's body thudded to the ground, blood flowing from the corners of his lips.

"You were asked a question. Answer it."

Markov spat blood and a piece of a tooth onto the cold tile floor. "Yes. She has received a medical injection," he murmured.

Freya stood over him. "And what was in this so-called medical injection?"

"A combination of certain benzodiazepine drugs. For the purpose of sedation."

Freya looked at Hugo. "We can't leave her here. We just can't."

Hugo clenched his jaws. Taking the drugged woman along with them would certainly delay them and maybe even lead to their discovery. He thought through the various options, then turned to Markov.

Hugo's eyes flashed. "Give her something that will wake her up," he said. "Do it now—and if she doesn't wake up, then this will be the last thing you'll ever do."

The doctor clumsily pulled himself up by the doorframe and staggered to the metal cabinet. He removed a small, transparent bottle, then took a syringe, stuck it in the top of the bottle, and pulled the needle back.

With a furtive glance at Hugo, Markov injected the woman with the syringe and took a step back.

"There. She will wake up soon."

Not ten seconds passed before the young woman began to move. She moaned, and Freya put a hand gently against her face.

"Hey, are you awake?"

The woman opened her eyes with apparent effort, blinking several times before focusing on Freya.

She mumbled, "Who are you?"

"My name is Freya. What's your name?"

"Anna."

Hugo put his hand on Freya's shoulder and said, "Okay, new plan. We're taking Anna with us. You hold onto her, and I'll handle Markov. Okay?"

Before Freya could answer, a man roared from above them.

*

It was impressive. Mikko watched with admiration as Sussie directed the drones from the computers lined up in the back of the white van. Three additional monitors had been connected, and they flooded the van's interior in a faint greenish glow.

"Check this out," she said.

A second later, one of the drones swept down onto the roof of the villa and aimed at two men hiding behind a shed. Their bodies displayed angry red on the screen from the drone's powerful infrared camera.

"And tada!"

A thin, metallic drumming filled the air as a torrent of ammunition pummeled the shed. The targeted men threw themselves behind a tree and then took off running.

Mikko chuckled. "You control them pretty well."

"Hell yeah, I do. The issue isn't with how to control them, though; it's more about understanding how much is enough. I don't want to scare these guys away. We need to draw them to us, not push them back against Hugo and Freya."

"True."

Suddenly, there were three more men on the screen. One pointed, then they all aimed weapons and opened fire on the five drones swarming outside the villa. Mikko raised his eyebrows.

"They don't seem to be in panic mode, even though we caught them off-guard with a surprise attack." He checked his watch. "It's time, Sus. Be ready to pull them back—slowly, so they can see which direction it's coming from."

Sussie clicked her teeth. "Roger."

With expert precision, she directed the small cloud of drones toward the roof in a wide circle and emptied the last of the magazines. When the rounds were gone, she kept holding the trigger, creating a buzzing sound that sounded over the area. On the monitors, Mikko watched as guards poured out and pointed their weapons into the air. They had swallowed the bait.

"Good," he said.

Sussie steered the cloud back in a kind of controlled chaos, and Mikko opened the back door to allow access to the drones' storage chambers. Twenty-eight seconds later the first drone softly flew down and landed in its cage.

"One in. Four to go."

Cries echoed from far away as Sussie steered the remaining drones back toward the van, and Mikko thought he heard the faint sound of revving snowmobiles. Stepping out into the snow, he lifted his binoculars toward the villa—then dropped them, startled.

"We've got company, Sussie!" he shouted. He scooped up the binoculars from the ground and jumped back into the van. Pulling the door closed, he said, "Time to go. Four or five guys are heading this way, and fast. All the drones home safe and sound?"

"Yep, we're good," Sussie said.

Mikko slammed the rear doors closed. The first part of the plan was done, at least. He pulled out an emergency light, lit it, and threw it out the van window against a tree. The burning phosphorus illuminated the surroundings in a reddish gleam.

Sussie jerked her head toward him. "What the hell are you doing?"

Mikko chuckled and hopped into the driver's seat. "Giving them something to aim for," he said with a wink. Then he stepped on the accelerator.

*

They froze as the voice above them thundered again. A deep, primal scream. Hugo grabbed hold of Markov's arm and dragged him forward. Freya followed closely behind with her arm snugly around Anna. Anna, pale and weak, held on to Freya with a grip that turned her knuckles white.

This might not have been such a great idea, Hugo thought as he watched Anna stumble along. But really, it had been inevitable. Freya was never going to leave the woman behind.

Another shout, this one even louder. Whoever was doing the screaming had to have been completely mad with anger.

Hugo yanked Markov to the door, spun him around, and demanded, "Who's screaming?"

Sweat was streaming into Markov's eyes, and he rubbed at them and grimaced. "How am I supposed to know? One of the guards must have discovered you."

Freya looked at Hugo, and Markov, sensing a moment's uncertainty between them, snickered triumphantly.

"Not so victorious now, are we?"

Hugo swung a fist and hit the scientist so hard that his forehead thumped into the doorframe. Markov whimpered but said nothing more.

They were going to have to improvise. That's the kind of thing that happened during secret missions—circumstances changed, and you could either change with them or go down in flames. From further up the stairs, a door slammed open and a man stuck his head out and shouted something. Markov yelled in response, and Hugo hit him again. This time, Markov cried out in pain. Ahead, the man stepped into the stairway with a long, dark weapon.

A second later, a series of heavy bullets slammed into the door frame next to Hugo's head. He grabbed Markov's arm and threw them both backward into the lab room. They collapsed in a pile beside Freya and Anna; Markov tried to scramble to his feet, but Hugo lunged for him and pinned him down.

"Not so fast, my friend."

Markov pursed his lips and spat in Hugo's face. With the back of his arm, Hugo wiped away the bloody saliva and threw a look at Freya. She was hunched over, protecting Anna with her body. When the long salvo was finally silenced, Hugo glanced at his wristwatch—only three minutes left to get out of here. If they didn't escape, they'd be dead soon.

The gunman at the top of the stairs shouted in glee. "Stay where you are. You aren't going anywhere."

Hugo clenched his jaws. It was now or never. His pulse throbbed in his ears as adrenaline drove through his veins like a high-speed freight train. He jumped to his feet, lifted his weapon, and set off up the stairs. Flying up three steps at a time, his legs pumped like pistons.

From the top of the stairway, their assailant cried out in surprise. He raised his weapon again and pulled the trigger. A long, hazy sound echoed through the stairwell, and Hugo felt something pelt him in the shoulder and face. Still, he didn't stop advancing.

At the door less than a second later, he reached out and grabbed the barrel of the man's rifle. It burned his fingers, but he ignored the pain and yanked the weapon away. The man screamed in words Hugo didn't understand; in response, Hugo tiger-leaped forward and thrust the butt of the rifle into the man's face. A muted thud mixed with a sick crunching noise as the man's nose was crushed and he staggered backward.

Only then did Hugo stumble to the side, reaching for his shoulder. The warm wetness that met his fingers confirmed that he'd been hit. Freya shouted from the bottom of the stairs.

"Hugo? Answer me!"

Hugo took a few deep breaths and regained balance. "Yeah, I'm here," he called back. The coast is clear. Bring them up."

Markov and Anna came first, with Freya right behind them, pointing her Desert Eagle at the back of Markov's head.

When she saw Hugo leaning against the doorframe, she said, "Christ. You're hurt."

Hugo grimaced. "Yeah. Went right through the shoulder."

"Okay. When we get to the van, we'll patch you up."

A long burst of machine-gun fire exploded in the distance, and they stared at each other, wide-eyed.

"Time to go," Freya said.

Hugo looked at the time. "Forty seconds left. We definitely have to get out of here now. Take Anna; I'll take care of Markov."

"Sure you can?"

"I'm sure. Go."

The small group moved through the deserted house and, after what seemed like a lifetime, pushed themselves out through the massive door. In the distance, explosions and a long, drawn-out burst of gunfire rang out. Hugo smiled crookedly. It seemed that Mikko and Sussie had successfully given the villains something to aim for.

He pointed. "There. Let's move." He and Freya put Anna and Markov in front of them as they headed to their meeting point, and Hugo sent up a silent prayer that the plan he'd orchestrated would succeed. This was always the most sensitive part of a collaboration—the first assignment.

The seconds passed, and a cold feeling began to spread in Hugo's stomach. But when he finally heard the sound of an engine approaching, he relaxed. It was the van, with snow spraying high behind it.

"Excellent—let's move. Our ride is here."

Without coming to a stop, the white van slowed and the passenger side door slid open in front of where they stood. Hugo and Freya pushed Markov and Anna inside, then jumped in after them. In the distance came the renewed sound of shouting voices.

*

He regretted it the second he gave the order to land. Xi gripped the armrest as the helicopter pilot performed evasive maneuvers, dipping and turning sharply to escape the firestorm beneath them. Xi stood from his seat and swore as the helicopter dived, fighting to keep his composure. He got a clear look at the ground through the side window as again the pilot abruptly changed direction.

A dozen little dots below scurried around, shooting their weapons into the air toward the helicopter. The helicopter's runners hit a treetop, and Xi growled, "Get us out of here, goddammit! Now!"

The pilot said nothing but immediately changed course again. Xi turned to Miguel, who was a sickly green color but produced a wan, distorted grin that reminded Xi of a shark's mouth.

"That Russian scientist is a popular guy," Miguel said in a quivering voice.

"The men on the ground are looking for something. It looks like someone got here before us."

"You think?"

Xi shrugged. "They don't seem particularly interested in talking, do they? Shoot first and ask later. I'm thinking it isn't likely that Markov's still in his lab."

Miguel was going to reply when the pilot once again threw the helicopter in a cross turn. He sat in his seat, arms wrapped around his knees, and closed his eyes.

"So what are we going to do, then? Landing here would be pure suicide."

The hair on Xi's arms stood up. It was true. "Pilot," he said, "ascend. Take us the hell away from this nightmare."

The helicopter climbed sharply, pressing Xi back down into his seat. Ten seconds later, it leveled out, and Xi pulled a pair of heat-seeking glasses from a black box under his seat. He pulled the equipment onto his face, turned it on, and scouted the area below them. Thirteen little red ants scurried around on the ground. He lifted his gaze toward the villa in the distance.

"Take us closer."

More red-and-gold dots appeared as the helicopter approached the property. Xi counted five—and four of them were moving quickly away from the villa. He knew immediately that one of those insolent dots was the man he had met in Malmö.

Under his breath, Xi grumbled, "Now you, you moron—you're finished."

*

It's always better to get away and live to fight another day. As Mikko slammed his foot on the accelerator, Hugo's injured shoulder rammed into the edge of his seat. He moaned, and Freya grabbed hold of him.

"How is it going?"

"I'll manage."

Sussie looked up from her laptop. "What's going on? You hurt?"

Hugo nodded. "Yeah, took a round to the shoulder."

Without a wasted moment, Sussie retrieved a first aid kit from the wall of the van and tossed it to

Freya. She caught it and rifled through the contents.

"Well," she said, raising an eyebrow, "that's convenient," and pulled out a package of hemostatic gauze. With a knife, she cut a hole from the fabric around the wound, exposing Hugo's skin, then tore open the gauze pack and pressed the bandage hard against Hugo's shoulder. The color drained from Hugo's face.

"Looks like it went right through, like you thought," Freya said.

Hugo let out a sigh of relief. "Good. Give me something for the pain, and just do your best to fix it."

Freya found a bottle of disinfectant and some ibuprofen in the first aid kit. "Just ibuprofen?" she griped, shaking her head. "There's hemostatic freaking gauze, but nothing stronger than ibuprofen?" She sighed and turned to Hugo. "Hold on. You're going to feel this."

Hugo emptied his mind, swallowed the pills, and felt a vague burning sensation as Freya worked on his shoulder.

The van swung hard to the left as Mikko turned onto the snow-covered forest roads. "Hold on!" he shouted. A second later, the van took to the air, hitting an enormous pothole like a roughly constructed ramp. Hugo flew forward, almost landing on top of Freya, but she managed to hold him down. White-hot pain surged through his shoulder; Hugo clenched his jaws and endured it.

"There," Freya said after a few minutes. "Not quite like new, but it'll be good enough for now."

Before Hugo could reply, Freya pulled a thin syringe from the box and stuck it in his leg.

"I found something stronger," she said with a half-smile. "This will make you feel better."

A wave of fire streamed through his body, and his eyes glistened.

"Holy— Wow. What was that?" he asked breathlessly.

Freya blinked. "Just our special energy mix."

The van drove over another bump, and from the back seat, Anna groaned. Her skin was blanched and clammy, but otherwise, she appeared unscathed. Freya crawled over the seat back and sat down, wrapping her arms gently around the young woman.

"Easy. Take it easy. It's over now."

Anna lay in her arms and began to sob.

But through the sound of her cries, the van's engine, and the road rushing by beneath them, Hugo heard something else—a deep, rhythmic sound. He knew what it was the second he heard it.

"Helicopter," he said.

Mikko cried out, "We've got company! Again!"

A long burst of gunfire echoed through the air. Ahead of them, Hugo saw the snow being whipped up as high-caliber rounds pelted the road in front of them. A bullet went through the windshield and shattered it. Mikko screamed as a shard of glass sliced his face. He slammed the accelerator, and Hugo cursed in the crippling cold gusts that blasted through the van as they sped down the slick roadway.

*

It had been way too close. Xi hit Miguel on the shoulder.

"Jesus, not so close! Markov's in the car. We need to stop them, not kill them."

Miguel's face reddened, and he spat, "Don't you think I know that? Tell the pilot to keep the chopper still."

Xi groaned. Miguel was a brilliant mercenary; he'd have been outstanding if it weren't for that temper that tended to made him unsteady.

"Okay, now. Put a few rounds in the bridge in front of them."

Miguel aimed at a wooden bridge forty meters ahead of the van. The heavy bullets demolished the wood, and Xi smiled. That would stop them.

*

It may not have been the best time to have a chat with the manager, but Hugo put on a headset.

"Ready."

Sussie worked fast. The van was approaching a wooden bridge, and in the same second that Sussie gave thumbs-up, the bridge exploded in front of them. Massive chunks of wood trusses tore off and fell to the river below.

"Hold on!" Mikko yelled.

The voice in Hugo's ear spoke, but he couldn't make out what it said. Everything happened so fast, and adrenaline made his body perceive everything without filters: the sharp salves from the helicopter, the crashing of bullets hitting the bridge, Mikko's roaring, Anna's hysterical screaming.

A second later, the van slid onto the collapsing bridge. It listed alarmingly to the left, and Mikko pressed the accelerator to the floor.

"We're going to make it!" he shouted.

The wheels spun beneath them as the once-level bridge became a slanted incline. The icy river rushed heedlessly beneath the disintegrating structure. Finally—miraculously—the tires found purchase and the van lurched forward, clearing the threshold with a roar and leaving the destruction— and merciless helicopter—behind.

"Yes!" Hugo thundered.

The voice in his headset repeated its question. "What's happening? Who is this?"

"Hugo! It's Hugo!"

"Hugo? This is Madeleine. How's the mission going?"

Hugo gave a dry, nervous chuckle, then hashed out a quick summary of the last half hour. Madeleine listened patiently.

"You said you have Markov?"

"Yes, he's lying here on the floor of the van."

Now Madeleine chuckled. "Great job, Hugo. I knew you were the right man for us."

"Let's not get ahead of ourselves. We still have an angry helicopter chasing us, and they're not giving up. And yeah, we have Markov, but we didn't find an antidote or a scanner."

"Gotcha. Get to runway B as fast as you can. I'll see if I can arrange for a little help to be waiting for you there. And you're heading to Helsinki later?"

"Yeah. Markov's assistant is there. And the antidote and scanner. How much time do we have?"

"Before the London press conference?"

"Right."

"Twenty-two hours—a little less, actually. Make sure you get a move on."

Additional rounds screamed by, hitting the surrounding pines.

"We're doing our best," Hugo replied. "Over and out."

15

The beauty before him was stunning. The gold coins scattered across the table glittered as Klaus Horst stared at them. This was his great pride in life—his gold coin collection. All eight of them—all high-quality, some extremely rare—were strewn on a luxurious length of black velvet. Ever since Klaus was a boy, he had found peace and order in coin collecting. And the gods only knew that he needed peace and calm now when so much was at stake.

He picked up a 1920s Indian gold coin. His fingers slid over its surface, and he shivered. The phone on the desk vibrated, and he laid the coin back down on the velvet cloth.

"Yes?"

The voice on the other end crackled, cut apart, barely making it through. Klaus pushed the phone harder to his ear.

"Yes? Hello?"

"It's Xi."

"Xi? It's about time. You have something to report? Do you have Markov?"

"No, not yet. I'm pursuing him in a helicopter now."

Klaus bit his lip. "You disappoint me, Xi. I knew you weren't the best, but you came recommended. A young, up-and-coming assassin. That's what we heard, and that's why we hired you. Was it a mistake?"

"No. We have them in sight—the van Markov is in. Some people got to Markov's villa before us and took him."

"Who?"

Xi hesitated for just an instant, then said, "It's him. The man from this morning. The man who was outside Novus. Hugo."

Klaus' heart skipped a beat. "Are you sure?" he asked.

"Ninety-nine percent."

Klaus got up and started pacing the room. The thick, dark-green carpet muted his steps, and the amber lamps spread a discordantly warm glow. "Okay," he said. "Make sure you get hold of Markov. Do what you need to do. *Anything* you need to do."

Xi said something, but his voice broke up.

"What?"

"I said I talked to the pilot. We're right behind them. Trust me."

The call cut off then. Klaus stared at the silent phone, trembling. There was so much at stake here. His entire time at QuantumCorp had led up to this day. All the planning, all the hours he had spent preparing his ascent to the throne. All the humiliating missions he'd had to perform on Heidi's behalf. He walked over to his palatial desk, set the phone on its glossy surface, and sat down. He glanced over the gold coins and his feeling of content joy slowly returned.

*

The impact was hard—hard enough that Hugo groaned in pain as his shoulder bumped into the seat in front of him.

"Sorry!" Mikko steered the van with a skillful hand, and it came loose from the snowdrift it had become stuck in. The tires sprayed snow as they sped up once more. The faint rumble of the helicopter came closer, and Hugo rolled down his window and stretched out his head, searching the clouds for the approaching threat.

"There! Behind us, to the right," he shouted to the others. "About a hundred meters away."

Mikko called out, "Shit! We haven't got that far to go. We can't die now that we've almost escaped!"

Freya grabbed one of the M249 machine guns. "This might scare them off," she said. She crawled to the open window with the big rifle in one hand. She flipped the safety and stuck the barrel out through the window. In the same second, Mikko swung the opposite way. Freya fell back into the van and dropped the gun, cursing. Mikko checked the rear-view mirror.

"My fault! That was my fault!"

Freya muttered under her breath in response, then grabbed the rifle again and crawled back to the window. She tried to get a good view of the helicopter, but the pilot seemed to perceive the threat and maneuvered the chopper strategically behind the van.

"I don't see it! Mikko, do something!"

"I'll try. Hold on!"

Three seconds later, they reached a space of flat ground, and the hard-packed snow made the van slide like Bambi on ice. Freya tried in vain to get herself into a shooting position. As she fumbled, a long volley of shots from the helicopter hit the van's side door, punching softball-sized holes in it. Anna yelped, and Markov covered his head with his arms.

Hugo saw the look of determined focus on Freya's face. She was dirty and bloody, and her sweaty hair was glued to her forehead. But in her eyes, a fire burned. Some people got that way when they were placed in a life-threatening situation, and some didn't. Those others went down, but not Freya.

She grabbed hold of the doorframe and held the heavy weapon in a firm grip. "Turn right when I say so!" she called to Mikko.

"Roger!"

"Three, two, one . . . now!"

Mikko veered right, and the van slid forward. As if in slow motion, the helicopter slid forward into Freya's field of view. She lined up the sights and gently squeezed the trigger. The blast of the machine gun echoed off the metal walls of the van, and Hugo saw Freya's muscles thump as the bullets flew from the weapon.

Freya's battle cry joined in with the chaotic noise of the machine gun. A dozen bullets struck the rear of the helicopter, and a thin cloud of smoke began to spread behind it.

Sussie shouted triumphantly, "You got it! Awesome shooting!"

Freya's and Hugo's eyes met as she pulled the weapon back inside the van.

"Good shot," he said.

She winked. "No problem."

Mikko yanked the steering wheel and straightened up the van. "Nice, Freya," he called back. "Seven miles to go."

Hugo fell back into the seat, his heart pounding. He took a few deep, measured breaths until his pulse fell again. On the floor beside him, Markov lay whimpering on the floor. Hugo leaned over, grabbed his blood-stained collar, and pulled him up to sitting.

"Your discovery. Tell me about it."

Markov stared at him blankly. "What do you mean?" he stammered.

"Exactly what I said. I want to hear everything about your invention with the drug and nanobots."

Markov swallowed hard and covered his mouth. "I'm going to throw up."

"No, you're not," Hugo said flatly. "You've managed to hold it in this long—you'll be fine. The worst is over. Now tell me."

Markov pulled his trembling hand down from his face. "All right. The treatment consists of two parts. The first is an injection of a hypnotic-type sedative mixture that prepares the brain to be receptive, and that is followed by another injection of specialized nanobots that access certain selected places in the brain."

Hugo listened as Markov went on about the scientific details of his "breakthrough." The more he talked, the colder Hugo felt inside.

*

The light led their way. Mikko slowed down a little as they approached the city and traffic increased. He pointed.

"There's runway B."

They passed through a gate and swung up onto the plowed runway. A lone black car sat parked just under a hundred meters away, and as the van got closer, the car's headlights blinked three times.

From behind Mikko's seat, Hugo said, "Okay, that was the signal. Drive over there."

They approached the black car, and as they got closer, all four doors opened at once. Three men a woman stepped out and stood next to the vehicle, looking in their direction. Once the van had come to a stop, Hugo opened the door and stepped out with a groan of pain.

The woman was around fifty, gray-haired and wearing a thick, faux-fur coat. Her thin, angular face was stern, but her eyes gave off the slightest hint of warmth at the very corners. She reminded Hugo of his high school chemistry teacher.

"We heard some of you are injured, is that correct?"

"Yes. I am, for one." Hugo gestured toward the bandage on his shoulder.

"My colleague and I can treat you before you leave." The woman paused and said, "If you're interested, that is."

"I'd certainly appreciate that."

Next to the woman stood a short man in a brown cap. He cleared his throat and said, "I'm an intelligence specialist. Madeleine called and told me I needed to be here."

Hugo studied the man. He had those special qualities that make a person completely unmemorable—the kind of guy whose face you'd never recall if you passed him on the street.

He tilted his head and asked, "Intelligence specialist for whom?"

"Like I said, Madeleine called me personally."

Hugo's eyes shifted to the woman. "Who is your friend?"

She shrugged and replied, "All four of us got the same call. We didn't know each other before this; we just came here to help as best we could."

Sussie stepped out of the van and laid a hand on his good shoulder. "Madeleine tends to operate like this," she said. "People only find out the bare minimum amount of information, and only just when they need it."

Hugo frowned. It had been a while since he'd been in this world of secret operations, but he was gradually finding his rhythm. He turned to the woman in fur.

"Okay. A young woman in the van needs medical help, too. The others can do whatever it is they're supposed to do."

The woman reached into the black car and pulled out a sizeable medical bag. "Lead the way."

*

The vibrations got more and more severe; Xi knew they wouldn't make it.

"I can put her down there," the pilot said, pointing

Xi cursed. This was the second time the man named Hugo had escaped him. And not only that, but he'd also got hold of Markov. Xi clenched his fists and pounded the armrest.

Miguel was checking his gun. He lifted his eyes to Xi and said, "Calm down."

"Don't tell me to calm down!" Xi hissed. "This is the second time the damn bastard has gotten away."

Miguel shrugged. "Yeah, but we have all of QuantumCorp's resources at our disposal, right?"

"True. What's your point?"

"We already know where they're going next. The report said Markov's assistant is in Finland, so that's obviously their next destination."

Xi fell silent and Miguel continued.

"Which means they'll have to charter a plane to Finland three hundred miles away. It takes almost an hour to fly there."

"Yes, and?"

"I know a guy inside QuantumCorp's data department. They have a direct connection to all QuantumCorp's satellites in orbit around the earth. If we can get in touch with him, then we can get hold of a little more firepower than we have access to right now."

Xi's ears perked up. "What kind of firepower are you talking about?"

"I heard they have access to some high-tech stuff—microwave weapons, drones, you name it. Quite experimental. If the password Klaus gave you works in the data center, we can have a party."

Xi thought about this for a moment.

"Okay, call him."

A minute later, Miguel handed his cell phone to Xi.

"Here. His name is Raj."

Xi took the phone. "Yes, Raj? This is Xi Liu. I work for Klaus Horst and could use your help."

The voice had a distinct Indian accent. "Good for you. I know Miguel, not you. Why should I help you?"

Xi took a deep breath. "Because if you help me, you'll be rewarded. And if you don't, I'll come for you when this mission is over."

"You can't talk to me like that."

"Of course I can. I'm in the middle of a secret operation and I demand that you help me."

Raj hesitated. "Even if I could help you, you have to enter a top-secret password to get access to the classified systems. QuantumCorp may be a private company, but our security is at least as high as the military's."

Xi licked his lips and said slowly, "Code name: red aluminum adder."

Raj fell silent. "I'll be damned," he murmured.

Xi waited, listening as Raj tapped on his keyboard. Thirty seconds passed.

"What do you need help with?" he finally asked.

Xi explained in detail what he had in mind, and when he terminated the call, a wave of anticipation rolled through him.

16

The wait is always the worst part.

Hugo scouted the dark sky with his binoculars but saw nothing. For the hundredth time this evening, he touched his wounded shoulder. What the doctor had done to him earlier had worked. His pain had lessened considerably, and though he could feel the stitches tighten as he moved, it felt leagues better than it had just an hour ago.

A hand touched his other shoulder, and Hugo turned to see Mikko beside him.

"Hey, buddy. You see anything?"

"No. They should be here any time now, though."

"Trust Madeleine. If she says she'll do something, she'll do it."

"Hope you're right."

Mikko chuckled. "You're used to this kind of waiting, right? Considering everything Sussie told us about you—and what you told us yourself—you're a super-soldier. Hugo lowered the binoculars peered sideways at Mikko, trying to determine if he was making fun of him or not. He decided the question was innocent.

"No," Hugo answered. "Not at all."

"Not at all what? Not used to waiting, or not a super-soldier?"

Hugo chuckled. "Neither. I'm not a super-soldier, and I'm not used to waiting, either. All the operations we performed were sanctioned at the highest level and always planned down to the smallest detail."

Mikko chuckled. "I see. So you're accustomed to having a little more resources than we have here, then?"

Hugo scouted the dark horizon once again. There—a dim light appeared in the distance—and was approaching. He pointed. "That has to be our ride."

Mikko didn't answer when Hugo turned.

"Listen," Hugo said. "With the resources we have available now, and considering what's happened in the last ten hours, I think we're doing an outstanding job. I mean, this morning I couldn't have dreamed that I'd be here, on the run from St. Petersburg with a group elite soldiers," he paused, "and a crazy Finnish guy."

Mikko burst out laughing and thumped Hugo on the back. Hugo groaned.

"Oh, God, buddy. Sorry about that. I forgot."

Hugo held up his hand and forced a grin. "Don't worry about it. Go ahead and tell the others our ride has arrived."

Mikko hurried off, and Hugo followed the slender private airplane with the binoculars as it slid in for a landing. Powdery snow sprayed in all directions as the heavy-duty wheels connected with the runway. He pulled out his cell phone and scrolled through his contact list to Lita's name. *I really should call her*, he thought, but still he hesitated. This just didn't seem like the right place to talk to her.

Instead, he wrote a short text message and pressed send. The yellow-and-blue lacquered aircraft taxied to their position and stopped. A stairway extended, and a man with round glasses and a wide smile stepped through the door and waved.

"Hey there, team. Time to leave."

A few minutes later, the four of them were sitting in comfortable seats and the aircraft was moving to start position. Hugo's eyelids, suddenly heavy as lead, fell closed as the aircraft began to accelerate.

"Ten minutes. Just give me ten minutes," He mumbled.

Mikko watched as, in the space of five seconds, Hugo's head listed to the side and he fell deeply asleep.

*

It was like a shadow in the night, almost invisible. A few hundred kilometers away, the giant C-8 drone made a forty-five-degree turn and increased its speed. This was the latest generation Cai Hong combat drone and was packed with high-tech equipment. Less than ten minutes later, its sensors registered the target and it activated its weapons.

Its encrypted communication with the control center confirmed the commander, and the drone shifted into attack mode.

*

It started as a faint trembling. A fraction of a second later, the wing had four holes in it as powerful machine-gun rounds made contact.

Sussie yelled, "What the hell was that?"

Hugo peered out the window and saw sparks flying from the engine. The aircraft began to shake harder.

"We're hit," Hugo answered simply. Sussie stared at him uncomprehendingly.

"What? Hit?"

Hugo pressed his finger to the window. "Hit. Someone shot us. They hit the engine."

Sussie gasped and hurried to the window. A faint smell of smoke spread through the cabin.

"No, no."

"Take it easy. We're not dead yet, okay?" Hugo looked Sussie in the eyes, willing her to keep a calm head. "Go to Freya and keep an eye on Markov and

Anna. I'll get to the pilots and see what's going on. All right?"

Sussie nodded, turned, and left. The plane rolled, and Hugo grabbed the seat back in front of him. Hoisting himself up, he ran to the cockpit door and pounded on it.

"What's happening?" he shouted.

On a monitor next to the door, the pilot's face was pale and distraught. "Someone's shooting at us. Or they hit us, I think. The number two engine is damaged."

"Yeah, it's burning! You need to activate its fire extinguisher."

"The pilot, clearly in shock, squinted as he thought about this. Then he jerked his head up and nodded. "Yes! You're right about that."

Hugo pounded on the door again. "Let me in. I can help you."

A few seconds passed as the pilot talked to his colleague in the copilot's seat. Then he said, "Okay, I'll unlock the door. Stay there."

Hugo waited until he heard the lock click, then opened the door and entered the cockpit. The pilot's eyes stared at Hugo blankly. Hugo stepped closer to him and slapped him sharply on the cheek.

"Hey, wake up! Someone out there is trying to kill us. We need you right now."

Slowly, the pilot touched his fingers to his cheek. He murmured, "Yes, you're right. I'll do my best."

The gray-haired copilot turned in his seat. "Thanks for that. I've been trying for the last few minutes to get him to focus."

"No problem. How do things look?"

The pilot, still slow but with clearer eyes, went over the situation. "The number two engine is out of play. The right wing is damaged, and oil pressure is dropping. It looks like our hydraulic systems are damaged too."

"How much further to Vantaa?"

The pilot read an instrument display and replied, "Fifty kilometers."

"Will we make it?"

"I don't know. It depends."

"On what?"

The pilot issued a shuddering sigh. "On whether or not you were born under a lucky star."

Hugo chuckled. "Do your best," he said. "Let's get down to the ground in one piece. I'll run back and tell the others to get ready."

The pilot nodded, and Hugo exited the cockpit and headed back to the team.

"Everyone prepare yourselves for a crash landing," he said when he had joined them. "It's going to be a little bumpy."

Freya helped Anna with her seat belt; once she'd heard the click, she hurried over to Hugo.

"What's the news?"

"One engine is dead—damaged hydraulics. We will come down; the only question is if we'll do it in one piece."

Freya's normally unruffled demeanor momentarily slipped as her eyes widened and her mouth fell open. The plane rolled again, and Hugo reached for her. Freya instinctively grabbed hold of his hand. A slight howl sounded from somewhere far away.

"I . . . understand," she managed.

"Take care of Sussie, all right? She looks pretty stressed. And Anna, too, for that matter."

Freya snapped out of it and returned to herself. "Obviously. Are you going to help the pilots?"

"Heading there now," Hugo replied. He grabbed Freya's shoulder. "We'll make it. Trust me."

He didn't wait for an answer but spun around and sprinted back to the cockpit. There, both of the pilots were struggling with the controls. With one engine dead, they had to give full throttle to compensate. After a couple of turbulent areas, the damaged wing lost altitude and the pilots had to fight to get it back up. Hugo held on tightly to the door frame.

"How can I help, guys?"

The pilot pointed out the window. "Look for the airport—I need to keep track of the instruments."

Hugo breathed a sigh of relief at the man's focused tone. The smack he'd delivered had apparently gotten him back on the right track. Stepping forward, Hugo gripped the tops of both pilots' backrests.

"Sure thing."

The pilot carefully adjusted the course. "Thirty kilometers," he said.

The copilot intoned, "Roger."

They inched closer as the seconds ticked by.

Peering out the side window, Hugo pointed. "I see the airport! Slight right, just a few degrees."

The pilots looked up and searched for the lights.

"Roger that. Three degrees right. Reduce throttle."

"Speed: three hundred and fifty knots."

The plane rolled a couple of times, but the skilled pilots managed to straighten it out. Sweat trickled down Hugo's back as he stared at the now-brilliant runway lights. A feeling of confidence swept through him—they were going to make it.

A second later, that delusion vanished as another burst of gunfire pierced the other engine, tearing it to metal shards.

*

The light flickered in the cockpit as the power disappeared. A few seconds passed before the light blinked on again.

"What was that?" Hugo asked.

"The ramjet was activated. It generates power from the hull."

"Okay. I just got a little nervous there for a minute."

The pilot's watery blue-gray eyes turned up at him, but he said nothing in reply. After a few minutes of silence, he reported, "Five kilometers. Height: three hundred. Hold her steady. We only get one try."

The radio crackled. "Flight four-four-two. What's happening? You disappeared there for a while."

"We're coming straight in. We've lost both engines. The ramjet is activated."

"Roger. The rescue corps is ready."

"Good. We're going to need it."

The runway lights loomed clear in front of them. Hugo strapped himself to the folding seat on the wall and watched the powerful lights get gradually closer.

The pilot yelled, "Hold on! Here we go!"

A fraction of a second later, Hugo descended into darkness as he struck the back of his head against the wall of the cockpit. A thundering train of cries, roars, and chaos rushed forward and swept over him.

When he woke up, he was greeted by a throbbing headache; the pain radiated from there, spreading down over his shoulders. He was on the floor. He tried to push himself up, but his wounded shoulder wouldn't allow it.

Another minute passed as he squeezed the flickering stars from his field of view. Searing smoke singed his nose. He forced himself to crawl to the pilots' seats. Both of them were dead—one stabbed through with a metal bar from the instrument panel, one lacerated from the face all the way to the torso and covered in blood. Hugo's stomach turned, and he doubled over and vomited.

Wiping his mouth on the back of his hand, he lumbered out of the cockpit. The interior of the plane was unrecognizable, like a giant had picked up the entire planet and shaken it. Debris was everywhere. He staggered through the rubble.

"Mikko!" he called out. "Freya!"

No answer.

"Sussie!"

A woman shouted, "Hugo! We're back here!"

He climbed over broken seats, the strong odor of smoke stinging his nose and eyes. "I'm coming! Stay where you are."

When Hugo reached the small group of people he'd spent the last few tumultuous hours with,

Sussie stood up on unsteady legs and stumbled to him.

"You're alive. Thank the good God."

Hugo hugged her. "How're you guys doing?"

"Markov is unconscious. Freya and Mikko are both a little bruised, but Anna—" her voice fell silent, "she's injured."

"How serious is it?"

Mikko got up and stood next to them. "If she doesn't see a doctor within an hour or so," he said gravely, "she'll die."

The rescue sirens came closer. Hugo lifted his eyes to Mikko and said, "Sounds like your prayers have been heard."

"What should we say to them?" Mikko asked.

"To who?"

"The rescue team, of course. We were shot down. We've got this kidnapped scientist on board. We'll be arrested!"

Hugo shook his head. "Don't worry. Think about what this will looks like to them. They're only coming to save us. We'll play the role of the ignorant, panicked, rich tourists who just survived a near-death incident."

Mikko blinked. Sussie stared at Hugo.

"You're kidding, right?" she said. "Shouldn't we tell the truth?"

"Sit down. I've got a plan," Hugo replied. He talked them through his idea, and two minutes later, emergency personnel rushed into what was left of the plane. One by one, they helped each of the injured passengers, loading them into the waiting ambulances.

Once inside his ambulance, Hugo sat down on the gurney for the ride to the airport hospital.

17

Klaus smiled stiffly when two of the board members' assistants passed in front of him and stopped a few feet away. They were in the hallway outside the room where the board meeting would soon take place. Klaus shook their hands.

A young man named Jack, with a hook nose and thick, square glasses, was the assistant to Donald Gold, a wealthy industrialist from Central America. Klaus had only met Jack once and remembered the weasel as a small, slippery type.

"Good to see you, Klaus. All is well, I hope?"

"Yes, thank you. So, anything new in the mining world?"

Jack snorted a laugh and slapped Klaus on the shoulder as if they were long-time pals. "Not that I can think of. Just the same endless struggle of fighting all the idiot environmentalists who are trying to shut us down. Those bastards are getting bolder and bolder by the day, I'm telling you." Jack pushed the glasses up on the bridge of his nose and went on, "The other day, they tried to storm one of our facilities. We just barely managed to chase them away."

Klaus scratched his cheek. "Yeah. I think I read about that. It was the mine that they stormed, wasn't it?"

"That's right," Jack said. Then his phone rang, and he held up a bony finger as he answered it. "Yes?"

He listened intently while Klaus watched.

"Okay, I'm on my way."

Jack grinned crookedly and slapped Klaus on the shoulder again. Klaus responded only with a stiff smile.

"Got to go," said Jack with a suddenly somber expression. "Donald needs me."

"All right. See you in there."

With that, Jack power-walked away, and Klaus pondered what this could mean. With Jack's reaction, it was probably serious. Donald Gold was one of the most powerful men in the world of mining. For the past twenty years, he had built up an empire that controlled huge wealth and had made Donald a very rich man.

But he, too, had been contacted by QuantumCorp to take a seat on its board. He'd accepted, and just like that, QuantumCorp had added another powerful member to its ranks.

Another man came barreling around the corner. When he reached Klaus, he handed him a cell phone.

"Here. There's an urgent call for you."

Klaus pulled his sizeable head back in surprise. "What? From whom?"

"I don't know. I was just told to give the phone to you as soon as possible."

A jolt of dread passed through Klaus as he took the device and held it up to his ear. "Yes?"

A raspy voice said, "This is Major Loush."

Klaus straightened up in an instant. This could not be good news. "Major Loush, what can I do for you?"

"We have a situation here that's going south real fast. Your name came up, which is why I'm contacting you."

A bead of sweat trickled down Klaus' temple. "Is that right?"

"About an hour ago," Loush continued, "one of my men in the drone department received a call from an external resource. The caller needed help taking an airplane down and communicated a level-seven code."

A cold lump spread in Klaus' stomach. *No, no, no.*

"Code name: red aluminum adder."

No!

Loush kept talking. "That code gave the green light for my man to activate all available resources to bring down the target. So he did." The major paused, then said, "But things went a little too fast. He activated a drone to shoot the plane, which crashed near an airport in Finland."

Klaus cleared his throat and tried to sound concerned, yet innocent. "Sounds very dramatic."

Loush's voice stayed even. "Yes. But when we checked the code, we learned that it belonged to the board member Heidi Leibowitz. As you are her assistant, I'm calling you to confirm that this was a sanctioned attack."

Klaus licked his lips and said, "Well, Mrs. Leibowitz is very busy at the moment preparing for a board meeting. I can ask her to—"

Major Loush interrupted; the calm had disappeared. "Listen up, pencil pusher. The plane crashed in Finland, and hundreds of people are on the way to the crash site. They will find out that the plane was shot down, so I need to confirm that the mission was sanctioned. Do you understand? I won't hang up until I've talked to Heidi. Is that clear?"

At that moment, a large woman entered the hallway from the bathroom. It was Heidi. Her painted lips pouted at him, and she blinked. Klaus smiled stiffly and cleared his throat again.

"Yes, well, thank you for calling. I'll let you know as soon as possible," he said and hung up.

Heidi came up to him. "Who was that? You don't look well."

"Ah, it was nothing important," Klaus said with a shrug. "Just one of the inspectors we worked with down in the mission in Cuba. Nothing serious."

Heidi took another step toward him, and he inhaled her powerful perfume. She leaned forward and whispered in his ear.

"It'll be cozy tonight. Just you and me."

Klaus forced a smile. "I can't wait."

Heidi moved her hand along his inner thigh, and he froze.

"But first," he said, "there's a board meeting. Work first. Then play."

Heidi spun around dramatically and entered the ornate meeting room, and Klaus followed behind her.

*

The silence was deafening. They stood still for several minutes while sweat ran down Klaus' back, soaking his tailored shirt. The clicking of a pair of heels echoed through the room.

The thin, white-haired woman was hunched forward as she walked, and her sharp eyes darted back and forth like a snake looking for prey.

A well-built man pulled out a chair, and the elderly woman sat down. Ten other people were seated around the oval-shaped marble table. Behind each seated board member stood his or her assistant. The hunched woman glanced over the congregation like a queen surveying her subjects.

"Good of you all to come. We have a lot to discuss tonight."

The assembled people nodded.

"But first, let's watch a video." She looked to her assistant and said, "Robbie, if you would be so kind."

The muscular man—every part of him thick and intimidating—walked to a panel on the wall and pressed a button. Hologram transmitters slid up from the table in front of each participant. Some of the members shifted uneasily, but none rose.

"There's no danger here, my friends. It's simply that a video is worth more than a thousand words. Robbie, you can start the show."

The holograms flickered. The scene showed two men in white coats working at a drill hole. A mining machine was hoisting something from under the ground, and the researchers were collecting it. They packed each item meticulously and made careful notes.

"This is from a rural area in Siberia," the old woman told them, "near our gold mines there. These researchers are environmental inspectors from Russia, and they document the levels of exhaust and pollution."

The hologram's display morphed to show a group of scientists going down into a deep hole below a mountain. The camera followed the researchers as they went further and further down, scraping soil samples from the walls of the hole.

"And this is from Chile, near our molybdenum mines. It's the same thing there—a group of researchers analyzes everything we do in the smallest detail. Not only that, but over the last two weeks, this kind of activity has increased daily. And it's not a coincidence. No, mark my words. We are being attacked!"

A thin-haired man from Canada cleared his throat. "But Madame Dinkel, can we be sure of that? Who would be so stupid as to attack us?"

Nova Dinkel spat, "Who do you think? Techyx, of course! They're the only ones who have the resources for something like this. This is a collective attack that they have launched to weaken us. They know they can't beat us directly, so they're trying to attack our resources, to hit us where it hurts the most."

Klaus' heart pounded. This was going exactly as he'd hoped. His instinct ten days ago had been right. He'd received a collection of reports describing the exact results Nova was showing them now—local environmental inspectors were suddenly acting much more aggressively, initiating raids to obtain evidence. Klaus had read reports like this before, and although each one was centered on a different localized problem, he knew they were symptoms of the same disease: Techyx.

This multinational company with huge resources at their disposal fought QuantumCorp in several arenas; the ceasefire last year between the two companies had been fragile at best. Techyx had also changed leadership a few months ago, and the new guy seemed intent on making his name known.

Nova pounded the table with her aged fist so hard that the people closest to her recoiled.

"And what should we do about it?" she asked. "Should we let those bastards do as they please without defending ourselves?"

Another drop of sweat ran down the center of Klaus' forehead. It was now or never. He swallowed hard and approached Heidi's chair. She twisted around in surprise.

"What are you doing?" she whispered. "Go back to your place."

Klaus pulled his lips back in a shark-like smile and replied, "Shut up."

Heidi's lips parted in shock.

Nova raised an eyebrow. "Mr. Horst, is there something you want to share with us?"

Klaus straightened and took a deep breath. This was his moment. "Yes, Madame Dinkel, I would like to offer my services. Let me explain."

Everyone's eyes were locked on Klaus.

REVENGE

18

The flashing lights were easy to spot even so far away. Hugo walked to the window and surveyed his surroundings.

The hospital building, tall and modern in its construction, extended to the right. Thick snowflakes fell, creating a thin blanket on the ground. Hugo's body, bruised in multiple places from the crash, ached dully.

A voice spoke from behind him, and he turned, clasping his hands together to conceal how much they trembled. He looked at the group. Mikko, seated on the hospital bed, took hold of the frame for support and stood up. He stretched and groaned.

"I'm getting too old for this."

Hugo put a hand on his shoulder. "You're a tough one, I'll give you that."

"You are too," Mikko chuckled. "We're all tough—and lucky."

Everyone had made it—or, almost everyone. The pilots were dead, and Anna was injured. At that moment, she was in surgery. They hadn't heard anything about her condition for more than an hour.

Freya walked over to Sussie, who was standing with her arms crossed, looking out at the distant twinkling lights.

"They'll see that we were shot down," Freya said dully. She turned to the others. "We won't be allowed to leave tonight."

Hugo thought of his brother, who was hovering between life and death at the hospital in Malmö. It was crazy how much had happened since that catastrophe. He shook his head. They had less than eighteen hours left before the planned attack.

"We haven't come this far just to give up now, right? he asked the team.

With a nod of her head, Sussie indicated the two policemen standing outside the door. "What about them?" she asked. "How do you suggest we get past them?"

Hugo's eyes flicked to Mikko. "I'm working on that."

"Okay, well, you'd better hurry," said Sussie. "If we already have a police guard, I can only imagine what it's going to be like when they figure out the plane was shot down. Then the cops will really pour in here."

Hugo's mind raced; it was now or never. "Okay. Let's try this."

Hugo laid out the pitch. Twenty seconds later, Freya raised a skeptical eyebrow.

"Okay, that sounds simple enough, but you know we're going to be chased, right? By all the Finnish police, I mean."

"I know."

Mikko burst out laughing. "You're one crazy cat—must run in the family. I say we do it."

Sussie agreed. "Yep. We have no choice."

Hugo looked to his left. "Freya?"

She shrugged and said, "We've come this far. We can't stop now."

*

She screamed as she fell to the ground. The guards rushed to look through the small square of glass and saw the woman lying lifelessly on the cold, white tiles. They pushed open the door and rushed in, and that's when Mikko and Hugo jumped from their positions.

Mikko's fist hit home, and the first guard went down. He blew on his knuckles with a pained grimace and cried, "Lord, I haven't punched a person in a long time!"

Hugo struck the back of the other guard's head, and as if a light had been flipped off, the man collapsed. Sussie got up from the floor and brushed herself off. The coast was clear—at least for a few minutes.

"Okay, come on. Let's get our gear," Hugo said.

The corridor outside was empty of people. Mikko and Freya slipped into the room next door, where their rescued equipment sat. It smelled of smoke, filling the small room with the noxious odor. Hugo and Sussie popped into the room next.

Freya moaned when she saw the meager three bags. "Is that all they got?"

"We'll make do," said Hugo. "Grab them. We'll head down to the parking lot and take one of the cars."

They moved quickly. Hugo's heartbeat pounded in his ears as the four of them ran down the stairs and stepped out into a bitingly cold evening. Snow swirled around them.

Hugo looked left and right. In the corner, a jet-black van was parked. A Peugeot. He looked at Mikko with a grin. "What do you say?"

Mikko's smile widened. "I think that'll work just fine. I love French cars." He rushed to the sleek vehicle and began to pick the lock. In a matter of seconds, there was a click and he shouted, "Come on!"

Swiftly, the team loaded the equipment that remained, and Freya jumped into the passenger seat next to Mikko. Hugo climbed into the middle row with Sussie. Mikko started the engine, and they started moving.

"That was surprisingly easy," said Mikko.

Hugo looked at Sussie. She was still shaken.

"Hey, you," he said.

"Yeah?"

"Can you call Madeleine? Give her an update on what happened?"

Sussie nodded. "Sure."

Sussie pulled an iPad out of one bag and turned it on. Her fingers worked like lightning, and after forty seconds Madeleine's face slid forward.

"Sussie! Hugo!"

Hugo took the tablet and asked, "Hey Madeleine, how's Felix?"

The words came so fast that he couldn't control himself. When his brother's name exited his mouth, it was like a floodgate within him was released. Tears ran down his cheeks.

Madeleine's mouth tensed. "He came out of surgery three hours ago. He's seriously injured, but he's hanging on."

"But is he alive, right?"

Madeleine's forehead wrinkled. "Yes," she said, "he's alive, but he's still in danger. He lost a lot of blood. The next twenty-four hours will be crucial."

Hugo tried to process Madeleine's words. Sussie, realizing he needed a minute to think, took the iPad back and said, "We're in Finland."

"Already? That was fast."

Sussie summarized the last six hours, and Madeleine whistled. "You've been busy."

"You can't even imagine. We're here to look for Markov's assistant. We had Markov, but he was injured in the crash, so they've got him in the hospital. If we're going to prevent the attack tomorrow, we have to find the antidote and the scanner. Otherwise, we're smoked."

"Okay. Do everything in your power to get there, and then get to London. There are seventeen hours left. And don't worry about the police—I'll take care of it."

Hugo leaned forward. "We will do everything we can. We're not giving up. Please keep an eye on my brother."

Madeleine gave a thumbs-up. "We'll do everything we can, Hugo."

Before Hugo could answer, the windshield of the van exploded in a sea of tiny shards.

*

Two hundred meters above them, a dark drone made a wide turn. Its advanced cameras scanned the area. It was airborne, but it was on borrowed time. The airspace above airports wasn't open for drones, but Xi didn't care.

He had to take down Hugo and his team. He *had* to. It was that simple. Xi wanted to be the best mercenary in the world, and you didn't become that by giving up.

Xi sat in a state-of-the-art aircraft at three thousand feet and looked at the monitor in front of him. The dark drone above the airport streamed live pictures as it approached the target.

"One more time. Shoot them."

A cold, measured voice answered, "Roger. Attack formation Delta."

The drone accelerated and moved into position. Its cameras automatically homed in on the black Peugeot driving along the fence that surrounded the airport. The van's headlights made it easy for the drone to follow. The sensors adjusted downward, and it sent a command to its controller.

The cold voice came back to Xi, "Approved to open fire?"

Xi pounded the table. "Yes! Shoot!"

A second later, the drone unleashed hell.

*

They were stuck. Mikko roared, "We have no more road!"

Hugo stuck his head out of the shattered side window, the frigid wind tearing at his hair. He turned his head, trying to see what was shooting at them. Finally, he saw it—a massive, dark shadow glided across the sky, and a faint growling bellowed through the air.

"Jesus. Whatever it is, it's big."

Seeing the look on Hugo's face as he settled back into the van, she said, "What is it? A helicopter? A drone?"

"Looks like a drone. A really advanced drone."

Mikko shouted again. "Fifty meters! There's no more left!"

Hugo crawled forward and squatted next to the driver's seat. The dark road was indeed about to end. A gate marking the exit was closed, and an armed guard stared at the approaching vehicle. Hugo pointed.

"There. Break through the gate and get us out on the rural roads, away from buildings. We need to neutralize the drone that's following us before we do anything else."

Mikko nodded once and gripped the wheel so tightly that his knuckles became white marbles. Freya crawled into the footwell.

"Hold on!"

A few seconds later, the Peugeot slammed through the tall metal gate, which was thrown off its hinges and flew ten meters into the air. The deafening bang disoriented Hugo; he looked up and saw Mikko struggling with the wheel.

"We did it! Holy shit, we did it!" Mikko cried.

"Well done, Mikko."

Another long burst of bullets screamed across the sky and churned up hundreds of tiny clouds as they hit the ground. Mikko swerved wildly, nearly ramming into a tree, but he managed to correct the course and keep it upright.

"Careful!" shouted Sussie.

Hugo went back to Freya and asked her, "Do we have anything we can use?"

Freya chuckled. "We have an M249 left in that bag—it's powerful enough to shoot down any drone." She pointed to one of the heavy fabric bags. Hugo ripped it open and pulled out the powerful machine gun. As he secured it, Mikko made another turn and Hugo fell into Sussie's lap.

"Hey!" Sussie pushed him back up. "Watch that thing!"

"Thanks for the assistance."

"Any time. Now what?" she asked.

"Open the back doors," Hugo instructed. "Make sure they stay open."

Sussie's eyes grew wide as saucers it dawned on her what he was going to do. They crawled over the seats to the back door.

"Ready," Sussie said and gripped the handles.

Hugo took a deep breath. "Okay, on three. One, two, three!"

She pushed hard on the door and it flew open. Hugo raised the gun as he scanned the skies for the target. He saw nothing. The van veered right, and the door slammed shut in his face.

"Come on! Keep it open for me!"

Sussie kicked the door and it flew open again. Once more, Hugo looked out and up, studying the darkness. Aha! There it was. The inky shadow in the sky was gigantic and growing bigger by the second as it quickly approached.

Sussie whispered, "Oh my God."

Despite everything happening around him, a calm settled on Hugo. It all became external to his sense of inner peace—the roaring wind in his hair, the dizzying snow that made his fingers numb.

He whispered, "Closer, closer." Finally, he exhaled slowly and squeezed the trigger, filling the van with deafening noise.

19

He slammed the screen so hard that the folding table rattled.

"Damn it!"

Miguel put his hand on Xi's shoulder. "Hey, take it easy."

Xi slapped his hand, and Miguel yanked it back.

"Shut up!" Xi spat.

Miguel didn't answer, but just rubbed his hand where he had been struck. That reaction hadn't happened before. Xi could be verbally tough—even cruel—but he had never slapped him.

Xi's eyes flashed, and he screamed, "That bastard, why can't he just die?" He knew he had to call Klaus. He'd promised to update him when he was approaching Finland. He was running out of time, and given how resilient Hugo had turned out to be, it all started to grind on Xi's nerves. He pulled his hand over his face and rose.

The plane rocked in the sky as it began its approach, and he stumbled. Miguel reached his hand out automatically, and Xi grabbed it.

"Thanks," he mumbled.

"Yeah, don't worry about it," Miguel answered sullenly.

Xi pulled a cell phone out of his pocket and stared at Miguel. "I have to report to the boss. Go back to the others and make sure they're ready.

After we land, it's full speed ahead to this Aino Salo woman."

"Roger." Miguel turned to go, but Xi reached out and grabbed his arm.

"We're going to finish this now. Okay?"

Miguel clenched his jaws. "You bet."

"Good."

Miguel went to the back of the plane and sat down with the others. When he was gone, Xi took a few deep breaths and felt a calm return to him once more. Then he dialed the number and raised the phone. It rang three times.

"Hello?"

"It's me."

"Yes?"

"It didn't work. They shot down the drone and managed to escape."

"You can't be serious."

"I am. They left the airport in a black Peugeot van—it looks like they were heading straight for the Finnish scientist."

"For Christ's sake," Klaus cursed, "this is the second time you've failed today. I thought you were a rising star, but I'm starting to think I made a mistake betting on you."

"It's not me, Klaus, it's that damn Hugo. He's good—much more skillful than we thought. And Markov was injured in the crash. I was told he was in for surgery, so it looks like it just Hugo and his team again."

"This is your last chance, Xi. Get the Finnish scientist and the antidote. Crush Hugo; do it now!"

The call ended, and Xi frowned. A drop of cold sweat slid down his temple. This was a new feeling for him—failure. It had never happened to him before, and certainly not twice the same day. He felt dizzy.

*

The discomfort came in waves. Each time they hit a pothole, Hugo grunted in pain. His wounded shoulder had taken a hell of a beating when he'd shot down the drone, and now, he was paying the price. Sussie crawled to the seat next to him holding a first aid kit.

"Well, here we are again."

Hugo forced a smile. "Lucky me."

Sussie rebandaged Hugo, then stuck a syringe into his shoulder. "This'll help with the pain."

"Thanks."

He leaned back and closed his eyes as the painkiller made its way through his veins. After a few minutes, that warm feeling spread inside, and the pain receded into a faraway place in his mind.

Driving along the deserted country road. "It's not far now," he called back.

Freya glanced out of the passenger window. "Midnight. They'll be asleep when we get there."

Hugo answered without opening his eyes, "Probably so. We can use that to our advantage."

"How are we going to do it this time?" Freya asked.

Mikko chuckled as they passed a huge lumber truck. "Hugo, my man!" he said. "You have a plan, right?"

Hugo opened his eyes and sat up. "Yeah—sort of. It's been a while since I did this."

Mikko slapped his knee. "I knew it!"

Sussie handed a laptop to Hugo. "Here, take a look."

Hugo opened it and set it on his lap. A pdf file sat open on the screen; at the top was the image of a round-faced woman with her hair pulled back into a bun at the base of her neck. Under her no-nonsense eyes were dark rings that gave her an anemic look.

"Aino Salo, forty-seven. Married. No kids. Researcher at the semi-state-owned lab Microdigital, which specializes in nanotechnology."

Hugo scanned the additional personal information about the Finnish researcher.

"But she has a secret," Sussie went on. "She's addicted to gambling. It's gotten her in trouble—she owes some very bad people a lot of money. That's what Markov took advantage of. That's how he got her to work on the nanobots he needed for his treatment."

Freya mumbled, "Not very chivalric of him."

"No. Chivalry isn't exactly Markov's bag. So, when we go in, we're careful, okay? No deadly violence. We take her, make her open up the lab for us, get the antidote and the scanner, and get the hell out."

Everyone in the car nodded in agreement.

"Roger that," Hugo said.

They continued toward the town center. Aino lived in the central part of Helsinki, and her workplace was close to her home. Hugo leaned back.

"Just give me a few minutes."

He closed his eyes, and Sussie made eye contact with Freya. They watched each other as the streetlights flicked by.

*

She didn't know what woke her. Aino Salo sat up in bed in her luxury apartment. Beside her, her husband Pekka slept heavily. Aino peered out the window. The snowstorm had picked up again, and the drifts swirled around outside, making her bed feel twice as cozy and warm.

She glanced at Pekka and contemplated going back to sleep, but she knew she'd only lie there at this point.

"Shit," she whispered. It had been like this for the past few months. She kept waking up earlier and earlier. This time, it was just after midnight. She slid gently off the bed, pulled the robe from her chair, and wrapped it around her body.

As she exited the bedroom, she closed the door lightly. In the kitchen, Aino turned on the kettle. A cup of tea sometimes helped, but deep down, she knew better. This particular waking moment had to do with her conscience. For the past month, she had been forced to work with that bastard Markov Tupolev.

The Russian researcher had tried to work out a collaboration with her a few times in recent years, but she had always deflected. At first, his interest had been flattering, but soon it had all turned nasty.

She had managed to hold him at bay, but then he'd found out her secret. How he'd done it she didn't know, and it didn't matter, either. Not now.

The kettle clicked, and she poured the boiling water over a tea bag. She added a teaspoon of honey, then leaned against the counter. If nothing else, the warm beverage at least gave her some relief as she stared into the whirling snowstorm.

*

Far below, the mangled Peugeot came to a stop. Heavy snowflakes settled on the hood, melting in seconds from the rising heat of the engine. Mikko checked his watch; it was half-past twelve. The pale glow of the streetlights glittered across the snow-covered ground, and the traffic lights silently and rhythmically alternated between *stop* and *go*. He leaned against the side door and looked up.

"We're here."

Hugo gingerly raised and lowered his shoulders as he pulled himself up into a sitting position. His wounded shoulder throbbed. "Get ready, people," he said.

With quiet efficiency, everyone in the van went through his or her equipment. They would take no firearms. The information available to them indicated that Aino had been forced into this. Hugo patted the two knives against his chest.

"We don't know how far behind us Xi is, so we need this mission to go fast. In and out, no frills. We enter through the main door, go up the elevator, and secure Aino. If her husband is there, we neutralize him. Then Aino takes us down to the lab, where we collect the antidote and scanner. Any questions?"

Sussie, Mikko, and Freya shook their heads. Soon, they were standing on the sidewalk in the freezing midnight air. They made their way to the main door; twenty buttons filled the surface of the control panel on the wall.

Mikko reached over and slid his hand down them all. A few seconds passed before three, then four, voices started talking. Then the lock clicked, and Sussie pulled the door open.

"Excellent."

They entered the beautiful hall, where a large crystal chandelier spread a pleasant glow around the space. The sound of their coarse boots echoed off the marble walls as they walked to the elevator. When the doors slid aside, they piled inside, and Hugo pressed the top button.

Mikko's smile widened. "This is going according to plan so far," he said gleefully.

Hugo took a deep breath, preparing to carry out the next step. The elevator came to a stop, and as they exited, he pointed down the hallway.

"There it is. Seven-A."

Freya and Mikko took up position on either side of the door, and Hugo placed his ear against it. He listened for two full minutes but heard nothing. Sussie stood by the elevator, and when the doors slid closed again and the elevator car disappeared, she froze.

"Come on now. Move," she whispered.

Hugo cast his eyes to Mikko, then to Freya. They nodded—they were ready. Hugo took out a lockpick gun and drove it into the lock. It was a particularly advanced type, one that could normally only be obtained by police. He pulled the trigger, and the lock clicked. Gently, he took hold of the handle and pushed the door open.

*

Aino tensed. The sound from the hall was muted but certain—the lock. She knew that sound. It had been disengaged. Aino lowered the teacup silently. She barely dared to breathe. With her heart pounding in her ears, she stared into the hall but saw nothing. The faint lamp was on, but she saw no movement. Had she imagined the sound?

No. She had heard it clearly. The hair on her arms stood up as the silent seconds passed. Then came another sound—the door. It had opened. Her pulse quickened as time seemed to slow down. Everything felt so surreal, like a dream. Inch by inch, Aino stood up.

The floor was cold under her feet. Tiptoeing around the kitchen island, she peeked into the bedroom. Pekka was in there, still sleeping.

A shadow fluttered past in the hall, and she turned her head sharply at the movement. Someone was there. Another shadow flicked by—there was more than one "someone" in her house.

Aino listened to them shuffle through the corridor. No one was speaking, but she could feel their presence. Feel their intrusion. She took two more steps toward the bedroom and stopped cold. A woman stood before her in the hallway, looking straight at her. A strong-looking woman. Aino barely dared to breathe. They stared at each other for what felt like an eternity before another shape appeared behind the female intruder. This one was a man—tall and fit. Both of them looked like soldiers, though they didn't appear to be armed.

Aino dug deep for courage and whispered, "Who are you? What do you want?"

The woman held up her palms, but Aino flinched, spun around, and ran toward the bedroom. A voice called out behind her to stop, and Aino heard rapid steps. She careened through the bedroom door and threw it shut behind her.

"Pekka! Someone's in the house!"

Pekka jolted upright just as the dark shadows swept into the bedroom. Aino screamed in terror.

*

The snow sprayed like a geyser as the heavy Mercedes hit the curve in the road too quickly.

"Careful!" Xi howled.

The driver skillfully straightened the car and stepped on the accelerator, and the powerful engine thundered. Behind them, two more black Mercedes came up fast. The short convoy sped up even more as it barreled along the outer edges of Helsinki. There was almost no traffic at this time of the day, so they could floor it with no trouble.

"Miguel, give me a status."

In the back seat, Miguel worked on a black tablet. "It looks like Hugo and his team have already gotten to Aino," he said.

"What? Already? How the hell did they manage that?"

Miguel shrugged and took hold of the grab handle as the car turned another sharp corner at speed. "I don't know," he said. "The surveillance cameras only stream real-time video. I don't have access to any of their backup systems."

Xi turned around. "Is that something you can fix?"

"Not from here. Not when we're mobile."

Xi swore. This mission had gone from simple to nightmarish. He hadn't expected this resistance, this Hugo interference. Xi hadn't slept for nearly thirty hours, and he was beginning to feel the effects of the deprivation. He was getting sloppy; he could feel his mind struggling to cope.

He took a small, round jar from his bag, shook out a couple of pills, and dry-swallowed them. He offered some to Miguel, who accepted.

"Thanks."

"How much further?"

"Almost seven miles."

Xi shook his head to clear his thoughts. "Okay, Tom," he said to the driver. "Full speed now, and no mistakes. We've had enough of them today." Then he lifted the radio to his mouth and said, "Jack, come in."

The radio crackled. "Jack here," the man answered from the last car in the convoy.

"Seven miles to go, so get ready. When we get there, we enter with full force. Kill everyone."

"Everyone? What about the researcher? Shouldn't we keep her alive?"

"No," Xi said coldly. "Kill everyone."

*

The fear exuding from the husband and wife was so dense, Hugo could almost touch it. Aino's eyes were as big as saucers. Hugo held up his hands to calm her.

"Take it easy. I know you're scared, but we aren't here to hurt you. We aren't going to do anything to either of you. See? We aren't even armed."

Pekka sat next to Aino with his arm around her. "What the hell is this?" he sputtered. "You've broken in. Who do you think you are? You'll never get away with this."

Hugo sighed. This was going to take some time, and time was something they didn't have. He had no idea how far behind them Xi was, but it probably wasn't that far. They needed to persuade Aino as quickly as possible.

"Okay. Look, I realize this may be confusing, but I'm telling the truth. We aren't going to do anything to you. We just need Aino to help us with one thing, and when that's done, we'll get out of here. There won't be a problem."

Pekka hissed, "No problem? I'll make sure you have a problem, you bastard."

Mikko, who had been standing next door, took a big step forward and yelled in Finnish as he stuck a finger in Pekka's face. *"Ole varastossa*, idiot!" (*Now shut up, idiot!*)

Pekka froze. Mikko continued in a slightly calmer tone.

"We don't have time for this. A group of assassins is on their way here right now, and they're not as understanding as we are."

Aino gasped. "Assassins? Coming here? What are you talking about?"

Hugo pulled up a chair and sat opposite the terrified couple. This wouldn't work if he didn't take the time for at least a little explanation. He spoke evenly but quickly, and two minutes later, he leaned back.

"You understand now? It's not you that we're after. It's the antidote and the scanner you keep in your lab."

Pekka leaned against Aino and whispered in her ear. The seconds ticked by. Hugo noticed Aino's hands begin to tremble.

"Okay," she said at last. "We'll do it—we'll take you to the lab and give you what you want. But you have to promise you'll let us go after that."

Hugo smiled. "You have my word."

Aino searched Hugo's face for signs of deception but found none. She nodded. "Let me put on some clothes, and I'll take you down."

Hugo motioned to Sussie and Freya. "Stay with her," he instructed. "Mikko and I will be with Pekka in the living room." He turned to Pekka and said, "Get dressed. It's cold outside."

Two minutes later, they all stood together in the living room. Aino had put on a pair of jeans and a thick sweater, and as she pulled on her jacket, she tensed.

"Wait."

"What?" Hugo said.

Aino rushed into the kitchen, and Hugo ran after her. She grabbed a gold-colored access card from the island. "Don't want to forget this," she said nervously.

Hugo thought through the next steps. It was two hundred meters to the lab. They would head down in the elevator, hop into the van, and drive there. Then, Aino would let them in. And then—

He interrupted himself. *Slow down, Hugo. One thing at a time.*

He clapped his hands together once. "Okay. Good. We're leaving. Let's head to the elevator."

Silently, the team and the anxious couple walked down the hall and onto the elevator. At the bottom, they stepped out into the great hall. The snowfall had increased in the last fifteen minutes, and a two-inch layer of snow had already covered the van. A plow truck, its lights flashing, drove past them and disappeared.

"All right," Hugo said. "Out here, we're exposed. Get in the van, and we'll drive to the lab." He turned. "And Aino, when we get there, it's your job to get us in as fast as possible. Got it?"

Aino pulled her jacket tighter and reached for Pekka. "Yes. Of course."

Mikko opened the door, and they headed out into the snow. Hugo opened the side door for Aino and Pekka as Mikko and Freya climbed in front. As Hugo was opening the other passenger door, a black Mercedes blared around the corner. A man leaned out the window with a semiautomatic rifle and started shooting. The rounds slammed into the door of the Peugeot, and Hugo threw himself down.

20

Everything around him slowed. The snowflakes descended so unhurriedly, it seemed they were suspended in the air. When the seventh bullet blasted the passenger door, Hugo hit the ground and rolled. He scrambled up to a half-seated position and saw two more black cars following the first one.

That's him! Hugo thought. He bared his teeth and kicked the passenger door shut. "Move!" he shouted at Mikko.

Mikko stepped on the accelerator, and the wheels spun. Snow shot up behind the van as it accelerated, and Mikko pulled hard on the wheel. The Peugeot made a U-turn, speeding around cars stopped at a traffic light.

Two more assailants stuck their heads out of side windows and began shooting. Hugo ran to close the wooden gate the van had left through—it didn't provide much protection, but it had to be better than nothing.

Hugo was more or less unarmed; all he had were the knives, and they wouldn't be much help here—not against three moving cars packed with armed men. He could only watch as Mikko accelerated. The large, damaged vehicle was too slow. It would just be a matter of time before the rest of the team was caught and killed. He pulled his body closer to the wall to avoid a fresh hail of bullets.

To his surprise, the van turned tightly again, and instead of attempting to escape, it headed straight for the three Mercedes.

"No! What are you doing?" Hugo shouted.

But Mikko couldn't hear him—that, or he ignored him; either way, it didn't matter. The van placed itself in the middle of the roadway and accelerated. The passenger side window opened and Freya stuck herself halfway out. She looked at Hugo, threw something toward him, and retreated into the van. The next second, she was hanging out the window again. The fronts of the cars were just thirty meters away now, with the distance closing rapidly.

Freya flung a dark object at the oncoming cars just before the Peugeot pulled a sharp right turn. Hugo threw himself toward whatever Freya had hurled at him, groping at the snow until he got hold of a pistol grip. He pulled the gun from beneath the snow and checked the magazine.

A second later, the whole world rumbled as the front of the first Mercedes exploded in a blast of fire.

*

Heat radiated through the windshield of the second car. Inside, Xi gasped at the enormous fireball in front of him.

"Jacky! No!"

Another dark object moved through the air, this time against his car.

"Grenade!" he shouted.

Miguel pulled hard on the steering wheel, and the heavy Mercedes veered right, hitting the curb square on and launching into the air. Seconds later, the car was rocked by the power of the explosion they'd barely missed.

"Shoot them!" Xi roared.

The two men in the back seat leaned out of their windows and opened fire with their machine guns. Xi watched with a mix of horror and elation as the rounds burst the tinted side windows of the black van.

It swayed as the driver tried to escape the inexorable storm of bullets. Xi passed the wreck of the first Mercedes, but there was no time to look for survivors. Narrowing his eyes, he instead turned his focus to the black Peugeot. He was able to see inside it now—a man and a woman were in the front, but it wasn't the same man he had fought before. It wasn't Hugo. Where was that son of a—

Just then, he caught sight of a shadow fluttering near the house, behind the wooden gate. It was him. Xi grinned sadistically.

"There you are, you bastard."

As soon as Xi saw him, the figure raised its arm and started shooting. Bullets slammed into the door next to Xi, and he yelled, "There, inside the gate! Take him down!"

His comrade opened fire, and Hugo threw himself back. The van swung around and sped away in the thickening snowstorm. Xi cursed. He was being forced to make a choice: Hugo or the Peugeot. Hesitation grabbed hold of him, and the van vanished into the night.

*

The thunderous noise of gunfire disappeared behind them as Mikko swung around the corner. Sirens echoed in the distance. He picked up the radio.

"Hugo, do you read me?"

The radio crackled. "Hugo here," came the breathless reply.

"We're going to continue to the lab."

"Roger. I'll hold them here as long as I can."

Freya threw a worried glance at Mikko but said nothing.

Hugo continued, "When you're finished, head to the airport as fast as possible. I'll be right behind you."

"You don't want us to come get you?"

Shots echoed from the radio, and Mikko flinched. Hugo's voice broke up with static.

"No! Don't come here! I'll go myself."

With that, the connection broke. Mikko held the radio in one hand and steered the van with the other.

Mikko looked over his shoulder at Aino. "How far?" he asked.

Aino, stiff with terror, stuttered, "To . . . to the lab?"

"Yeah, lady. The lab. How far?"

She leaned forward and pointed. "It's just over there. Three blocks away. To the left."

"Okay. Get ready."

Pekka's face was pale, but he maintained his composure. "Who was that in the cars?" he asked.

Freya checked the magazine on her rifle and answered without looking up, "Evil men. Those are the guys who are after you."

Aino closed her eyes. "Why? We haven't done anything."

"In their eyes, you're a target that must be eliminated, no matter the cost. These people are serious about killing you."

"Oh my God," Aino moaned. "What are we going to do?"

Sussie put her hand on Aino's shoulder. "Once we have the antidote and scanner, we'll head to a police station and drop you off. One of us will contact the police to explain that you need help. You'll be safe there for tonight."

Some color returned to Aino's face. "Thank you," she said, taking Sussie's hands in hers. "Thank you so much."

Sussie smiled. "Don't worry about it. One thing at a time. We're not going to let anything happen to you."

They drove the last few hundred meters to the lab. It was a modern office building that shared an entrance with a hotel. Aino leaned forward.

"Park in front, and we can go right in."

As instructed, Mikko pulled the Peugeot up to the entrance. They jumped out into the swirling snow and ran to the large glass doors, the biting cold turning their breath into streams of white vapor as they ran. Aino pulled out the gold-colored card and laid it against the scanner; the lock clicked, and Freya pulled the door open.

Once in the warmth and safety of the building, Aino led the way. She jogged to the elevator with the rest of the crew at her heels and pressed the *down* button. The readout above the elevator counted down; seven, six, five. Freya secured her weapon, and Aino and Pekka stared at her.

Freya shrugged. "You never know."

The elevator doors slid open, and once inside, Aino placed her card on another reader. She pressed the *B* button—the basement level.

"Almost there," she said, throwing a shaky grin to the others.

On the bottommost level, they made their way to a steel door. A code reader was built into the wall, and Aino placed her hand against it. There was a brief flash of green light, and a metallic voice spoke.

"Please enter code."

Aino tapped a series of numbers on the keypad below the reader, and the heavy metal door swung open.

"Slicker than snot," Mikko chuckled.

Aino hurried into the lab. "It's in the second room, in the safe." She dropped to her knees when she reached the safe, working fast to enter the code. The lock clicked, and she pulled out a compact, clear yellow bag.

"Here." Aino carefully placed the bag on a table opened it. Inside, there were three syringes filled with a gold liquid; beside the syringes was an electronic scanner the size of a mobile phone.

Aino looked at each person in turn. "This scanner looks for the unique signatures of nanobots," she explained. "It's effective up to twenty meters. And this," she paused, picking up one of the syringes, "is an antidote to neutralize the injections."

Mikko and Freya nodded at each other.

"Good. Well done," said Freya.

Before Aino could answer, the unmistakable rumbling of machine guns echoed in the distance.

*

Pain pulsated through Hugo's shoulder as he threw himself into the wall. He cried out and dropped to his knees. This shit was getting old.

He pushed the pain away from his mind. One of the Mercedes had followed the van, but the remaining one had stayed—and its passengers hadn't let up in their indiscriminate shooting.

A shard from the brick wall of the apartment building bit into his cheek, and he soon felt a trickle of blood running down his face. He had to do something—if he stayed there, he'd be dead for sure. The Mercedes made a U-turn, and the shooting temporarily stopped. Pushing himself back up, Hugo saw two men jump out of the car. One of them Hugo recognized instantly; with the dark hair that met his eyes and the narrow goatee, it was none other than the guy he'd fought this morning.

The man aimed his weapon at the wooden gate in front of Hugo and cried out, "Come out! Come out now, and your friends will live!"

Hugo checked his gun—three rounds left. He leaned forward and fired a shot through the slats, and instantly, the others dropped to their knees and began throwing lead in return.

There was a break in the shooting, and the man bellowed again, "It's over! Come on out, Hugo!"

Wailing sirens were growing louder; it wouldn't be long before the police were here. Hugo had to get out of there. Someone inside the Mercedes shouted something he didn't perceive.

The dark-haired man answered, "Wait. We have him."

Hugo glanced back at the door to the apartment building. It had been damaged from the shooting, barely hanging on with its only remaining hinge. He leaned forward again and fired another shot. His adversary screamed and dropped to his knees.

The men began shouting in unison and opened fire. The hail of ammunition blazed around Hugo's head. This wasn't going to work. He whirled around, ignoring his shoulder, and threw himself against the broken door. It fell in with a bang, and he landed on top of it. Rolling quickly, he jumped to his feet and ran into the foyer they'd passed through before.

The sirens were very close now. One of the men shouted, "We have to move!"

"Go on," came the dark-haired man's voice. "Pull back and rendezvous with the others. I'm not going to let that bastard get away this time."

Hugo glanced over his shoulder. Ten meters away, the Asian man stood in the gate wearing a wicked smile. Blood was running down his face from a gash on his forehead. Hugo slunk backward until he reached a door labeled "basement." He couldn't fight at this point; he had to flee—he had only one round left.

"You know it's over, right?" the man called out. Hugo turned to look; his opponent stood at the apartment door, staring at him wildly.

Hugo spat on the ground. "You're the one who shot my brother."

Xi moved closer. "Oh, was that your brother? The man from this morning?"

"If anyone here is going to die, it's you," Hugo said darkly.

Xi laughed. "Well, you can try. I just need to know one thing."

"What's that?"

"It made me immensely happy to kill your brother."

Anger shot through Hugo like a white-hot sword, but he held it back. Xi wanted him to make the mistake of rushing toward him. Hugo clenched his fists.

"Oh yeah, you will die, but not yet. You have to live just a little while longer."

Xi's smile faded at the tone of Hugo's voice. His eyebrows joined together in the middle in a look of murderous anger, and he raised his weapon. Xi began shooting, and at the same second, Hugo threw himself against the basement door.

*

Horror flashed in Aino's eyes.

"Lord God, they're here!"

Mikko ran to the door and cracked it open, listening. Another long streak of gunfire shook the metal slab in his hand, and someone shouted. It had to be the men from the car, and if they were here, that could only mean Hugo was dead—or, at the least, seriously injured.

He pulled the radio to his lips. "Hugo. Come in, Hugo." No answer.

Freya came up to him. "What's up?" she asked.

"He's not responding."

Freya took a deep breath. If they stayed here, they would surely be overpowered—these guys were armed to the teeth. "We need the heavy weapons in the van."

Mikko nodded, then tried to contact Hugo again. "Hugo, come in."

Still nothing. Aino and Pekka stood nervously watching the exchange from a few feet away.

"What's going on?" Aino asked.

"We've got a minor problem. We're considering the next step."

If they stayed here, they would die, so they had to move. The van was lost, so they would have to make do with what they had.

Freya spun around. "Aino, is there another way out?"

Aino stared at her for a moment before regaining composure. "Oh! Yes, over there. There's an emergency exit." Mikko slammed the lab door closed, then dragged a desk in front of it to block the way.

"Great," he said to Aino. "Show us the way."

Pekka stammered, "But—but what about the car? You said you were going to take us to the police station."

Freya grabbed the yellow bag from the table. "Not an option anymore," she said. "We'll do what we can with what we have."

Pekka started to protest, but Mikko groaned. "Quiet! Right now, just focus on surviving. We'll help you as much as we can. You can be thinking about where the closest police station is located."

Aino grabbed Pekka by the arm and spoke into his eyes, "We need to help. Pekka, listen to me. We have to do this together, okay? I can't do it myself."

Pekka looked at his wife for a long thirty seconds before answering, "Okay."

The gunshots were coming closer, and the numbers above the elevator began to count down.

"Time to run! Aino, lead the way." Aino pulled Pekka behind her, and they headed to a door on the other side of the room. They came out in a narrow hallway; above them, there glowed a green sign: emergency exit.

"This way."

They ran out the door, the gunshots behind them tearing the lab to pieces.

21

Shock waves of pain echoed through Hugo's body as he toppled down the stairs. He landed with a bang on the concrete floor, and the air was knocked out of him.

Get up!

Using every ounce of determination he could muster, he pushed himself up on his feet and looked around. He stood in a corridor that stretched both to the right and left. All he could do was guess; he chose right and started running as fast as he could.

Xi shouted from the top of the stairs. "Hugo!"

Hugo ignored him and the agony that echoed through his body with each step. Sharp fluorescent lamps along the ceiling bathed the hallway in a sterile radiance, and the damp air smelled faintly of mildew. As he ran, Hugo tried every doorknob he passed. Every one of them was locked. The corridor swerved to the right, and he followed it, pounding the concrete as fast as he could. He stumbled over his feet once, catching himself halfway to the ground.

"Mikko!" Hugo yelled into his radio. "Come in, Mikko!"

No answer.

Dammit.

Shots resounded behind him, and he jerked. Xi was shooting wildly from wherever he was in the corridor; Hugo tried to ignore it as he kept running and searching for a way out.

Finally, he saw a sign.

Parking.

He pushed the door open and found himself in a large, underground garage. About twenty parked cars stood scattered in the semi-darkness. Hugo ran, going as far as he could before he sank to his knees and hid behind a Jeep. Seconds later, the door he'd just come through was kicked open again, and Xi rushed out, weapon raised.

"Hugo!" Xi's shouts echoed through the space. "You're stuck! There's no way out!"

Hugo swallowed hard, trying feverishly to come up with a plan. Xi was barely fifteen meters away from where he hid. Lying on the ground next to Hugo was a small chunk of mortar; he picked it up, aimed, and tossed it toward a pair of parked cars on the other end of the garage. Xi spun at the sound and opened fire. The two vehicles were torn apart.

Ears ringing from the machine gun's blasts, Hugo waited and watched silently as Xi approached the decoys.

"Hugo," he yelled, "Are you there?" His face was twisted in an excited sneer as he reached the cars and began to search the area behind them. For a moment, all Hugo heard was the buzz of the ventilation system.

Then, "You fooled me, Hugo!"

Xi did an about-face and stalked back toward Hugo's hiding place. His pulse throbbed in his ears, and he tasted metal in his mouth. Carefully, he pulled a knife from the holster on his chest. It wasn't much against a machine gun, but he didn't intend to die without a fight—especially not against the man who had almost killed his brother. Hugo bared his teeth. Every muscle in his body was ready to pounce.

From somewhere nearby, a rumbling noise rose and quickly got louder. Xi turned in time to see the oncoming car headed straight for him. He opened fire, and the car's windshield shattered and collapsed inward, and the vehicle veered into a steel and concrete column. Whoever had been inside was most certainly dead.

Hugo had to do something. If he stayed there, he'd end up dead too. The world spun as Hugo got up on his feet, leaning forward to stay hidden. He shuffled further away from Xi, and when there were four cars between them, he stopped and noticed something on the ground a few feet away.

It was an old, rusty screwdriver. Hugo glanced up at Xi—good, he was looking the other way. He grabbed it, and then scanned the garage for the oldest car there. His eyes fell on an old, beat-up

Toyota. Staying light on his feet, Hugo rushed up to it and drove his left elbow into the box. He stretched inside, took hold of the handle, and opened the door. In a matter of seconds, he was inside; he drove the screwdriver into the ignition.

Come on now.

The engine began to cough. Further afield, Xi screamed, "Hugo! Are you there?"

Fast steps approached on the concrete. Hugo held the screwdriver in a death grip as the engine continued to cough. Xi came closer, shooting as he ran. The rear window burst as three bullets met their mark. Hugo swore.

"Come on!"

As if in answer, the coughing stopped and the engine came to life. Hugo threw the truck in gear, released the emergency brake, and stepped on it. Xi moved around a couple of cars and stopped, took aim, and continued to shoot. The thundering sound echoed through the garage.

Hugo swung around a concrete pillar and searched left and right for the exit. The gunman continued to pummel cars with bullets, screaming all the while.

Finally, Hugo found the exit. He held his foot down with all his might and veered up the ramp. Xi—a raging, mad dragon of a man—roared from where he stood in the garage as he emptied his magazine in the direction of Hugo's vanishing bumper.

*

The cold hit them as they pushed through the heavy door ran outside. Freya led Aino, and Pekka and Sussie came last. Gunshots echoed from the stairs as Mikko slammed the door closed again. Quickly surveying their surroundings, Mikko saw that they stood between two houses. The snow was a thick blanket on the lawns, and the snowstorm wasn't letting up. The freezing wind howled through the narrow side street.

"You guys see anything we can use to block the door?" he asked the group. They all hunted until Sussie shouted.

"Got it!" She pointed behind a dumpster; two thick planks leaned against the garbage receptacle.

"Perfect, Sus."

Together, Mikko and Sussie dragged a plank over to the door and wedged it underneath the handle. It was the best they could do—it would buy them some time, but not much. Sirens echoed off the walls of the houses, and flashing blue lights reflected in the surrounding windows. Aino looked wildly around as shots echoed from behind the closed door.

"Now what? What do we do?" she cried.

Freya, Mikko, and Sussie shared a concerned look and gave each other a nod. Time to move.

"Where's the nearest police station?" Mikko asked

Now it was Aino and Pekka who looked at each other.

"Just around the corner, I think," Pekka said uncertainly. Can we just get out of here?" Before anyone could answer, a long machine-gun blast echoed, answered with a series of single shots.

"I don't know about you, but it seems to me that the police are busy here. I don't think we should run straight into a firefight between the police and the villains."

Aino's shoulders dropped, but then she perked up again. She pointed and said, "I remember now. The police station is about ten minutes in that direction."

"Okay," Sussie said, "Then let's get there ASAP."

Together, they began to trudge through the deep snow. The going went slowly, and before they'd walked twenty meters, they were gasping for breath. A barrage of shots behind them forced them to bite the bullet and plod on.

They turned a corner and came out onto a wider street, where a massive snowplow was clearing the way for cars.

At that moment, the radio crackled. "Mikko? Come in, Mikko."

Mikko's eyes shot open wide and he grabbed the radio from his belt. "Hugo? You're alive!"

"I am indeed. Had a couple close calls, but I've managed to survive so far. Where are you?"

"We had to flee out into the open. We're on foot, headed to the police station where we can leave Aino and Pekka in safety. We're two blocks north of the lab."

"Did you get the antidote?"

"Yep. And the scanner too."

"Superb, Mikko. Good work. I'm on my way."

Mikko shook his head. "Wait, what?"

"I'm driving, heading your way."

"Where did you get a car from?" Mikko asked, but Hugo didn't answer. Seven seconds later, a Toyota approached, honking its horn. It skidded to a full stop, and Hugo threw open the passenger door.

"Get in!"

Freya and Sussie helped Aino and Pekka climb into the back seat. Mikko jumped into the passenger seat and chuckled as Hugo pushed the accelerator to the floor and the old truck began to pick up speed.

"You're one tough mofo, my friend."

Hugo grinned. "Just imagine what I'm capable of when paying off debt."

*

Xi heard the drawn-out gunfire and the following singles and cursed. This had gone awry so fast that he didn't know how to react. He lifted his radio.

"Miguel? Can you hear me?"

The radio came to life with the sound of yet another long blast.

"Xi? Is that you?"

"Yes, it's me. I'm on the north side. Where are you?"

"We're stuck with the police. I don't think we're going to get out of here." As if to prove the point, there was another long series of shots.

"Okay. Do your best. If you can't get away, then surrender. We'll come to get you later," he lied.

"Got it, Xi. Just make sure you nail that bastard."

"I will, Miguel. Good luck."

The connection was broken, and Xi shook with anger. He couldn't believe it—his team was out of play, and that damn Hugo had escaped yet again. He nearly pulled the trigger out of frustration but caught himself; he couldn't reveal his position. He took a deep breath and ran his fingers through his hair. He was alone in this now, but he could do it. He was a survivor.

Ever since he was little, he'd been a survivor. This trait had taken him a long way, all the way to becoming a top-trained assassin with missions worldwide. He reminded himself of these things and hopped on the balls of his feet a few times to pump himself up. Then he headed out into the snow.

As he pushed himself along, following the tracks of the truck Hugo had stolen, he thought of his brother Hai, who had died long ago. He thought of all the sacrifices Hai had made over the years, and the more he dwelled on the memories, the more fiercely the white-hot wrath burned within him.

He was going to have to inform Klaus about matters—and Klaus was going to go crazy. It was fully understandable and couldn't be helped. Xi sighed and pulled his cell phone from his pocket.

"Yes?"

"Klaus, it's Xi."

"Yes?" the voice repeated impatiently.

"We have some problems. We almost got hold of them, but the police showed up and our team split."

"What's the status?"

Xi mumbled, trying to find the words.

"Well?"

"Well, I'm trying to tell you, if you'd just listen." Xi let out an exasperated blast of air. "God, I don't have time for this." He regretted his words the second they came out.

Klaus answered coldly, "Continue."

"Hugo and his idiot team seem to have gotten their hands on the antidote. They're—"

"What?" roared Klaus. Xi ignored him and went on.

"They're fleeing the area by car. I'm on foot, alone. The others have been captured."

There was silence on the other end, and for a moment, Xi thought Klaus had hung up.

Then came the word, "Roger." The voice sounded clinical, robotic. It was almost more frightening to Xi than when Klaus was shouting. Silence filled the air between them again, and Xi waited, involuntarily holding his breath.

"You're dismissed."

Xi froze at the words. "I . . . I'm sorry?"

"You heard me. You are dismissed. Your assignment is canceled. Report back here at once."

Xi's heart felt like it had stopped. This had never happened to him before. Dismissed! What did that even mean? A weak sense of nausea began to spread through his guts. Report back? He was just supposed to cancel his hunt? After all that had happened? He took a couple of unsteady steps, stopped, and looked around. Silent snow swirled around his body as the walls of the surrounding houses pressed in closer to suffocate him.

*

Klaus felt sick. The conversation with Xi had been alarming—no, more than alarming. Disastrous. It was yet another failure, and this time, it was a huge one. Enough was enough. There was far too much at stake to continue like this.

He rubbed his temples. Now, more than ever, Klaus needed to keep a cool head. He hadn't slept in a long time, and the lack of sleep was starting to take its toll. He had to lie down, even if it was for just a few hours. Then he'd have the strength to take care of the second part of his plan.

He was still in a bad mood from tonight's presentation. He'd gone through his plans to the board, everything he wanted to do with Techyx. That's when Heidi realized he'd been cheating on her—professionally, anyway. But this was a venture, and he wasn't going to be an assistant for the rest of his life. Klaus would reach the top, no matter the cost. Still, despite all his preparation, he wasn't one hundred percent sure he was making the right move.

He reached his apartment—an apartment no one else knew he had. Now it was time to get rid of Heidi's shadow. Slowly, he removed his clothes and changed into a pair of velvet pajamas. The luxurious material helped him relax.

He sat on the edge of the bed and soaked in the silence.

A moment later, the door opened, and Klaus turned to stone as Heidi entered the room.

"Klaus."

He kept his face unfazed, but inside, everything turned upside down. Somehow, Heidi knew about the apartment. And like a complete idiot, he'd forgotten to lock the door.

"Heidi."

"That really wasn't a bad show performed for the board today. Very impressive."

"Thanks."

Heidi pulled off her sleek black coat and laid it over a chair, then started pacing the floor in front of him.

"You just need to know I'm not mad at you, Klaus. You are a capable man, which was why I chose you to be my assistant to begin with. You've been a big help to me for the last two years."

Klaus tried to seem unmoved. She was taking his betrayal alarmingly well.

"But," she went on, "you should also know that I'm already aware of your small, shady plans."

He shrugged. "I don't think you do, actually."

Heidi stopped pacing and stared at him, hands on her hips.

"Oh, really? I know you hired Xi Liu, a highly paid mercenary, to attack Novus in Sweden. And that you initiated a plan to use a Russian scientist's mind-control technique to launch an attack against Techyx tomorrow."

Klaus gulped, and he felt sweat begin to bead up on his forehead.

"You knew about all that?"

"Of course."

"Why didn't you say something?"

Heidi sat down next to him on the bed. "Because it's a natural development; I've always been waiting for you to do something like this. Within QuantumCorp, this is how you become initiated into the innermost circuits—by showing that you're willing to go beyond any and all boundaries to reach your goals. It's part of nature, the will to give everything, to risk everything, to achieve everything."

Klaus sat quietly as she spoke, feeling like a schoolboy who got caught cheating on a test. He shook his head.

"I can't believe you knew. How long have you known?"

Heidi shrugged. "It doesn't matter. What matters is that you've proven yourself to be made of the right material."

"But then, the board?"

"What about them? I'd already prepared them, and they played their role exceptionally well. You know this isn't the first time we've gone through something like this."

Klaus squinted, trying to grasp what she was saying, but it was so hard to wrap his head around this.

Heidi smiled, stood up, and snapped open the top buttons on her blouse. "Now you'll get your punishment."

A moment's panic rushed through him as the grin on her fleshy face.

22

He couldn't sleep. Dr. Mustafa Boon lay in bed and looked at the clock for the twentieth time. Half-past three. It was nerves, he knew that. Anxiety about tomorrow. Tomorrow, he had to be at his very best. It was a typical reaction, he knew—when you most needed sleep, that's when it most often escaped you.

He pulled the blanket off and tossed it to the end of the bed, then sat up and put his hand over his face, squeezing his weary eyes. He wasn't going to fall asleep. Might just as well accept it.

Mustafa slipped his robe on and turned on the shower. A long shower would be a lovely way to pass the time. The press conference was tomorrow—eleven in the morning at the hotel. And here he was, at the exclusive Mandarin Oriental hotel next to Hyde Park in London. Only the best was good enough, as Techyx saw it. Mustafa was one of their top researchers and, for the past three months, the head of the research group assigned the QuantumCorp abuses. Their job was to document every infraction the company committed; it was dirty work, but what QuantumCorp was doing would be politically explosive. It was of the utmost importance that everything was documented as accurately and in as much detail as possible.

He turned the channel of the hotel room TV to CNN. The end of a news summary rolled by, and when it faded away, a news anchor leaned forward over her desk.

"And, welcome to Update; I'm Olivia Karlsson. This morning, we begin with excitement in London. In recent weeks, there have been rumors of a big reveal in the corporate world. At eleven o'clock, we will be live covering a press conference at the exclusive Mandarin Oriental hotel—and who has called it?"

Karlsson paused dramatically.

"None other than Techyx, one of the most successful multinational companies in modern history, having skyrocketed among industrial firms exponentially over the past two years."

A sling whipped through Mustafa's heart. *And I'm the one to keep it that way.*

Karlsson continued, "As we all know, Techyx has a few competitors out there, but their biggest one by far is QuantumCorp. We are eagerly awaiting the presentations at this morning's press conference." She gave a strangely seductive smile, and then said, "And now, other news."

Mustafa turned off the sound and tossed the remote on the bed. Steam was pouring into the bedroom from the bathroom's open door, and he removed his bathrobe and stepped into the sizeable shower. Almost instantly, the heat relaxed him and he sat down on the built-in bench. After a few minutes, he lay down on the tile shower floor and placed his feet on the wall. The hot water was hypnotic as it beat against his body, and he didn't notice the tiny insect that flew into the bathroom.

And this was no ordinary insect. Its exoskeleton was light and strong, and its interior was packed full of advanced electronics. In a smooth motion, it steered itself up to the glass shower door, registered the heat radiating from Mustafa's body, and continued over the top. Deftly avoiding the jet of water pouring from the shower head, the little bug aimed downward. It landed imperceptibly on its target's foot—a surface that would work just fine for its goal. A narrow needle—thinner than a strand of hair—punctured Mustafa's deep brown skin, injecting into his bloodstream an advanced drug. When it was finished, the insect flew back the same way it had come.

Mustafa didn't detect anything except a minor itch on the top of his foot as he stood and left the shower.

*

Some distance away, parked behind a truck, stood a midnight-black, ultra-modern, extended van.

Inside, a highly specialized group of workers made final preparations. Dr. Michael Zepp, white-haired and sporting a pot belly, spun around in his chair.

"Well done, QC. Very good. The target noticed nothing."

In the next seat, a man who went by the hacker name QuicksilverChaos—but was called QC for short—shrugged his bony shoulders.

"Yeah, thanks, it was no problem. Easy-peasy."

Dr. Zepp stood up and stretched. It had been a long night. He went off to the coffee maker at the back of the van and poured two cups into white, disposable plastic mugs. He handed one to QC.

"Well, I don't think it's all that easy," Zepp said. "Controlling these experimental miniaturized robots is tricky, but you succeeded. Well done."

"Thank you," QC repeated. He took the coffee and offered an awkward salute of appreciation.

Ten monitors were installed along the van's walls, five on either side. Above each group of monitors sat a controller. The screens showed the Mandarin Oriental hotel—some displayed the exterior, some the interior. This group had spent the past week smuggling a hundred mini cameras into the hotel, installing them on each floor. Every angle of any interest at all was covered by the latest generation of cameras, which sent military-level encrypted video streams to the monitors in the van.

251

"It won't be long now."

QC shrugged his shoulders again. To him, time was a relative concept. He'd be earning as much this week as he would after ten years in his old job as a system administrator.

"It's quiet. We still have the other two scientists to prepare."

Dr. Zepp sipped his coffee as he went through the checklist. Soon it would be over and he could leave this damn van. He rolled his eyes. He hated this—this the van, these people he was stuck with. But there wasn't much further to go now.

He'd promised dear and holy to himself that when he got out of here, he'd give up the gambling for good. After all, that's what had put him in this situation. Those two thugs had shown up ten days ago, pushed their way right into his apartment. Zepp had been dialing the police until the men declared they'd been sent by his bookie. The month prior, he'd been quite unlucky—everything he had played on had lost, and now he owed more than a million.

Zepp looked around him, at the cramped van, at these people he was consigned to lead, and sighed. Soon. Soon it would be over. He rolled his chair to the nearest monitor and calibrated the last of the parameters for the next injection.

"Okay, QC, where's the next victim?"

QC grinned and let fly another one of his nearly invisible miniature pets.

*

Fatigue had long ago turned to complete debilitation. Madeleine stood up and stretched, her body stiff and sore from too many hours in the conference room. This space was filled with the members of Novus who had survived the attack the day before. Most of them had small wounds here and there; some had arms and legs in bandages. That wasn't stopping any of them from giving their all in trying to restore Novus. The strike they'd received had been hard—more than half of the employees were either dead or horribly wounded.

Madeleine went to the window and looked down at the collection of journalists still standing there despite the weather. The snow blew in gusts outside. When she appeared in the window, ten of the reporters immediately pointed their cameras in her direction, and she quickly ducked away again.

Henrik went to her. "Are they still there?"

"They sure are."

"Impressive. They're not quitters, anyway."

"No," Madeleine replied, "but that's their job, I guess." She sighed and said, "It would just be nice to have a little break, just a few hours."

Henrik put his hand on her shoulder.

"How long have we known each other, Madeleine?"

She turned to look at him. The corners of her mouth turned up. "Two years, I think," she said.

Henrik, as the contact for the Swedish Armed Forces, had used Novus many times and had more or less always been satisfied with the outcome. The fact that an external group had carried out this type of terrorist attack on Swedish soil—and had caused so many deaths—gave the situation an extra dimension for him, made him feel even more connected to the company and its people.

"You know I'll do everything I can to help, right? Both me and the SAF—we're here for you."

She touched his hand affectionately. "That means a lot to me, Henrik. It really does."

"Good. It looks like we'll be able to restore some of the communications and operations we're running."

"Thanks—that's helpful and impressive. But I'm still worried."

"About Hugo and the team?"

"Right."

"Have you heard something?"

"Sussie called an hour ago. She said they were heading to the airport again to find a flight."

"A flight to where?"

"To London."

"London?"

Madeleine nodded.

"They're headed to the press conference? To Techyx's press conference?"

"Well, she didn't say that explicitly, but I imagine so. The call was cut off—we only got to talk for half a minute."

"They showed something on the news about an attack in Finland," Henrik said. Think that has anything to do with them?"

She shrugged. "It's possible."

Henrik crooked his hand over his mouth as he thought. It was important to support Novus as much as possible—especially now, when they were so exposed. But at the same time, no brutality was to be allowed on foreign territory.

"So now what?" Henrik asked

"Only one thing to do. I have to help them."

Henrik nodded. "I understand. Should we start finding a flight?"

Madeleine smiled slyly. "I've already done that."

23

He couldn't think. Xi shook his head to get the flow of thought going again. The icy snow and wind bayonetted his clothes, and he shivered. But what was far worse than the cold was the mental and physical paralysis caused by the fact that he'd been disconnected from the mission.

He had no clue how to handle it. Xi had heard of clients who withdrew an agent from an ongoing assignment but had always believed that the employee must have made some unpardonable mistake and deserved it. But now, now that it had happened to him, he realized how wrong he had been. A wave of uncertainty rolled through his body.

He grumbled wordlessly, a deep, guttural sound. He had to do something. He couldn't just stand here and freeze to death in the middle of a snowstorm in Helsinki. He had to get out of there and demand revenge. Yes, he would. If it was the last thing he did.

He'd have his revenge.

A yellow, flashing light got closer as a plow truck approached. Xi trudged through the knee-high snow toward the arriving plow truck and aimed his weapon at the driver. The driver stopped the truck and raised his hands.

Xi motioned with the gun for the driver to open the door and come out.

"What are you doing?" the round-faced driver asked once he, too, was standing in the snow. He chuckled absurdly. "Are you going to rob a plow truck?"

Xi cocked the weapon. "Give me the keys."

The driver shook his head in confusion and pointed back up at the truck. "They're in the ignition, ya crazy bastard. Tell ya what—why don't you take over my work for the night while you're at it?"

Xi scowled at the man. "Shut up. Just be happy that I haven't shot you yet. Now get out of here if you want to live."

The driver looked around him, then back to Xi and the barrel of the gun, and scoffed.

"Fine. Great," he said with a bewildered shrug. He turned and lumbered through the snow until he reached the road he'd just plowed. He turned back and looked at Xi.

Xi lifted the gun to the sky and fired a round, shattering the soft, snowy silence of the night, and the driver turned again and started running. Xi jumped into the driver's seat, slammed the door closed, and put the weapon on the passenger seat.

"Here we go," he muttered. He released the brake and stepped on the accelerator, and the heavy plow truck began to move. A faint smile

danced on Xi's lips as the truck got up to speed,
and he looked for a sign for the highway. There
wasn't much time left—the press conference in
London would be starting at eleven, and he was in
another country. He pondered his next step as he
steered the plow toward the abandoned highway.

*

One man's death is another man's bread, they say.

When Hugo and the team were finally on the
highway, the pickup skidded and drove straight
into a snowdrift.

"Goddammit," he murmured. Pushing away the
pain in his throbbing shoulder, he threw the truck
into reverse and shouted, "Come on!"

The wheels spun. Mikko opened the door.

"I'll push." He jumped out, got into position at
the front of the hood, and pushed for king and
country. Nothing. The others jumped out to help as
well, but the truck didn't budge. They were truly
stuck.

"Super," Hugo groaned. He opened the door
and joined the others. It was a miracle that they'd
managed to make it this far in the old Toyota.

"We're just going to need to find another
vehicle," Hugo said. The four of them stood on the
on-ramp to the deserted motorway—deserted of
people, that was. Several cars sat abandoned

around them, but they were all buried under feet of snow.

"Look for something we can drive all the way."

Mikko looked back toward the road in the direction they had come. "Remember that Jeep a while back? That would do it."

"Right! Good memory, Mikko."

"Stay here and I'll get it." And with that, he spun around and started running.

The snow eased as they saw Mikko fade into the distance.

"Now what's the plan, Hugo?" Sussie asked.

Hugo flexed his jaws. "We'll head to the airport and hope that Madeleine arranged transport. Then we get to London as fast as possible."

Sussie checked the time. "Less than nine hours left. Any chance we'll make it?"

Hugo shrugged. "Yeah, there's a chance—and as long as I'm alive, I will fight for it."

Sussie and Freya looked at him and nodded. There was something natural about how he'd said it, without any doubt or hesitation. The women looked at each other and shared a knowing gaze; they had accepted him as their leader.

A few minutes later, a faint whistle cut through the air. From down the road, the thick tires of an extended-cab Jeep cut through the snow. It stopped in front of them and a thick cloud of smoke drifted past them.

Mikko flung opened the door and grinned. "Anyone need a ride?"

The other three jumped in, and Hugo sat in the passenger seat.

"Well done, Mikko."

"No sweat, buddy."

They drove up the freeway, and Freya made a quick estimate.

"Great—ten kilometers to the airport. Just make sure not to run into the ditch and we'll probably make it."

Mikko couldn't drive faster than fifty because of the roads; the trip was going to take a while. Hugo pulled out his cell phone and scrolled to Lita's number. It rang eight times before a sleepy voice answered.

"Hello?"

He cleared his throat. "Hey babe, it's me."

The voice was instantly wide awake. "Hugo!" She burst into tears.

"Hey, it's okay," Hugo said.

Lita took a deep breath, sniffed, and said, "I wasn't sleeping—just resting. I've been waiting all night for you to call or text."

"Sorry, sweetie. I've been thinking about getting in touch with you all day, but it's just been crazy here. Sorry."

"You don't have to say sorry. Not now. We can take care of sorries later." She hesitated. "How are you doing?"

"Well, it's been an exciting day so far, that's for sure. I'll tell you more when I get home. I just wanted to call and say I'm okay. We're all okay."

"Thank goodness." Lita exhaled hard.

"How are you?" he asked her.

"I got Jennifer to come over earlier. We talked all evening, and she's sleeping on the couch now."

"I'm glad you have your best friend there with you. Listen, we're on the road, so if the call is lost, it's because we're out of range."

"I understand. Can you tell me where you are?"

"No, babe. No details. You know that."

Lita sighed. "Yeah, I know. What time is it?"

"A little after four. If all goes well, I'll be home tomorrow."

"Tomorrow? Like tomorrow *today,* or literally tomorrow *tomorrow*?"

Hugo laughed. "Tomorrow tomorrow."

"All right. Hugo, be careful."

"Always, Lita. You know that. Always. I love you."

"I love you too."

Lita hung up, and Hugo stared at the phone. Freya leaned over to him.

"You think we're going home tomorrow?"

Hugo shook his head as they continued down the snow-covered highway. "Who knows?"

*

They continued in silence. A snowplow had come through not too long ago, and Mikko kept the wheels on the plowed roadway. After a while, they passed a sign—seven kilometers left. Sussie tapped away on an iPad.

"It looks like they're having a hard time confirming our flight."

Mikko rubbed the inside of the immense windshield with his sleeve, then stopped short and turned on the defroster.

He grinned at Hugo. "Forgot this ride had one of those."

"Why can't they confirm the flight?" Freya asked.

"The blizzard is preventing all take-off and landing."

"But this is an emergency," Mikko murmured. They have to give us permission."

Hugo frowned. "It's not that easy. Airports have strict rules, and snowstorms can cripple an airport for several hours. Even the most powerful plows can have a hard time in a real blizzard."

Sussie tapped the iPad. "Hugo, a colleague in Malmö just sent a message saying that you need to call Madeleine."

"Got it." He grabbed his phone and dialed her number.

"Hey," Madeleine answered.

"What's up? It's Hugo."

"Thanks for calling. What is your status?"

"We're on our way to the airport—five kilometers away. We had some problems with our previous transport, so we had to find a new one. We have the antidote and the scanner in our possession."

"Great, Hugo. But we have some problems on our side. We're struggling to get the permits to lift off in the snowstorm."

Hugo knit his brows. "Listen, this day has been insane. But it's not over yet—now we're in the endgame and we still have a chance to win. We can't give up now."

"I know, Hugo. We're doing everything we can."

"Do more. We'll be there soon—I expect a plan to be ready." His voice came out icy, surprising even himself. Without waiting for a response, he ended the call.

Nobody in the car said a word for a few minutes. Sussie shifted in her seat.

"Everything good?"

Hugo stared out at the whirling snow. "Yeah."

When they arrived at the airport, massive plows were driving around the outside, bathing the entrance in yellow, flashing light. Mikko applied the brake, but the car slid in the icy snow and drifted onto the sidewalk, where it came to a stop.

"Oops. Sorry."

Hugo opened the door.

"Everybody out and into the terminal."

They ran inside and found the place deserted. A couple of janitors washed the floor, and a short man sitting at the closed café stood up brusquely. He waved and began to run toward them. He was breathing heavily when he reached them.

"Are you from Novus?"

Hugo glared at the man. "Perhaps. Who are you?"

"Madeleine sent me. I'll show you the way."

Hugo studied the man through narrowed eyes. Madeleine hadn't said anything about having a person meet them, but it did make sense; how else would they get to their flight?

"Do you have some credentials you can show us?"

The man fumbled with his wallet and pulled up a driver's license. Hugo pretended to investigate it. He had to talk to Madeleine about these details later.

Handing it back, he said, "Okay, looks good. Lead the way."

The man burst into a smile. "Come on. There's no line, so we've got a straight track there. Follow me."

They jogged after the man and through the security check, their steps echoing as they ran. The man pointed at a terminal. "This way."

A modern Learjet was parked outside, its lights flashing. Another man walked up to them and shrugged. "We're still waiting for permission," he said dully. "You can go ahead and board, but it might be a while."

24

The aroma was delectable. Mustafa approached the host, who greeted him with a well-practiced smile.

"Good morning, sir. What room number?"

"Forty."

"Excellent. Welcome." The host motioned for him to continue into the dining room, and Mustafa found his two colleagues already there, sitting at a table.

"Good morning," he said as he approached them.

Tanya Lipton coughed as she swallowed a piece of bread; after drinking half a glass of orange juice, she looked up, cleared her throat, and smiled. "Morning, Mustafa. Sleep well?"

He pulled out the third chair. "Just fine, thanks, Tanya. Good morning, Ben. How are you all?"

Ben Chimes chewed and swallowed, smacking his lips. "Great. Their bacon is fantastic."

Mustafa chuckled. "Good. I think I should take some with me, then."

Ben and Tanya were his colleagues, but more than that, they were his friends. Both of them were brilliant researchers who had given up underpaid research jobs when they'd been invited to Techyx.

And it was under his leadership that they were performing their most important work to date.

It was today, this very afternoon, that the world would know about their discoveries. It would be beautiful. Their work had resulted in a well-documented report that described in detail all the offenses and violations QuantumCorp had made in their search for minerals and mining deposits all over the world.

It had been a difficult job, but they had done it. And today, they would reap the fruits of their labor.

"You guys are making me even hungrier," Mustafa said. He got up, fixed himself a plate of roasted eggs, bacon, and toast, and went back to the table.

"So," he said through a mouthful of food, "ready for the press conference?"

Tanya sipped her juice, then said, "Yep, everything's ready. We'll start with your introduction as planned. Then we'll each take three minutes, and then we end with the video."

"Good."

"It will be beautiful."

"And what about security?"

Ben frowned. "There are hundreds of people here. QuantumCorp wouldn't arrange anything here—it would be suicide."

Mustafa reached down and rubbed his shoe to get to the itch on the top of his foot. "But you never know," he said. "They could send in a maniac with a gun."

Tanya glared and nodded toward a table full of thick men in suits. They weren't eating, but their eyes moved constantly over the room.

"Anyone who tried will never get past our guards."

Ben scratched his neck. "Right—have you seen their weapons? Those are some real cannons they've got there."

Mustafa wolfed another slice of bacon and said, "You may be right. But to be on the safe side, make sure everyone's up to date on the details. Okay?"

Tanya and Ben looked at each other and shrugged.

"Okay."

*

The wait was unbearable. Hugo looked out the window for the twentieth time.

Sussie stood up and wandered up and down the aisle. "Come on now," she grumbled.

"Madeleine's doing everything she can," said Hugo, leaning back in his seat. "We can't do anything now except wait."

The Learjet had been ready to leave for twenty minutes, but they still needed take-off clearance. The snowfall had eased over the last ten minutes, and Hugo hoped that all the available snowplows were out there, busting their butts to clear the runways.

"I know, I know."

The minutes slunk by. Finally, the door to the cockpit opened, and a young man came out with a wide smile on his lips.

"Okay, guys, we're ready. We'll start taxiing in a minute, so take a seat and buckle up."

Mikko and Sussie raised their fists in the air, whooping with excitement.

"Here we go!" cried Mikko.

Three minutes later, the pilot gave full throttle, and the Learjet accelerated along the runway. Even though the snowfall had eased, visibility was still poor. The plane sped up and climbed into the air.

Hugo closed his eyes while his thoughts churned. His shoulder—and his entire body—ached, but he couldn't rest. Not yet.

Sussie pulled out a laptop and turned it on.

*

It was now or never. Xi veered past an abandoned car and stepped on it. White-hot rage surged through his body. He would get his revenge.

When he reached the airport, he almost slammed into an abandoned Jeep at the entrance. He jumped out of the plow and ran into the airport.

He continued until he reached the security check. Two female guards were talking in front of the metal scanner. It was a gamble, but he saw no other way. He had no more time. Xi took a few deep breaths and forced himself to calm down.

He walked up to the security check and smiled. "Hi, how's it going?"

The women looked up; the one on the left, the younger one of the two, smiled back.

"Not much to do now that they've closed the runways," she said.

"Oh no," Xi said, his smile unwavering, "Have they really? But I have a flight to catch—look, I have my ticket and everything."

He pulled a piece of paper out of his pocket and waved it. The guard on the right—the one who hadn't returned his smile—reached for it, took it from him, and looked it over. She tilted her head in confusion, and in one swift motion, Xi pulled out a knife and thrust it into the woman's exposed neck.

The younger woman didn't even have time to scream. She could only shut her eyes in terror before Xi pulled the knife from her coworker's throat and stabbed her with it.

Both of the guards fell to the floor, and Xi scanned the area. No one had seen. He wiped the knife clean and hurried on. He knew there were hundreds of cameras at the airport; his deed would be discovered before long. But if he could get just a few minutes, he'd have a chance.

He hurried on through the terminal. Most stores were closed, but a few here and there were open. He went further, scouting out the windows at the different aircraft outside. Xi had heard that a Cirrus SR22 might be there—a powerful composite aircraft that would work perfectly for his needs right now. It was his last hope.

He saw it parked outside a terminal, and his heart fluttered with excitement. When he stopped to look more closely, a man in a uniform came walking toward him. He was short—shorter than Xi, even. His name tag said "A. Liss, Pilot." Xi thanked his lucky stars. He approached the pilot with a smile, stopping inches from his face.

Alarmed by Xi's proximity, he leaned back and asked, "Yes, may I help you?"

Xi pulled out his knife and laid the blade against the pilot's stomach. "Not a word," he whispered. "Follow me."

The pilot's face turned ash gray. "What do you want?"

"You and I are going to take a little flight."

25

Klaus woke up with a jolt, drops of sweat running down his forehead like a spring rain. He sat up in bed and was met with the sound of Heidi's snoring. Klaus pulled off the blanket and twisted out of bed. He reached for the clothes on the floor and pulled them on.

"Where are you going?" came her sleepy voice.

He spun around. Heidi peered at him with one eye open. He shrugged.

"I was going to make some coffee. It'll probably be a tough day."

Heidi sat up, and the blanket slid down, exposing her fleshy breasts.

"Good idea. Run down to the kitchen and fix some coffee for us. I'll be right there."

Klaus' shoulders drooped, and he left the room. The big clock in the hall read quarter after nine— less than six hours left. In the kitchen, he turned on the coffeemaker, and soon, the pleasant aroma filled the air. He poured two cups just as Heidi came in.

"Here you go."

"Thanks, darling." She took a sip. "Come now. We have a lot to talk about."

They sat down on the couch; Klaus realized his head was pounding. Before he could say anything, Heidi put her hand on his leg.

"I know what you're going through, dear. I know."

"You know . . . what I'm going through?"

"Of course. When you're young, you're eager—you think you will live forever, and you take risks that would seem crazy to you when you got older."

Klaus sipped his coffee and shrugged. "Yes, you may be right."

"I know I am. You've been my assistant for two years now, and I know I've taken advantage of you. But I have seen you grow as a man, and I must say that I'm very impressed with your development."

"You are?"

Heidi chuckled. "Yes, I am. And I know that you don't prefer women, but you have fulfilled your duties to my utmost satisfaction."

His head spun. "Thank you," he paused, "I guess."

"You don't have to think about it anymore. Today is your day. Your exam, so to speak. You have planned this for a long time, and you need all your energy to focus on the day."

"You're right."

"This reminds me of when I was young," Heidi went on. "I went through a situation like this. I had also planned a secret operation, but my mentor found out about it and knew as much as I did when it went down."

Klaus frowned. "Did it succeed?"

"No. No, it didn't."

"How did your mentor react?"

Heidi took a sip of her coffee and gazed off, losing herself in the memories. She blinked and turned her eyes to Klaus. "I had to kill him."

Klaus froze. "Ah."

A smile widened on her full face. "But let's not focus on that. Talk me through your plan instead. I want to know everything."

So Klaus took a deep breath and explained everything he had planned for today. Heidi soaked in every word. When he fell silent, she nodded.

"I see. Then there's only one thing to do."

"What?"

"Go to London. At once."

"But I could supervise the operation from here—"

"No," Heidi interrupted, "that's out of the question. I'll arrange a private flight to London so you can be in place if something in the plan needs adjusting."

Klaus' shoulders slouched at the words. He knew it was pointless to argue with Heidi. A cold drop of sweat ran down his spine, and he repressed a sudden urge to shiver.

*

The plane shook as it passed through violent turbulence. Hugo peered out the window at the approaching city of London.

Mikko patted him on his shoulder. "Not far now."

"It'll be tight. The press conference will be starting soon, and we still need to get through London traffic."

"Good point."

"Was Madeleine able to call and get them to cancel the press conference?" Hugo asked hopefully.

Mikko spun around. "Yeah, Sussie, did Madeleine catch them in London?"

Sussie grimaced. "She got hold of them but couldn't persuade them."

"No? Why not, for God's sake?"

"They said they wanted proof before canceling," Sussie said. "Too many VIPs."

"What idiots," Mikko spat, throwing his head back in his seat.

"I agree, but if you look at it from their point of view, you can understand how it sounds farfetched. You know, that there's someone programmed to attack them without even knowing it."

London's glittering lights glided by outside, and Hugo tapped the window. "Yeah," he said, "but given who Madeleine is, they should have taken her more seriously."

Sussie opened her laptop. "I think we have bigger problems than that right now, anyway. Check this out."

The others gathered around Sussie as she produced a map on the monitor. A hundred icons moved over it.

"This shows all the aircraft in Northern Europe," she said. "And here we are, the green dot. We've passed Scandinavia and are approaching London."

Hugo leaned forward. "And why are we looking at this?"

"Because of this." Sussie zoomed in on the Baltic Sea and scrolled down toward Finland. A red dot was heading away from Helsinki; Mikko pointed at it.

"That?"

"Yep. Madeleine just sent a message saying they intercepted a hijacked plane that had taken off from Helsinki half an hour ago."

Hugo instantly knew who it was. "Xi."

"You got it."

Hugo stood up and shook his head. "That guy doesn't give up! He's going to follow us no matter what."

Sussie raised her eyebrows. "He's dedicated, I'll give him that."

"Sure is."

Freya put her hands on her hips and said, "So what does this mean? Should we do something?"

Sussie shook her head. "No, not now. Madeleine is communicating with the authorities, and they're doing everything they can to intercept the plane."

Hugo turned and looked out the window again. Far out there in the dark void, he knew that Xi was on his way. He could feel it. They had to get to London fast, get to the press conference and find out—somehow—who it was that was programmed.

"Okay," he said, turning back to his team. "We can't do anything about Xi now, so let's focus on what we can do. Let's take a look at Tupolev's scanner."

Freya pulled the yellow bag from under her chair and opened it. The unusual machine lay on a bed of foam-cut rubber. She picked it up and weighed it in her hand.

"It's heavy," she said. "So how does it work?"

Hugo studied the device. It was rugged, with a carrying handle and rounded, reinforced corners. A monitor on the side shone green with the text: *Scanning ready, press to activate.*

"I think you just point it at the person you want to scan and press the button," he answered.

"And then?"

"I guess you get some kind of message on the screen."

Mikko tilted his head. "Didn't Markov say it can also be used to deactivate any nanobots it senses?"

"That's right," Freya said. "How you do make it do that?"

Hugo shrugged. "No clue. You guys remember if Markov said anything about it?"

Freya shook her head. "No. He just told us it had that function, not how to activate it."

Hugo, Freya, and Mikko continued to examine the scanner while Sussie sat a few seats away, absorbed in the work on her computer. Hugo flipped the scanner upside down and pointed its underside. "Aha," he said. "I think I have it."

He held up the scanner and pointed to two metal contacts on the bottom. "Here's what I think: if the scanner shows positive for nanobots, you can deactivate them by sending a signal through these contacts. You hold it to the person's skin, and it sends a signal through their body."

"Does it hurt them?" Mikko asked.

Hugo chuckled. "How should I know? I didn't build it. Hopefully not."

Sussie suddenly stood up from her seat and joined them. "Hey, gang. Hate to say it, but they're having problems."

Hugo handed the scanner back to Freya, who replaced it in the yellow bag.

"Who is?" he asked.

"Eurocontrol. They're having trouble making contact with the hijacked plane. They're working on sending up a few planes to intercept it, but they're short on time. Even with the Rafales in northern France that can take off in ten minutes, it's going to be close."

"Can't the British send someone to meet the plane?"

"They could, but Eurocontrol is having trouble persuading them that the plane is on its way to London. For whatever reason, the British don't agree with that assessment."

Hugo groaned. "Come on."

"I know. But at the moment, there isn't much we can do."

The lights of London were even closer and clearer now, but Hugo couldn't calm down. Not so far behind them, he knew, a madman was coming with death and annihilation marked for them.

*

Now, there was no going back. Xi stared out the side window and watched Stockholm slide by.

"André, readjust the course. What, you don't think I can tell that you're trying to change course on me?"

Pilot André Liss swallowed hard. "Changing course."

Xi raised his gun to André's temple. "Do it again and it'll be the last thing you do."

A drop of sweat ran down André's forehead. He wiped it away and stammered, "Understood. It won't happen again."

They continued on, leaving Stockholm behind and passing Sweden altogether. The sky burned in a kaleidoscope of blues, oranges, and reds.

"Just keep heading straight for London. Got it?"

André nodded. Xi laid the gun on his knee and put his face in his hands. How had it come to this? How had he gotten here? Xi, who had for so long been one of the world's most formidable mercenaries, had come so low as to be a simple aircraft hijacker. He wallowed in self-pity until the plane's radio crackled. He jerked his head up.

"Unidentified flight. Come in."

André picked up the radio, took a breath, and said, "This is S-R Two-Two."

"This is Control, S-R Two-Two. You do not have permission to proceed on your current course. Order to land."

A shock of panic jolted André's eyes open wide. "Roger that, Control, but I cannot comply. As I explained earlier, this plane is on an alternative course."

The voice on the other end became sharper. "S-R Two-Two, if you continue, we will deploy fighter jets to intercept you."

Xi pulled his hand over his face, and André tensed.

The pilot licked his lips and brought the radio to his mouth again. "Acknowledged. Over and out." He laid the radio back down again and stared straight ahead.

Xi peered out the window. "Are they really going to send fighter jets after us?" he asked.

"I don't know. I hope not."

Xi flexed his jaws and whispered, "Come on, you bastards."

The plane shook, and Xi grabbed his weapon. He aimed it at André. "What are you doing?"

André glared at Xi. "I can do a lot, but I can't control whether there's turbulence, you know."

The plane shook again. "Stop that. Stabilize the plane."

"It isn't me, I swear. It's turbulence—it will pass soon."

"You think I'm stupid? You think I don't know what you're doing? This is a trick."

"No, no, believe me. I'll change altitude and see if that helps."

Xi stared out. There wasn't a cloud in sight. "How can there be turbulence when there aren't any clouds?"

André twisted toward Xi and glowered. "It's called clear-air turbulence. Would you like me to change the altitude?"

"Yes. Take us lower and slow down."

"Okay."

André adjusted the altitude, and the plane dropped a few hundred meters. The turbulence eased.

"Well done."

Before André could reply, the aircraft shook again, this time even more forcefully. Xi stumbled, panicked, and grabbed his gun. In his fumbling hand, he pulled the trigger and the shot thundered through the tiny cockpit.

André threw himself aside and screamed, "No!"

Xi stared as André sank down and grabbed at his shoulder.

"I— I didn't mean to!"

André sat up, moaning in pain. "You shot me, you idiot!"

Xi's hands shook and he hurriedly set the gun back down. He looked at the pilot and cried, "It was your fault! You're the one who made the plane shake."

"It's turbulence! There's nothing I can do about turbulence!" He pulled his hand away from his shoulder and gawked at the blood. "You shot me."

Xi leaned in toward André and examined the wound. "It just grazed you. You'll live. Just get us to London.

Tears streamed down André's pale face as he again took command of the aircraft. "Don't shoot me again," he said in a small, but decisive, voice. "If I'm going to get there, you have to hold off that damned gun. Okay?"

Xi tightened his lips into something resembling a smile. "You have my word."

*

He got permission. Bernard Poche lit the afterburner for both of the Snecma M88's engines. The air was squeezed out of his lungs as pure aviation fuel was injected into the afterburner chambers and ignited.

The violent force pushed the slender Dassault Rafale fighter plane as if a giant had picked it up and thrown it. The engines produced over seventy-five thousand kilonewtons. Bernard tightened his stomach as the plane accelerated along the runway.

Eight seconds later, its wheels eased into the air, and he flipped the switch to retract them. With a shriek, it headed for the sky.

"Flight tango-tango-foxtrot continues to target."

"Roger, tango-tango-foxtrot. You are cleared to continue at the highest available speed toward the goal."

Bernard's wing mate came up next to him, his black helmet shining.

"Let's speed up."

"Roger."

Both fighters had been given permission to accelerate toward the unidentified aircraft as quickly as possible. Eurocontrol had sent a lightning-fast request for help in intercepting the small plane that had left Finland without permission and set course southwest.

Bernard accelerated.

*

He saw the end. Xi squinted at the sparkling lights lined up along the horizon.

"London."

"Yes, but now what? We'll never be allowed to land."

Xi took a deep breath. "Don't worry about it. I'll take care of that."

André shook his head. "You know we'll never get permission, right?"

"Why do you think we took this plane?" Xi asked him.

André's face turned even more gray.

"You can't be serious."

"Sure, I can."

"Oh my God."

Xi scanned the horizon. It wouldn't be long now. He pointed out the windscreen and said, "Keep heading straight to the center, toward Hyde Park."

André stared directly ahead. "Somehow, I knew it would come to this, but I was also hoping you had planned something else."

Xi smiled. "This is the end station for me, André. I've reached the end of the road. Just take us to Hyde Park and slow down as we approach."

Xi pulled out his phone and scrolled through the list of contacts. When he found the one he was looking for, he pressed the icon.

"Hello?"

"Hey, cousin. It's Xi."

"Xi?" The voice hesitated. "Why are you calling?"

Hurriedly, Xi explained the situation. "And that's how it is. Do you understand?"

"Ah— Yes, of course. We'll help you. For the family."

"For the family."

Xi hung up and fixed his gaze on London. Next to him, André pushed the pain away from his pounding shoulder and prepared for his worst nightmare.

*

"The target is in sight," Bernard reported. "Flying closer."

"Roger, tango-tango-foxtrot. Hurry—you're approaching the British Airspace border." The two Rafale planes screamed across the sky, approaching the goal of six hundred meters per second. The slender planes soared like attacking eagles toward their target.

The radio crackled.

"Unknown aircraft, this is tango-tango-foxtrot. Requesting a reply."

No answer. Bernard repeated his attempt a few times but received no response from the plane that slowly, but steadily, was approaching London.

"We're getting closer."

"Roger."

Bernard's heartbeat pounded in his ears. Seven kilometers. He tried again. "Unknown aircraft. This is tango-tango-foxtrot. Requesting a reply."

Still no answer.

"We'll fly up alongside and see if we can get in touch with the pilot."

Ten seconds passed as the fighter pilots turned off their afterburners and their speed decreased. They needed to match the speed of the civilian plane; otherwise, they would fly right over it.

Bernard was pressed forward into his seat belt as he decelerated. The Rafales came up on either side of the SR22. Bernard glanced to his right and saw that there were two figures inside. The one in the pilot's seat waved.

"Unknown aircraft, this is the tango-tango-foxtrot. Reply now!"

To Bernard's surprise, the radio crackled.

"We cannot turn around now."

"This is no game. You are not permitted to continue your current course. Land immediately and surrender to the authorities at once."

"Roger."

A second later, Bernard gasped as the little plane's nose dipped down and dove straight for London.

*

So close, yet so far away. Xi kept his eyes fixed on the large green area that was Hyde Park. He glared at André.

"Stay on course. Don't force me to shoot you again."

André gritted his teeth. "I can't believe I'm doing this. I'm going to spend the rest of the year in jail."

Xi grinned. "No, you can blame me. After all, I forced you into this."

"No kidding."

As they approached, Xi made a quick calculation. "Slow down in twenty seconds."

"Roger."

London's famous landmarks lay scattered. Butterflies filled Xi's stomach; it was time. His fate was approaching. Ten seconds. His heart pounded in his chest, and a wave of dizziness swept through him.

"There. Get in as steep as possible. Slow down . . . now!"

André groaned and pulled back on the speed controls as much as he dared. The plane dropped, and Xi pressed forward. He counted down.

Three, two, one. Now!

He reached up, grabbed the red lever on the ceiling, and pulled hard. A fraction of a second later, the nose lifted, and the increased wind resistance caused the velocity to fall even further. A hatch on the plane slid to one side and a parachute fell out. André screamed, but Xi ignored him as he approached his destiny.

26

The water was warm and comfortable. Mustafa Boon washed his hands, dried them, and spun around. The door opened and Ben came in.

"How you doing? All good?"

"I'm good—some jitters. This is going to be big. We put in a lot of work."

"You can say that again," Ben replied. "There's a hell of a lot at stake."

Mustafa adjusted his tie. His stomach gurgled audibly, and he wished he hadn't eaten so much bacon. Ben chuckled.

"Too much breakfast?"

Mustafa grimaced and patted his stomach. "Yes, but you know, bacon is an essential part of the good life."

"So true, so true."

"See you in the prep room later so we can go through the presentation, okay?"

Ben gave a thumbs-up. "Sounds good."

Mustafa left the bathroom, and Ben entered a vacant stall. As he sat there, he took a series of deep breaths until his heart rate had dropped. He was nervous, too—there would be a lot on the line over the next few hours. The information they'd be sharing with the world about QuantumCorp's damage to the environment was mind-blowing.

Lost in thought, Ben didn't notice the miniature insect that slid in through the ventilation grille in the ceiling and set a course straight toward him. It flew down without a sound and landed on his neck, where it performed its mission.

When it was finished, it lifted off and disappeared through the vent again. Ben left the bathroom and made his way to the prep room—a conference room Mustafa and Tanya had secured to go through the presentation one more time. He entered just as Tanya was motioning toward the big screen.

"And as you can see here, in Chile and Peru, we have documented hundreds of different violations, like pollution, as seen here," the film showed large pools of dirty water, "where they use cyanide to extract gold. It's a process that has been used for many years, but there are also rigorous safety regulations that must be observed. QuantumCorp has not followed these standards. In more than seven gold mines, QuantumCorp uses insufficient security systems to prevent dangerous contamination."

Mustafa theatrically raised a hand. "And what does that mean, exactly?"

Tanya smiled awkwardly as Mustafa played reporter.

"It means that contaminated water leaks straight into the groundwater and spreads. It's a disaster every time something like this happens, but what we see in QuantumCorp's case is on a completely different scale. The contaminated water has spread to at least twelve different aquifers. The consequences of this are extremely serious. And that's just Chile," she said and paused. "In the western part of South America, we have found over sixty-two mines in which QuantumCorp works the same way."

Mustafa shifted his weight. "You have proof that there is misconduct at sixty-two mines?"

"We do. In all of these mines, QuantumCorp approaches safety in the same way, giving rise to very serious consequences."

Ben clapped. "Bravo. Very striking."

Tanya pointed to the monitor. "Are we sure about this data, guys? There's no doubt it was sixty-two?"

Mustafa shook his head and answered, "Absolutely sure. We have triple- and quadruple-checked the numbers. They are rock-solid." Before anyone could say another word, a siren passed by outside on the street. As it faded away, another one came and went.

Ben went to the window and looked down at the crowded street. In the distance, a police car's flashing tail lights disappeared around a corner. A police motorcycle with its siren blaring followed behind it.

"Something must have happened."

Tanya came up next to him. "Did you see anything?"

"No, just the cops passing through."

They had good views of the park from there; Ben stood on tiptoe, but still saw nothing of interest.

Mustafa shrugged and said, "All right, let's finish this so we can get a cup of coffee before it's time. It's almost ten o'clock—one hour left."

*

The phone vibrated in Hugo's pocket, and he pulled it out. A picture of Lita's smiling face sat in the center of the screen. He answered the call.

"Lita?"

"Hey, babe." She hesitated. "Sorry, I know I shouldn't call."

"No, it's okay."

"But . . ."

"But what?"

"I'm just wondering . . . is it going to be like this from now on? You've only been home for a few months, and now— Are you just going to storm off on assignment again?"

Hugo tried not to sigh in exasperation. *Be understanding. See it from her point of view.*

"I hope not," he replied.

"But that's what you did, you know? You just left."

Jesus. This wasn't the time to have this conversation.

"Lita, can we talk about this when I get home? We're headed down to London now."

"London?"

He cursed silently. "Can we do this later?" he repeated.

"But Hugo, this can't wait. We need to solve this—I just can't accept it."

He pulled his hand over his face. Mikko came up to him, but he waved him away.

"Okay, sure, you're right. We have five minutes before we land."

He listened to her as she talked. Mikko came back and tapped on his wrist. Hugo nodded.

"Lita, I hear what you're saying, and you're right in a lot of ways. But listen, sweetie, I really need to go, okay? We'll have to finish this conversation when I get home."

"Hugo, this is important."

"I know. I love you."

"I love you too, but—"

He hung up. Mikko put his hand on Hugo's shoulder.

"Relationship problems?"

Hugo shook his head. "She's right—Lita. This is the weekend that I'm finally home, and I'm out here trying to catch a supervillain."

Mikko chuckled. "You hadn't imagined that one, huh?"

"Nope, not at all."

"It's time, buddy. We'll be landing in a few minutes. Novus called ahead and paved the way for us, so getting through security should be a breeze, but we still have to get a move on."

Hugo considered the next step and nodded. "Okay, we go through the security check, find our ride, and then go full-speed toward the hotel."

"That's it. Easy, right?"

Hugo laughed humorlessly. "Especially with London traffic. How are Sussie and Freya doing?"

Mikko grimaced. "As well as you might imagine. They're both starting to look a bit worse for wear. But . . ."

"But what?"

Mikko pulled a box from the inside pocket of his jacket and opened it.

"A little something to keep you alert?"

Hugo tightened his jaws. He had used stimulants during assignments before. Sometimes it was necessary as a last resort. He wasn't thrilled about it, but he accepted a small, white tablet and swallowed it. Mikko did the same.

"I'll see if the girls want one."

"Don't call them girls, Mikko," Hugo called after him as he disappeared into the back of the plane.

Alone again, Hugo closed his eyes. This was the endgame, and now it was all about keeping things together, not fumbling the ball. His shoulder thumped in pain, but he ignored it. The plane rolled.

Come on, Hugo, hold on.

*

For the family. That was the only thing that mattered: family. Teng Mao flung the wardrobe door open and grabbed the two machine guns hidden behind the hanging clothes. Xi was his cousin, and when he called for help, Teng had to say yes. That's how it was in the family.

"Hong! Hurry up!"

A chubby young man came panting into the room. "Do you have them?" Hong asked.

"Yes, here. Take one."

Teng handed a gun to Hong, and Hong almost dropped it.

He snorted a little laugh. "Wow—it's heavy."

"Do as I taught you. Both hands, aim, and squeeze."

"Are we really going to do this?"

Teng's eyes flashed darkly. "If our cousin calls and asks for help, it is our duty to help him, you understand?"

Hong hesitated. "Yeah, but it's not just us, right? Who else is coming to help?"

"I got at least four men, maybe more. They'll be here in a few minutes. Now head down to meet them—I'll be there soon."

Hong didn't move.

Teng yelled, "Now!"

Hong spun around and bounded out of the room. Teng went back to the wardrobe, got down on his knees, and pulled out a box. Opening it gently, he removed five hand grenades and a grenade-carrying vest. After he'd pulled the vest on and attached the grenades, Teng stood and looked at himself in the mirror. He grinned coolly. He looked like a real soldier.

He popped his knuckles and whispered, "For the family."

Teng ran down the steps and ripped open the door. Hong stood just outside; his weapon raised high.

"Lower the gun, you nitwit. You don't want all the neighbors to see you."

Hong lowered the weapon. "Sorry."

Just then, two vans, a white one and a red one, swerved onto their street and slowed in front of their house. Two men jumped out and ran up to Hong.

"Shall we do this?"

"Yes. Xi called me from a plane saying he needs help. And we will help him. His enemies will land at Heathrow soon; what we're going to do is intercept them on their way into London."

A light-haired man of about twenty-five laid his hand on Hong's shoulder. He always reminded Hong of the quintessential California surfer, even though he was pretty sure Mike had never even been to the ocean.

"You know we'd do anything for you, bro."

"Thanks, Mike, you're a true friend. How many guys do we have?"

"Two in each van. That's what we could scrape together."

"Weapons?"

Mike shrugged. "I grabbed what was available. It wasn't much—two pistols and a machine gun. That's all."

"Okay, it'll do. Let's go."

They jogged to the vans. Teng went to the red one and gestured to Hong.

"You get in the white one."

"But Teng, I want to go with you."

Teng sighed. Some things never changed. Hong wasn't the most intelligent kid in the family, but he was loyal to a fault.

"Okay, come on."

Hong burst into a big smile and followed his big brother into the red van. Once inside, Teng turned to the man sitting next to him.

"Hey, switch to the other one instead."

"Sure." He glanced at Hong, then hopped out and ran over to the other vehicle. Both vans revved their engines and set off for Heathrow.

27

The cold made his bones ache. Hugo walked down the stairs with two large, dark bags in his hands. The snow made the steps slippery, and he nearly lost his footing. He made his way slowly, and when he reached the bottom, he looked back up at Mikko. Behind Mikko stood the familiar contour of Heathrow Airport.

"Now what?"

Mikko pointed to an approaching passenger van. "Right on time. I told you Novus was effective."

"Great."

Freya and Sussie followed behind Mikko as the van drove up to the bottom of the stairway and stopped. A young man with red, spiky hair jumped out of the driver's seat, ran around the front of the van, and opened the side door.

"Were you the ones who ordered the pickup?"

Hugo walked up to him. "Yes, thank you for coming so soon."

The young smiled and said, "No problem. My boss said it was important?"

"Yes, it is."

Hugo said no more but motioned for the others to load the gear into the van. Then he jumped into the passenger seat.

"Okay, let's go. Take us into the Oriental Mandarin."

The man started to protest but fell silent when he saw the expression on Hugo's face.

"It's just that there was an accident on the M4 earlier. There's still a lot of traffic, so it'll probably take a while."

"Okay, I understand."

Hugo turned to Sussie. "Do you think you can work out a faster passage to London?"

"Let me see."

Hugo beckoned to the young man to start driving. "We'll just take it as it comes. Get us to the hotel as fast as you can."

"On it."

*

The van picked up speed. Teng removed a laptop from his backpack and opened it, and the screen flickered. The driver pulled the wheel, nearly causing the computer to slide off Teng's lap to the floor.

"Take it easy!"

The driver shrugged. "Sorry."

Teng snorted. He worked fast and opened the email from Xi.

Thank you, cousin. Your help is very valuable. You know you've always been my favorite in the family. The people I'm after are extremely competent, so don't make the mistake of underestimating them. They are armed. Attached is the tracking signal I managed to attach to one of them.

Teng typed in the signature Xi had attached, and a map flashed onto the screen. A red, flashing dot appeared in the middle. He lifted his head and pointed out the front window.

"They're driving north on the parkway away from Heathrow. Get on the M4 at Cranford Parkway Bridge so we can intercept them."

The driver pressed harder on the accelerator, and Teng smelled the odor of rubber burning.

"What is this piece of shit car you got hold of?"

"It was the only thing we could get on such short notice."

Teng glared at the man but said nothing. Hong leaned forward and put his hand on Teng's shoulder.

"Is everything all right, Teng?"

Teng patted his brother's hand. "Yeah, don't worry about it. We're about to go hunting, so get ready."

Hong leaned back, raised his weapon, and smiled. "I'm ready."

*

The van swayed when the young man pulled too hard on the wheel.

"Sorry!"

Hugo looked at the clock. It was a little after ten.

"What's your name?" he asked the driver.

The young man's focused face cracked into a toothy smile. He looked over at Hugo. "It's Tim."

Hugo nodded at the road. "Tim, do you have a girlfriend?"

"Yeah, her name's Andrea."

"Tell you what. If you can get us to the Oriental before eleven o'clock, I'll arrange for you and Andrea to get a luxury trip to the Maldives next month. How does that sound?"

Tim's smile grew until it covered his face. "It sounds like an offer I can't resist. I'll do my best. Hold on."

Tim slipped into the crowded traffic on the M4 and glided in and out between the cars. The traffic was dense but moving. The snowfall had eased, and the multitude of cars had effectively plowed tracks in the snow. Hugo twisted around and made eye contact with Sussie.

"Are you online?"

"Yep."

"See if you can get us some press cards or something so we can get into the press conference."

Mikko nodded. "Smart thinking."

Hugo shrugged. "We should have thought of it sooner. It's been a busy day."

Freya sat quietly, her hands fiddling with the weapon on her lap.

"Hey," Hugo said. "You okay?"

She shrugged. Her eyes were glazed over. "Yeah, I'm fine," she said.

Hugo recognized that gaze. When a person approached the edge of exhaustion, they often got the look Freya had right now.

"Good. Go through our weapons and make sure they're locked and loaded. We want to be prepared if we get into a firefight at the hotel."

Before Freya could respond, a burst of bullets hammered into the rear of the van.

Hugo shouted, "Look out! They're shooting!"

Tim pulled hard on the steering wheel and veered past a truck in the inner lane.

"What was that?" he cried.

Hugo turned to Freya. "Give me a weapon."

Freya tossed him a rifle; he caught it and checked the magazine. It was full.

"Tim, whatever you do, don't stop, okay? If you stop, we'll all die."

303

Tim's eyes were as big as saucers, but he nodded and stared at the roadway ahead. Hugo checked the side mirror. One—no, two vans crossed through the traffic behind them. In the closest one—a dented, white van—a man hung out of the passenger side window and pointed a gun at them.

Hugo shouted, "Take cover! Turn right, Tim, now!"

This time, the burst of bullets lasted longer. A dozen rounds breezed past them as they changed lanes, striking the truck that had been in front of them. Cars honked and pulled to the side as the chaos on the freeway took hold like a rolling storm. Hugo rolled down his window and leaned out. The van swerved, and he fell back onto his seat. He crawled out again and tried to find a position.

"I don't have a clean shot. There're two of them, a white one and a red one."

Mikko crawled to the other side, rolled down the window, and stuck out his head. "They're close. The white one's thirty meters away. What do we do?"

Hugo's brain went into overdrive. The police must be on the road, considering how many people had witnessed the shooting.

Snow exploded into the air when a car drove into another with a violent crash.

"Whoa!" Hugo shouted. "Shit! I hope they're okay." He turned back to the driver. "Tim, how much further to the hotel?"

"A little more than seven kilometers."

"Get in the emergency lane. See if we can put some distance between us and our pursuers."

Tim didn't need any more instructions. He yanked the van into the emergency lane, and a white cloud appeared behind them. The two vehicles chasing them skidded and sped up. Forced to drive single-file in the emergency lane, their overall visibility of the Novus team's van decreased, and so did the rate of fire.

Tim called out, "Guys, the engine's doing its best, but I don't think it can go any faster."

Freya leaned forward and grabbed Hugo's arm. "Now what? Are we going to drive into London with them in tow?"

Hugo shook his head but didn't respond. There was no time to hash out the details of this problem. He looked around for his target but saw nothing. Nodding toward the road, he said, "Go on, Tim. I'll tell you when it's time."

Another bullet hit the back door, and this time the rounds drilled into the interior of the van. Sussie shouted and fell forward.

"Sussie!"

The van lurched again, and Sussie slid onto the floor. Hugo froze as he watched her fall seemingly in slow motion.

No!

A second later, he exhaled as she crawled up and groaned. She reached for her head.

"I actually think I got hit."

Mikko pulled her hair away from her face and saw a stream of blood running down her temple.

"You did, but it looks like the bullet just barely nudged you."

Sussie whimpered, "The luckiest girl in the world, I guess."

The last barrage had slammed a dozen holes in the door, and Hugo saw the swirling snow through the hole. The red van was close now; there was no time to lose. He turned his eyes to Tim. The young man was pale but held the steering wheel with a grip so sturdy that his knuckles were pure white. A symphony of honking cars contributed to the chaos.

"You're doing a great job, Tim. Just a little longer."

Hugo scouted ahead and pointed to a boxy Royal Mail truck driving in the middle lane. "Tim!" he shouted. "Drive past the mail truck and get in front of it!"

Tim's face resembled a question mark. "And then?"

"And then we'll give them a surprise."

Tim's face went even paler when he understood what Hugo meant.

*

It was time. Teng swapped magazines. The warm weapon was like a living force in his hands. He pointed to the escaping van.

"Get us closer! They're injured."

The driver stepped on it, and a faint smell of smoke began to fill the cabin. They gained on their target. The van in front of them had been hit, and a faint vapor swirled behind it.

Hong shouted, "Teng! Are you going to shoot them?"

Teng bared his teeth. This had already taken too long. The police were surely on their way. They had to finish this now.

"Yes, hold on."

Teng leaned out of the side window and started shooting. The long hail of ammunition thundered into the window of a sedan driving next to the Novus van, and it exploded in a cloud of shards. Hong cried with delight.

"Again, more!"

The driver glanced in the rearview mirror and shook his head but said nothing. Teng swapped out the magazine once more and again hung out the side window. The cold wind tore at him, but he aimed carefully.

This time they wouldn't get away. As Teng was about to squeeze the trigger, his target punched the accelerator and sped past a long, red Royal Mail truck. Teng motioned for the driver to follow.

"Get us up in front."

The driver started to turn the wheel, but in the same instant, Teng watched in horror as the van's brake lamps turned on; a fraction of a second later, the brake lights of the mail truck also lit up.

After that, everything happened at half-speed. When the truck's brakes locked, it started to slide, pulling three cars along with it. The cars were pushed aside but avoided crashing as their speed was so low.

But the speed had been high enough to overturn the truck. It collapsed onto its side like a butterfly knife on the slippery road. A white cloud rose, and a long, crashing sound echoed across the highway.

*

They left the chaos behind them. A cloud of rushing snow flew into the air as the huge truck tipped over with a crash, blocking the road.

"It's okay, Tim," Hugo said.

Tim grabbed the wheel so hard Hugo thought the bones would penetrate his skin. His voice broke.

"You never said we were going to overturn a truck."

Mikko burst out laughing at the unexpected comment, and his laughter swept over the others. They shrieked with laughter at the stunning fact that they had survived. Life was always at its sweetest after you'd come close to death's awful breath. Sussie wiped away tears. Her bloodstained face was streaked.

"That was impressive, Hugo," she said. "Very impressive."

"Thanks." Hugo looked at the clock. Half-past ten.

"What do you think, Tim? Will you and your girlfriend be going to the Maldives?"

Tim forced a smile. "Yes, of course we will. If we survived the last fifteen minutes, the rest will be a child's game."

Hugo pulled out his phone. "Madeleine," he said into the receiver, "it's me."

"What's up?"

"Do we have permission to enter the press conference?"

Madeleine's voice disappeared for a few seconds. When she returned, she replied, "You do. The press conference starts at eleven o'clock, and there are two access cards for you at the receptionist's desk."

"Only two?"

"That's all we were able to arrange."

"Okay. Thanks. Any other information?"

"Yes," Madeleine said. "We've received reports that an airplane has entered English airspace and done some sort of controlled crash landing."

"Controlled crash landing?"

"Right. It's hard to interpret the report because it's missing a lot of information. But it seems that an aircraft was hijacked in Tallinn and set course for London."

A chill rolled through Hugo.

"Xi."

"Yeah. He seems to be a tough one."

"You can't even imagine."

Madeleine gave Hugo some more updates, then said, "That should be everything for now."

"Thanks for the help. We'll get back to you when we can."

"Good luck."

Hugo peered out through the cracked windshield. The large glassed, high-rise buildings stretched upward to space as they approached central London. None of the team noticed the red, bulky van keeping its distance behind them.

28

Klaus pulled the seat belt so tight that he could barely move, but it didn't help. When the helicopter rocked, his stomach nearly came up through his mouth.

"How far?" he groaned.

The pilot pointed. "Not far at all. London Heliport is ten minutes away."

Klaus winced and said, "Okay, just be sure to get us there as softly as possible."

The pilot gave a brief nod. He'd seen it before— wealthy businessmen who wanted to impress their girlfriends by taking them up in a helicopter. It's a wonderful trip until it ends with the businessman throwing up all over himself.

"Absolutely, sir. As softly as possible."

Klaus fixed his eyes on the Shard, London's iconic skyscraper. He'd heard that it helped to fix your gaze on something when you were feeling motion sickness. Keeping his eye on the building, he pulled his phone out of his pocket and dialed a number. It rang twice before a female voice answered.

"Hello?"

"Hi. It's me."

He was met with a hesitant silence, and then, "Are you there yet?"

"Not yet. Almost."

"How do things look?"

"I went through everything on the way here, and it all looks good," Klaus said. "The operation is continuing according to plan."

"Good. Call me when something new happens."

"Will do."

He hung up and breathed as deeply as he could with the seat belt restricting his midsection. When he lifted his hand, he noticed it was trembling. So much was at stake; he must not fail now. But he wouldn't. The men stationed in the van outside the hotel had sent him continuous updates, and everything looked good. No, it would be fantastic. Weeks of planning would reach their peak within the next hour, and what would take place would dominate world news for the foreseeable future. He shivered with anticipation.

*

Heat boiled within him. Mustafa touched his forehead and found it sopping wet. He took a few steps toward the bathroom but had to stop. Tanya rushed over to him.

"Mustafa! What is it?"

He tried to speak, but no words came out. He got down on his knees. Tanya stroked his back.

"Mustafa, talk to me. What's going on? Are you sick?"

The truth was that Mustafa Boon had never felt anything like this. It was as if his interior was on fire and lava was streaming through his veins. Every movement thundered as unrelenting pain echoed through his muscles. He gasped for air.

"I need— Take me to the toilet. I'm going to— Something I've eaten . . ."

But he knew better—this wasn't food poisoning. It was something else. He inched forward, crawling on the floor to the bathroom. He pushed open the door and continued inside. Tanya followed him helplessly.

"Mustafa, should we call for an ambulance?"

He shook his head. "No, not now. Press conference must continue."

Someone from QuantumCorp must have poisoned him, Mustafa thought. It had to be. They were the only ones who had something to gain from the press conference being canceled. His knees burned like fire as he crawled along. When he arrived at a stall, he pushed the door open, threw himself over the toilet, and vomited.

Black blood and bile poured out of his body. Currents of spasmodic pain washed over him like waves on a beach, and small, blinking stars danced in the corners of his eyes. His abdominal muscles cramped, and he slipped and fell hard, hitting the toilet seat with his chin and biting off his tongue. Torrents of blood poured from his mouth.

Somewhere far away, he heard his name being called. He tried to focus on it, but it drifted away into nothingness. Faster and faster, the darkness rushed forward, enveloping him, and finally taking him down.

*

He thanked God. Klaus Horst jumped out of the helicopter and wobbled as his feet landed on the icy ground. Snow swirled around him as the powerful rotor spun slowly. He took a few deep breaths and wiped the cold sweat from his forehead. Someone shouted at him, and he turned and looked at the pilot, who was knocking on the window.

The pilot pointed, and Klaus followed his finger. Two dark BMWs were driving toward them. They stopped, and three jumped out of each car. They were all armed. A muscular man with dark, cropped hair approached Klaus.

"This way, sir. We'll take you to the liaison center."

Klaus followed him. This was something QuantumCorp was a champion in—transport and logistics. When a company had operations across the globe, as QuantumCorp did, it was almost impossible to not become a specialist in those things. The cropped-hair man handed an iPad to Klaus.

"Here's the latest status report," he said.

Klaus skimmed it. The three nanobot injections had been performed according to plan. The targets didn't seem to indicate that they knew anything.

Goal 1: Mustafa Boon. Injections 1 and 2 performed. No reactions.

Goal 2: Tanya Lipton. Injections 1 and 2 performed. No reactions.

Goal 3: Ben Chimes. Injections 1 and 2 performed. No reactions.

Klaus lowered the tablet as they passed two taxis in the middle lane. He glanced over at the people outside on the sidewalk, who all went about their own affairs without knowing what he was up to. Without a clue that he was headed to his fate, to the moment he'd been waiting for his entire life. Now, at last, was his chance to shine.

The cropped-haired man raised a walkie-talkie. "Nest, this is Runner. Come in."

The radio crackled. "Bird's nest here. Come in, Runner."

"We have Tiger in custody. Moving on to you. Estimated arrival fifteen minutes."

"Roger, Runner."

"Runner over."

Klaus tensed his jaws to suppress a giggle. *Tiger.* He liked that code name.

It had started to snow again, and the thin snowflakes filled the air outside. Klaus grinned to himself, feeling warm inside.

29

Time was almost up. They skidded around a parked car as they approached the Oriental Mandarin, and Hugo pointed.

"There!"

Mikko stepped on the brake, nearly causing the van to crash into a parked car. Hugo threw open the door.

"Move it! It's almost eleven!"

He, Freya, and Sussie rushed into the beautiful hotel and to the receptionist's desk. A faint exquisite jasmine scent welcomed them. Behind the desk, gorgeous receptionist beamed at them as they entered, her row of perfectly white teeth glittering like diamonds.

"Welcome to the Oriental Mandarin. How can I help you?"

Hugo cleared his throat. "We're here for the press conference."

"What's the name?"

"Hugo Xavier."

The woman smiled, showing off her perfect teeth again. "One moment, please."

She disappeared, and Hugo turned to Freya. "What do you guys think?"

"The lobby looks okay, no threats that I can see," Freya said. "Sussie, do you see anything?"

"Nope, nothing."

The woman came back and pulled out an envelope. "Here you go, Mr. Xavier."

Hugo took the envelope and ripped it open, and two access cards with attached lanyards fell out. He gave one to Freya and nodded to Sussie.

"Find somewhere you can observe the entire lobby, okay? Freya and I will go to the press conference. Let us know if you see anything suspicious."

Sussie put an earpiece in her ear and nodded. "Roger." She spun on her heel and disappeared into the elegant lobby.

"Freya, are you ready?"

"You better believe it."

"Good. Let's take it nice and easy. If you see anything suspicious, let me know before you act. Got it?"

"Obviously."

They put the access cards around their necks and approached a sign that said in bold letters,

Techyx Press Conference

They showed their cards to the two guards, who gave brief nods and let them through.

"Welcome. The press conference will be starting soon."

"Thanks," Hugo said as he opened the door for Freya. She stepped in, and Hugo followed. A dozen pairs of eyes turned and examined the new arrivals. After a few seconds, they turned back to their notepads and tablets.

"There are two seats over there," Hugo said in a low voice. "You go grab them. I'll see if I can circulate a bit."

Freya walked away and sat down in one of the vacant chairs in the back of the room. Hugo turned right and strolled around the room, assessing the participants of the press conference.

Small, seated groups of men and women whispered to each other, but Hugo couldn't hear what most of them were saying. A couple of white-clad figures stood talking to each other in the back of the room. Hugo headed back to Freya.

"It looks okay for now. I don't see any threats."

"Neither do I."

He glanced down at the yellow bag between her legs.

"Make sure to keep that close. When something happens, shit will go down fast."

*

Pain echoed through his body as he crawled forward and stood up. He swayed for a few seconds before a man rushed up to him.

"Oh my God! I saw everything! Are you hurt?"

Xi blinked and tried to regain his orientation. He was in a park. He must have landed in a tree and slid down to the ground from there. The stranger continued to speak to him in a distressed voice. Xi shook his head slowly. He had to get to the Oriental Mandarin as quickly as possible. He turned to the babbling man.

"What time is it?"

The man fell silent and shifted his weight. He hesitated but checked his watch.

"A little after eleven."

"Goddammit," he cursed under his breath. The press conference had already begun. "Which way to the Mandarin Hotel?"

The man took a step back, a little more suspicious now.

"Why?"

"I have to get there; my family is there."

The man frowned and a few seconds elapsed. More shouting voices came from further away. As they came closer, the man lifted his arm and pointed.

"It's that way. Just under a hundred meters."

Xi smiled and bent down. The stranger was still standing there; he never noticed the knife until it impaled the soft underside of his chin. He fell backward, and Xi pulled the lifeless body deep into the snow-covered bushes.

The hiding place wouldn't stop the guy from being discovered, but it would give Xi a few extra minutes to complete his final mission. This was his destiny. He would show them just who they had betrayed.

Xi took a couple of stepping steps in the direction that the now-dead man had pointed.

*

They swung around the corner, and Klaus caught sight of the dark van.

"So close?"

The cropped-hair man—the one with the code name 'Runner'—shrugged. "The range isn't that far, and this was the best place."

Klaus groaned. The magnificent Mandarin Oriental was a hundred meters away. He had preferred a little more space between himself and the press conference, but he couldn't do anything about it now.

"Okay, get me into it."

Runner leaned forward to the driver. "Frank, park over there. Tiger and I walk over to the van."

"Roger."

The dark BMWs turned in behind a garbage truck that was idling at Knightsbridge. They jumped out, and Klaus pulled his coat around his body as he met the cold air. They hurried over to the van.

"Nest, we're on our way. We'll be with you in ten seconds."

"Bird's nest, Roger."

The rear door opened the moment they arrived. Two strong hands reached out and pulled Klaus up, and Runner climbed in and closed the door.

An older man with a trim, white beard set down a plastic coffee mug and stood up.

"Welcome, gentlemen. Welcome."

Klaus walked up to him and shook his knuckly hand.

"Dr. Zepp. Good to see you. Everything all right?"

Zepp motioned for them to follow him. "Absolutely. As you can see, we have complete control over the situation. The press conference is just starting."

A man sitting in front of a monitor swirled around on a chair and faced Klaus.

"Oh, hello there," said the thin man with dark-rimmed glasses. Klaus immediately recognized him.

"QC! Everything good?"

QC shook his head and said, "No, not quite."

Dr. Zepp froze. "What? Two minutes ago, you said everything was fine."

QC's mouth became a thin line. "Yeah, but that was then, and now is now."

Klaus held up his hand. "Enough. What do you mean, QC?"

"This. Look." QC pressed the keyboard, and on the screen, the grainy image of an office glided forward. A dark-skinned man was lying down on a couch, and a man and a woman were standing next to him. The woman had her arms crossed in front of her; the man on the couch wasn't moving.

"Who is that?"

"That, my friends, is Mustafa Boon."

Dr. Zepp gasped. "What? What is he doing there? Why isn't he out at the press conference presenting?"

"Something must have happened to him in the last five minutes, of course," said QC.

Klaus turned to Zepp and glowered. "This is unacceptable. This is your responsibility—you were supposed to make sure everything went smoothly."

"I don't know what to say. I apologize."

"Well, it's too little, too late, isn't it?"

QC worked on the keyboard. "Wait, I'll see if I can get some sound."

A few seconds later, a hidden speaker came to life.

"Mustafa, can you hear me? Mustafa!"

"Check his pulse."

"Did you call an ambulance?"

"Yes, it's on its way. God, his skin looks like ashes."

Klaus frowned. "Okay, we'll have to make do without Mustafa, that's all there is to it. It won't be as effective, but we'll do the best we can with what we have."

Dr. Zepp picked up an iPad. "Here," he said, showing it to Klaus. "The other two targets are ready. Everything looks green."

Klaus took the tablet and went through the information. Everything looked good. His heart pounded in his chest as he again thought about how all his planning would bear fruit.

Fifty meters away, a rusty red van sat parked, its engine running.

*

Panic raged within her. Tanya looked over the assembled journalists and froze. The sea of eyes looking back at her seemed endless as she stood on the stage next to an office table and chairs. All three of them would have sat there, but Mustafa had fainted in the hotel manager's office.

She ought to go up to the mic and say something, but she didn't know what. Everything had happened so fast, and now she stood handcuffed like a petrified deer. Ben entered and walked up to her. He leaned in close to her ear.

"He's not waking up. It looks serious. He's out cold."

"Have you tried everything?"

"Yes, everything I could, but nothing's working. The ambulance is on its way."

"What do you think it is?" Tanya asked.

"My guess is as good as yours. It looks like acute poisoning, but still," he said and paused, "he ate the same things we did, but we feel okay."

Tanya flinched when one of the journalists stood up.

"Excuse me, is there a problem?"

Tanya shook her head. "No, not at all. We're just discussing a few last details."

The journalist sat down, glancing over at the big clock on the wall.

Tanya grabbed Ben's arm. "We have to do it ourselves."

"But what about Mustafa?"

With a sharp edge in her voice, she replied, "He's not here, is he? And he specifically didn't want us to cancel. We should tell it like it is—our honorable colleague has become acutely ill, but that he is a vital part of the project."

Ben pondered for a few seconds. "You're right. We should do it."

"Okay, then. Ready?"

"Ready."

Tanya tensed her jaws, took a deep breath, and spun around.

"Hello, everyone. We're ready to begin; thank you so much for your patience."

She and Ben went up on the stage and sat down. Ben poured two glasses of water, and Tanya nodded.

"Honorable journalists, welcome to this press conference, where we will walk you through the work we've been doing for the past year—namely, the work of documenting the systematic environmental offenses committed by the multinational company QuantumCorp"

30

"This means that contaminated water leaks straight into the groundwater and spreads. It's a disaster every time something like this happens, but what we're seeing in the case of QuantumCorp is on a completely different scale. The contaminated water has spread to at least twelve different aquifers in this region alone. The consequences of this are extremely serious. And that's just in Chile." Tanya paused, shifting her eye contact with the journalists before continuing. "In the western part of South America, we've found more than sixty-two mines in which QuantumCorp works the same way."

A dozen hands rose into the air. Tanya pointed to a woman in the middle of the room, who stood up.

"Lisa Lert, NRT News. Are you sure about that number? Sixty-two?"

Tanya smiled grimly. "Absolutely sure. After the press conference, we will distribute an information booklet containing all the data we're presenting today."

Lisa Lert sat down, and Tanya continued.

"Our investigation has shown that this atrocity is happening in other parts of the world, as well as illegal mining operations, all under the auspices of QuantumCorp. We have gathered evidence cases from Zimbabwe and Liberia, for example. Take a look."

Tanya nodded to Ben, who pressed a button on an iPad. A projector in the ceiling lit up, and a video flickered behind them. It showed a group of men without protective gear working in a large, muddy hole. Using axes and shovels, they filled bucket after bucket with muddy soil that was then dragged out of the hole. Whoever was filming slipped, and the scene moved erratically. A few seconds passed before it stabilized again. Someone shouted, and people started to move away from the edge of the hole.

There were more shouts, and some of the men tried in a panic to climb up along the muddy walls. Their hands couldn't find a hold, and one by one, they slid down. As if in slow motion, one of the sides collapsed, first haltingly, then faster until all the sides came crashing down. The screaming voices were cut off when the miners were buried alive. A couple of journalists cried out, but Tanya raised her hands, calling for quiet.

"This video was taken in Liberia a month ago. As you can see, the poor men in these countries work under terrible conditions. They risk their lives for less than a dollar a day."

Suddenly, the room spun before Tanya's eyes, and she fell silent. Most of the journalists didn't notice her gently swaying back and forth, since their attention was still directed at the video. She grabbed the edge of the table to make the room stop spinning.

A weak voice echoed in her head, and she thought she was experiencing some type of audio illusion. She shook her head to make it disappear.

Now. Do it now. Now. Do it now.

Ben whispered, "Tanya, what is it? Are you okay?"

She cleared her throat. "Yes, I'm fine. Super fine."

Ben frowned at the strange comment. Tanya rubbed her temples, and light flashed in front of her eyes. The voice inside her head grew louder.

Now. Do it now. Now. Do it now.

A drop of sweat ran along her forehead and she wiped it away. She abruptly stood up. Several of the journalists had, by now, switched their focus from the film to her and were staring at her curiously.

"I apologize," she said shakily, attempting to chuckle. "We've had a big week. Let's move on."

Now. Do it now. Now. Do it now.

She walked around the table, and panic intensified in her mind as the voice grew more and more forceful.

Now. Do it now. Now. Do it now—kill them!

She fell silent and closed her eyes. The whole room was staring at her now. Ben stood up, walked over to her, and put his arm on her shoulder.

"Tanya, are you okay? Do you need to take a break?"

Tanya opened her eyes, and Ben took a step back when he saw how they glittered.

*

So close. Xi entered the Oriental Mandarin's exquisite lobby. A group of people came down the steps, and Xi stepped aside to let them pass. Pain pounded through his right leg with every step he took, but he ignored it. That didn't matter right now. He pushed it from his mind until it was nothing but a distant memory. He headed up the stairs and found it—a sign that said *Techyx Press Conference.*

A couple of guards stood in front of the doors leading to the room where the press conference was being held. Xi watched as two women walked up to the guards, held up a pair of access cards, and entered. Xi swore. He had to get hold of one of those cards, but how? He stepped aside as the seconds ticked by, frustration growing within him.

A man opened the door and came out of the conference room appearing agitated. He grabbed one of the guards.

"Where's the bathroom? I have to get some water for one of the presenters. Something is wrong with her."

The guard pointed to the left, confused, and the man ran in that direction. Xi grinned—his chance had arrived. He followed the man into the bathroom. Inside, the room smelled like a mixture of flowers and detergent. As Xi entered, the man was filling a small plastic bottle at one of the sinks. At first, he took no note of Xi, but when Xi made no effort to go into a toilet stall, the man looked at him in the mirror.

"Yes?"

"I'm going to need your access card."

The man frowned. "Excuse me?"

"You heard me. I need your card. Give it to me now and I'll let you live."

The man glared at Xi. "Get lost before I call the guards."

Xi lowered his head and took a step forward. "You're right," he said softly. "I don't know what came over me."

The man shot Xi a bewildered look, turned off the water, and screwed the top back on the bottle. Just then, Xi let his knife slip into his hand from his sleeve, and in a sweeping motion, he sliced the man's throat wide open.

The pulmonary vein pumped blood like a fountain with each heartbeat, and the man pressed his hands against his throat in a futile attempt to stop the blood. Before long, he dropped to his knees. Xi stood over him and pulled the access card from around his neck.

"You should have just given it to me."

The man's eyes rolled back, and he fell over. Xi washed off the blood-stained card and lanyard, then pulled it over his head. As he walked out of the bathroom, he grabbed a yellow 'wet floor' sign and put it in front of the bathroom door. He took a quick breath and approached the guards at the door.

Soon. He could almost taste it.

*

Something was wrong. Hugo got up and took a few steps to the side to see better. The female researcher stood on the podium and swayed. Her male colleague held his hand on her shoulder and said something to her.

Freya leaned toward Hugo and whispered, "What's happening?"

"Something's going on."

The two researchers made no effort to stop the press conference. A couple of journalists rose.

"What is it? Is everything okay?"

The male scientist gave a thumbs-up and someone to the right laughed. Hugo shook his head. He watched as a wave of anxiety began to slide over the people closest to the stage.

"He's lying. Something is wrong."

Hugo's brain went into overdrive. He scouted around to find out what his instincts were warning him about, but he couldn't pick up on any threats. The video on the wall had stopped, but the researchers still did nothing. Another journalist stood.

"Are we going to continue or not? I don't have time to sit here all day."

Something inside Hugo clicked. It more of a feeling than a thought. The last twenty-four hours had been like a fog, and he was struggling to give himself time to process everything they had been through. And that was probably why he hadn't seen it before.

What now flashed through him was like a white light of realization. If you were going to carry out the perfect attack—not just a bloody coup, but a spectacular act—it would require willpower beyond the ordinary. It would require a mind for detail and the ability to form a plan that would place all blame on the innocent. And who is more innocent than the victims?

The female scientist turned to her colleague and let out a blood-curdling scream.

*

The whole room froze as one. Tanya's voice went up an octave, and her screams increased in intensity. The journalists in the front row took a frightened step back when Tanya took a tiger-leap toward Ben.

Ben stumbled backward with Tanya on top of him, screaming and clawing. People screamed and shouted around them, and Hugo gasped.

"They're the assassins themselves!"

He rushed forward, passing two men who stood like statues staring at what was playing out in front of them.

He stumbled onto the stage, and the two scientists, who had been in complete harmony only a few minutes ago, now fought for life and death. The woman clawed long, bloody wounds into the man's face, and he screamed.

"No! Tanya, no! Help me!"

Hugo rushed forward, and a couple of journalists broke out of their paralysis when they saw him running toward danger. They also began to move toward the struggling scientists. Hugo leaped over a chair, past two screaming women, and jumped toward the white-clad woman who was using her long nails like weapons.

He caught a whiff of blood as he soared toward her. He hit her high up on the shoulder, and the two of them tumbled back. The woman shifted focus from her colleague to Hugo. She got onto her feet as smoothly as a panther, and Hugo her eyes glitter in a way he had never seen before.

"Stop!" he roared.

The woman either didn't understand what he said or didn't listen. But it didn't matter. She licked her lips, and to Hugo's dismay, she ran her fingers into her own forehead and ripped downward. Blood streamed down her face, and the people in the room let out a gathered gasp of horror.

Hugo knew that the scientist was beyond all ability to communicate. The only thing they could do now was to try to immobilize her until the police arrived. Both of the journalists Hugo had passed had now come up behind her but were clearly unsure how to proceed.

Hugo thundered, "On my signal! Three, two, one, now!"

But a fraction of a second before they jumped on her, the other scientist roared, and the room froze to ice once more.

31

It was a sound Hugo had never heard a human make before. It had come from somewhere deep within the male researcher's throat, and it was equal parts primal and terrifying. The man squatted and began to rock back and forth. The two journalists who had rushed forward to help Hugo found themselves standing between the two rabid scientists, and they hesitated. And that hesitation was enough.

The woman, her face covered in gore, leaped and began tearing into one of the men. Hugo saw the attack coming and threw himself at her but found her to be inhumanly strong. He tried in vain to grab hold of her arms but failed. She waved her arms like weapons, and the blood that dripped from her face made every part of her skin slippery and impossible to get a real grip. One of the journalists turned and retreated as his courage betrayed him.

Hugo yelled, "Come on! Help me!"

But the man hesitated and took a few more steps back.

"Hugo!" Freya rushed forward with the yellow bag in one hand. She threw it to the terrified journalist, who swallowed hard and then threw himself toward Hugo and the screaming woman.

They struggled to get hold of her until finally, Hugo managed to wrap his legs around her waist and grip her in a headlock.

Freya tried to hold the woman's flailing arms. The scientist got one arm free and sliced Freya on the cheek.

Freya reacted instinctively and punched the woman in the face, which made her calm down. But the calm only lasted a few seconds. Her powers returned, and she roared so loudly that Hugo felt his eardrums vibrate.

"The bag!" he gasped. "Now!"

Three meters away, the man stood just there, staring uncomprehendingly at Hugo.

"Now! Give it to me!" came Freya's booming voice. That got him to move. He ran forward and threw the bag onto the floor next to her.

"Can you hold her?" Freya asked.

"Yes—get the machine out!"

Every muscle in Hugo's body was stretched to the limit as he held onto the manic woman. It felt like a rusty dagger was lodged in his shoulder. Freya leaped to the bag, ripped it open, and took hold of the scanner. She pulled out the two metal sensors and tried to hold them against the woman's head. The crazed researcher pushed it aside.

"Hold her!"

Hugo tasted blood in his mouth. "Okay—now!" he shouted.

Freya brought the metal plates back, and this time they made contact. Freya pressed the button, and a low hum emanated from the machine. A few seconds passed, and as the scanner buzzed, the woman's frenzied screams subsided and her body began to relax.

Hugo saw small, flashing stars as he slowly let her go. The woman went limp and dropped to the floor, moaning. Freya stumbled onto her legs and reached down to Hugo.

"Hey. Are you okay?"

He grabbed her hand and pulled himself up. "I hope so. I think so. A bit sore, though."

At that moment, another abysmal noise bellowed through the room. Hugo and Freya spun around to see the other researcher rushing toward them.

*

Xi couldn't believe his luck. A roar pierced the conference room door, and both of the guards tensed. They hesitated for a few seconds, and Xi studied them. Another bellowing sound rumbled from the other side door, and Xi flinched.

The voice—if that's what it was—didn't sound human. It sounded like whatever was screaming was in unimaginable pain. As Xi watched, one of the guards mustered some courage and opened the door. He stuck his head in, then turned and said something Xi didn't hear. He pulled out his weapon, fully opened the door, and shouted to his colleague. Then the two men rushed into the room. Xi saw a piece of the utter pandemonium through the doorway.

What was going on in there? But now was not the time to hesitate. Not when he'd come so far. Xi tightened every muscle. This was his moment. He held his knife close to his body and barreled through the open door. Nothing could have prepared him for the chaos that met him inside. About thirty people stood back a considerable distance from a man in a white lab coat who shrieked as if possessed. Chairs lay overturned. The white-clad man ran straight toward some journalists standing next to a woman (also in a lab coat) who was lying on the floor. The woman's face was covered with dark red blood, and she wasn't moving.

Xi recognized the screeching man as one of the researchers who was supposed to present to the assembled journalists today. Xi flinched at the sight of the scientist's insane eyes, then took an involuntary step back. At the front of the room, one of the people attending to the unconscious woman stood, bounded toward the deranged researcher, and tackled him to the ground. As both men collapsed, it struck Xi who this challenger was: it was Hugo.

A shock passed through Xi's body. His instincts had been right, after all. Hugo was here. The scientist and Hugo rolled around on the floor, and a woman nearby shouted.

"Hugo, look out!"

Both of the guards were rushing forward, weapons drawn. "Stop!" they commanded.

Hugo pulled his fist back and landed a straight right on the researcher's jaw. The man kneeled, swayed, and nearly fell, but managed to remain upright. Then, unexpectedly, he turned away from Hugo, as if he'd lost interest in the fight.

"On the ground! Now!" shouted the guards. They took a step forward, but the scientist made no effort to listen. He lifted his hands as if to pray and then began to tear at himself on the neck. Blood was soon streaming down, staining his white coat bright red. Xi blinked in surprise.

The guards came closer. "Now! Get down!"

As if the bloodied scientist finally heard them, he slowly turned toward them and exposed bloody teeth. Everything was still for a moment; then he rushed toward the guards, screaming. Immediately, they opened fire. The bullets lifted the wounded man's bloody body into the air like a tattered mitten. He flew back, crashed to the floor, and moved no more.

Hugo grabbed hold of one of his comrade's extended hands and pulled himself up. Just a few feet away, a wave of white-hot rage flooded Xi's mind. He barreled toward the guards, punching one of them in the throat and bringing him to his knees. Xi hurdled him and struck the other between his legs; that one dropped, too.

The people in the room cried out as the violence flared up again. Seeing Freya, Xi grabbed for her, but she slipped away. Hugo took a step forward and measured a blow to Xi's midsection.

Xi grimaced but stood strong and stared into Hugo's eyes. "Do you remember me?" he asked.

Hugo chuckled dryly. "Of course I do. It's not every day a person gets a chance to exact revenge so quickly. You're going to die, I promise."

"Come on, then."

Xi turned his body toward Hugo, took a step to the side, and slid his knife into his palm. Opposite him, Hugo also pulled a knife from his chest holster. The two men circled each other. Moving like a panther, Xi made a series of lunges at his opponent until, finally, he made contact. Hugo stumbled back, a long cut drawn from his bicep to his forearm. Blood dripped steadily where he stood.

Xi grinned. "This is going to be easier than I thought," he taunted.

Hugo said nothing but moved to counterattack. He pushed Xi back and managed to land a cut on his cheek. A thin streak of blood ran down his chin.

"Not so cocky now, are we?" Hugo said.

Xi glanced at the motionless guard on the floor ten feet away. His weapon was hidden underneath him, but Xi could see the protruding handle. In one move, he slid to the side and pounced. He landed hard, rolled, and grabbed the weapon. Wasting no time, Xi lifted the handgun and shot. Hugo shouted and threw himself back.

Xi turned to Freya and raised the gun again. A shot rang out. Xi's expression morphed from rage to confusion as he looked at the small cloud of blood that sprinkled up from his right shoulder. He spun around, saw the guard who had shot him, and put a round in his head.

Voices sounded from outside the room.

Police! In there! Hurry up!

Xi turned toward Hugo's motionless body and spat. He laughed; this part was finished, at long last. Only one more thing remained to be taken care of: Klaus. Xi left the chaos behind and ran.

*

Things went wrong so fast. Sweat dripped from Klaus' forehead, and he wiped it away. On the monitor in front of him, he watched Xi shoot Hugo. He watched Hugo fall to the floor and not get up again.

Klaus buried his face in his hands. "No!" Then he reeled around and grabbed Zepp's collar. "This is your fault. It was your responsibility to ensure that the programming happened correctly." He paused, pursing his lips, and pointed at the screen. "But look now. Look at this disaster. That was not how it was supposed to go!"

Dr. Zepp stepped back. "You know, it might not be such a total disaster. I mean, the scientists went crazy—not just against the journalists, but more against themselves. Their credibility is destroyed now, right?"

Klaus tightened his jaws and punched Zepp hard on the chin. Zepp's hands went to his face and he staggered back a few steps, bumping into the monitors. The rest of the crew watched silently.

"That wasn't what we had planned, was it?" Klaus growled. "Or are you saying that all those weeks don't matter?"

"No, of course not. You're right. This is a failure, and I take full responsibility," Zepp said.

Klaus threw his hands up in the air when he saw Xi bolting from the press conference room. "It doesn't matter now."

He turned from Zepp and sat down. He had to get away from here, had to get himself to safety. What had Heidi said? Something about an apartment on the other side of Hyde Park. He glared at Runner, who had been sitting quietly for the last quarter of an hour.

"Time to go," Xi told him.

Runner opened the door. "Okay. Where?"

*

The ice cold hit him square in the face. Xi stumbled outside, leaving the pandemonium behind him. His shoulder burned with pain, and he whimpered.

Police officers came rushing up the steps, and Xi stepped aside. Once they were gone, he scouted the area. Klaus was nearby, he was sure of that. The surveillance range wasn't very long, just under a hundred meters.

He spotted it. A large, black van sat parked seventy meters away, and Xi started toward it. When he was halfway there, the back doors opened, and a man with dark, close-cropped hair stepped out. A second later, Klaus followed. Xi smiled. This was indeed a day of happiness.

Xi started running in Klaus' direction. After a few paces, however, his feet found a slab of black ice, and he hit the ground hard. He wailed in agony.

As he picked himself up, Xi saw Klaus and his friend staring at him. Xi pulled back his teeth in a shark-like smile. He smacked his lips and sensed the taste of metal. The two men were less than thirty meters away. Despite the pain, he started running toward them once more. Runner grabbed Klaus' arm, and they took off toward the park.

"Klaus!" Xi called after him. "Stop!"

They didn't turn around but instead ran faster. Pain resounded through Xi's body with each step he took. He put his hand inside his jacket and felt for his shoulder; when he pulled it out again, his fingers were red and sticky.

But he couldn't give up now, not when he was so close. Klaus and his companion disappeared into the park, and Xi followed.

*

Stars flashed before him, and he blinked hard to make them disappear. A voice permeated the fog that lay over his consciousness.

"Hugo. Can you hear me, Hugo?"

Hugo tried to open his eyes, but they were stuck together as if with superglue. He jiggled an arm, and someone grabbed hold of his hand.

"Yes," he mumbled. "I can hear you."

"It's me, Freya. Can you open your eyes?"

Hugo strained with all his might and finally forced them open with pure willpower. Freya smiled at him.

"Hello."

Hugo groaned as he slowly sat up. A nurse sitting next to Freya pulled a bandage from a first aid kit.

"Here we go. Take it easy." The nurse carefully wrapped the bandage around his head.

"Do you have anything for the pain?" Hugo said, his voice low and wobbly.

The nurse looked from Hugo to Freya and back again. She hesitated. "Yes, I do. But I need you to stay there until we get a gurney."

"No. Give me what you have. Please."

The medic hesitated again, but Hugo's flashing eyes convinced her. She pulled out a small disposable syringe and stuck it in Hugo's arm. Warmth spread through his arm and toward the rest of his body, and he relaxed.

"Thanks."

Hugo reached for Freya, and she helped him up.

"And now what?" she asked.

Hugo looked around. The two motionless scientists lay on the floor, covered with white blankets.

"Call Madeleine and update her on what's happened here," he instructed.

"What are you going to do?"

Hugo's voice became cold as ice. "Claim my revenge."

*

Safety. It was within sight. Klaus' foot caught on a root, and he stumbled and fell, hitting the ground hard. Runner stopped and helped him up.

"Come on! We're almost there."

Klaus groaned as his fingers slid across the icy ground. He got back up on his feet and continued to run. At the edge of the park, they kept running across the street; cars honked, but Klaus ignored them.

"Here! Hurry up."

They had arrived at a beautiful gate. Klaus stared at the handsome numbers. Twenty-three.

He ran to the doorbell and pressed the name Heidi had told him. A few seconds later, a voice answered.

"Yes?"

"Yes, hello, it's Klaus Horst. I need to come in."

No answer.

"Can you hear me? This is Klaus Horst. Let me in, please."

Still nothing. Panic slid grabbed hold of his heart, and his voice went up an octave.

"Listen, you bastard. If you don't let me in, I'll make sure you regret it for the rest of your life."

Four seconds later, the big gate clicked and slid open. Runner pulled out his phone.

"We're in. Number twenty-three. Get here as soon as we can. Right now, we're exposed."

Klaus rushed in through the gate, and when he entered the beautiful hall, his anxiety began to drift away. Intricate murals and statues lined the walls. They hurried on to the elevator. The doors slid aside, and they stepped in.

"Top," Klaus instructed.

As the elevator began to move, Klaus felt the tension in his muscles begin to ease one by one.

*

So close! Xi stood on the other side of the street and watched Klaus disappear through the elaborate gate. He cursed.

The cars sped by him as Xi studied the property. It was a beautiful old Victorian mansion with four floors. The only question was how he'd get in. When there was a gap in traffic, he ran over to get a closer look. Xi examined the windows carefully until—there. A series of windows lit up on the fourth floor. With a half-grin, he ran around the corner and scoured the area.

A large scaffolding hugged the side of the house next door, following the wall all the way to the top. He judged the distance between the two houses. It looked to be just under three meters, possibly four. It would be a challenging leap, but he had fared worse.

He jogged over to the other house, jumped the fence, and started to climb the scaffolding, his shoulder thumping with his heartbeat. When he reached the top, Xi walked to the edge and stared down at the abyss that opened under him. He yanked away one of the protective barriers and threw it to the side.

Now. It was time.

He took charge and tightened every muscle, then sprinted and jumped out into the darkness.

32

Something burned within him. Hugo stepped out into the frigid air, and the hair on his arms stood up.

A voice called out, "Hugo!" Mikko came running up the stairs to meet him. "What's going on?"

"It was a trap," Hugo said. "It was the scientists themselves who were the assassins. It was them."

"What?"

Hugo shrugged. "I'll explain later. The important thing right now is to get hold of Xi before he disappears again."

Mikko turned and pointed to the park. "I don't think you need to worry about that. I saw him run in there. With fire in his eyes."

Hugo narrowed his eyes. "What? Xi Liu ran into the park? He didn't have a waiting car?"

"Apparently not. He came out of the hotel five minutes ago and ran that way. I think he was following two guys who jumped out of that dark van and also ran into the park."

Mikko pointed at the van. Its windows were tinted, so Hugo couldn't tell if anyone was sitting in the driver's seat, but as he stared at it, he got the distinct feeling that something about the van was wrong. He couldn't put his finger on exactly what it was, but something had gotten his inner warning system going.

There was something else, too. His gaze glided over the surroundings and landed on the buckled red van that had pursued them on the highway. He froze.

"Mikko, look behind you. It's the red van."

Mikko's eyes widened, and he pulled out his phone. "I'm calling the cops," he said. Then, a moment later, he said into the receiver, "Yes, we need some help. There's a red van sitting on the roadside, and the people in it are armed. Can you send a patrol at once to check them out?"

A few seconds passed before Mikko clicked off the call and put the phone back into his pocket. "They're on their way," he said.

Soon, a police patrol quietly surrounded the van. Hugo heard the harsh voices of the police officers.

"Open the doors! Come out with your hands in the air!"

Hugo tensed, expecting chaos, but nothing happened. Instead, the driver's door opened, and a man stepped out and raised his hands. A couple of other men stepped out after him. Hugo glanced at Mikko.

"All right," Mikko said, raising his hand for a high-five. "One down, one to go."

Hugo slapped Mikko's hand passively and said, "Call the police and see if they can surround the black van, too. Do it as imperceptibly as possible. It's of the utmost importance that we don't let any of these guys get away."

"And you?"

"I have another task," said Hugo. "See if you can get Sussie to search the area around Hyde Park for any room or apartment that has a connection to QuantumCorp. Have her send what she finds as quickly as possible."

"Got it. Good luck."

Hugo descended the stairs, and when a hole in the traffic arose, he ran across the road and into the park. The pathways were covered by a thin layer of snow, but he kept good speed. Xi was five minutes in front of him.

Hugo could only gamble that Sussie would find a lead he could use. He started to run faster, and before long, he spotted tracks in the snow. Judging by the step length, two men had run through here. Hugo followed their footprints, continuing through the park until he had reached the other side, straight across from the Oriental Mandarin.

His phone vibrated in his pocket. It was Sussie. "Hey."

"I might have something," Sussie said.

"What did you find?"

"There's an apartment not far from where you are now. The rent is paid by a company in the Caribbean called Entanglement Limited." Sussie chuckled "Which means—"

"I know what it means—intertwining," Hugo interrupted. "It must be a reference to QuantumCorp."

"Exactly."

"Good job, Sussie. Text me the address."

"Sending it now."

"Great. How are Mikko and Freya doing?"

"Mikko has got hold of a police officer, and it looks like the cops are surrounding the van now."

"Excellent. Make sure you support them as much as possible."

"And you?"

"I'm going to fix this once and for all."

Hugo ended the call. He ran across the road and proceeded to the address Sussie had sent him. When he arrived, he stared up at the gorgeous, handcrafted gate.

Now what?

He yanked on the gate, but it was locked. He let his hand slide over all the buttons next to the doorway. A voice responded.

"Who's there? Who is this?"

Hugo cleared his throat. "I'm from the pizzeria. I have a delivery."

"Not for me—you must have the wrong apartment."

Before Hugo could protest, the voice vanished. He cursed under his breath. He had to enter the gate now, before Xi got too much of a head start. He saw movement through the glass and saw two elderly women come out of the elevator, each carrying a small dog.

Hugo stepped aside as one of the ladies opened the gate and tried to get her dog out. Hugo took a step forward and smiled.

"Here. Let me help."

He held the gate open for both of the ladies, who nodded appreciatively.

"Thank you very much, young man."

Hugo let the gate close but positioned his foot so that the lock wouldn't engage. The old ladies disappeared around a corner, and Hugo pushed the gate open and slid through.

*

The pain echoed up and down his legs. Xi got up into a crouching position with a pounding headache. He must have fainted, he realized. His knees seared with pain from rolling after the landing. He stood and limped to the edge that looked over Hyde Park.

He leaned over the low wall. Far below him, cars swept past, unaware they were being watched. He leaned further out and saw the light still shining from the house's top row of windows. Xi went through his options; none was better than the other. Klaus and his friend knew that Xi was on his way, and they'd had time to prepare. So no matter what, this was going to be difficult. He stared at the traffic, thinking, then turned around with a gleam in his eye. He knew what to do.

*

The smell of his sour sweat irritated him, and he groaned as the damp shirt stuck to his back. Klaus secured the weapon in his hand and weighed it. It was an excellent semiautomatic with enough power to stop a raging elephant. The door opened and Runner came in.

"Our men are on their way here. I've sent them the address—they should be here any time."

"Good. Go through the apartment one more time and make sure everything is as it should be."

"Sure thing."

Runner closed the door behind him as he left the room. Klaus was in the office, and along one side was a large stone fireplace. A fire crackled in the hearth, spreading a warm glow. Klaus got closer and sat down in one of the armchairs in front of the fireplace. The heat stretched over him, and he rubbed his hands together until warmth slowly returned.

He thought through the last hour. It might not have been so disastrous anyway. After all, the researchers had gone crazy. And they were probably dead. And the fact was that after this, QuantumCorp's reputation in the industry would be destroyed for years. They would have a hell of a time getting other organizations to collaborate with them.

As Klaus went through the situation in his mind, he became more and more convinced that it might have actually been a success. After a few minutes, he found that he was enjoying himself. But the smile on his lips faded as the office door slammed open. Klaus sprang to his feet in a panic as Runner rushed into the room.

"What?" Klaus asked, wide-eyed.

"I just talked to our men. They're delayed. They're stuck in traffic."

Klaus rolled his eyes. "You idiot! You scared me with your damned theatrical arts."

"I apologize."

"Leave me. Only disturb me if it's of utmost importance. Understood?"

But before Runner could answer, a windowpane exploded in a thousand tiny fragments as a black-clad figure came crashing through it.

*

So close. Xi rolled and got up onto his legs as softly as a panther. The pain was still there, but it was just background noise now. Klaus stood there like a statue, unable to move. Xi took a few steps toward him, and the broken glass crunched under his feet.

He hissed, "So, you think you can dismiss me?"

Klaus' face was pale as a sheet. The dancing flames in the fireplace reflected in the glass on the floor, spreading a kaleidoscope of colors that would have been beautiful, given different circumstances.

"No, no—it was a mistake. Believe me."

Xi bared his teeth. "No, you're the one who's going to believe me. Believe me when I say you are going to regret it."

The knife slid into his right hand, and Xi brought it toward Klaus' face. Runner, who had thrown himself aside when Xi made his entrance, now rushed forward with his weapon raised. He fired a shot into the ceiling, and it blared in the room.

"Stop! Stay where you are!"

Xi froze and glared at the man. "Who are you?"

"Don't worry about who I am. Just stay where you are, or I'll shoot!"

Runner took two big steps and grabbed Klaus by the collar. "Time to go," he said. "Move!"

357

Klaus stumbled to the doorway.

"You won't get away," Xi spat at him. "You know you'll never get away."

Klaus and Runner disappeared through the doorway and slammed the door.

*

From the corridor outside the apartment, Hugo heard crashing sounds. Voices shouted from behind the door, and he pressed his ear to it. There were at least two different voices, maybe three. Someone screamed, and glass shattered. Someone fell to the ground. Then came two loud bangs from a gun.

Now! Hugo kicked the door once, twice, but it didn't move. It must have been reinforced, he thought. More shouting came from the other side of the door, and he kicked again. Nothing. Then, running steps. To Hugo's surprise, the lock disengaged, and the door opened. A man with cropped, dark hair stuck his head out.

"Are you Hugo?"

Hugo stared in amazement at the tall, muscular man. "Yes, I am."

"Help us, for God's sake. There's someone after us. We have him locked in one part of the apartment, but he'll break out of there soon."

Hugo didn't need to hear any more. He pushed the door open and ran into the apartment. The beautiful sculptures and paintings along the walls stood in stark contrast to the chaos that ruled inside the apartment. Hugo rushed through the corridor and came to a doorway that opened into a massive library.

A man lay on the couch on his stomach with a gun pointing to a closed door. He turned his head when he realized he wasn't alone.

"You."

Hugo flinched. "Do I know you?"

"No. But I know you. I've been following you for more than twenty-four hours."

"What do you mean?"

Klaus bit his lip. "I am the person who arranged this entire coup. But we'll talk about that later. Right now, we have bigger problems. We managed to lock him in, but it won't last."

He pointed to the closed door, which shook a second later when someone threw themselves at it. Hugo smiled maliciously.

"Xi Liu?"

"How do you know his name?"

"You think you're the only one with access to information?"

Klaus gave a conciliatory nod. "You're right. So what should we do?"

The door stopped shaking and the seconds passed by. Hugo pulled out his phone.

"We make sure you get out of here."

"Are you going to let us go?"

Hugo held up his hand. "Sussie? It's me. Listen." Hugo told her what had happened, then said, "Get a police force here that can take care of the people who come out."

Once he had confirmation, he hung up.

"I want you to go straight down and wait in the hall. Do you understand? The police will be here soon to take care of you. And don't try to escape, now that we know who you are. Got it?"

Just then, another windowpane exploded, and again a black-clad figure rolled over the rug, landing heavily.

*

Runner grabbed Klaus' arm and pulled him out of the library. Hugo was alone with Xi, who slowly stood and brushed glass shards from his pants. Xi exposed his red teeth, and hair stood up on the back of Hugo's neck.

"Hello, Hugo."

Hugo took a few steps aside. "Yes. It's me again."

"You're supposed to be dead. I killed you myself."

"Not enough, obviously."

Xi's eyes flashed and turned black, and he moved in the other direction. The two men studied each other like two tigers in a pen. Hugo's entire attention was focused on the wiry assassin in front of him. After so many hours of hunting, it was a strange feeling to see Xi in front of him again.

Xi pulled out a knife, and Hugo did the same, both of the blades glittering.

"We doing this again?" Hugo asked.

"Didn't finish the first time," Xi answered, never taking his eyes from his target. Then, he lunged.

Hugo took a step aside. Xi mirrored his actions, and Hugo took a step to the other side. He felt every breath, every air molecule that came into his lungs.

"Is that the best you've got?" Hugo asked.

Xi didn't answer. Hugo knew he had to push him, make him lose his balance. Hugo blinked.

"You know the police are on their way, right? They'll be here soon, and then you'll be stuck."

Xi spat, "You idiot. Do you think you'll ever get me?"

Hugo took a few deep breaths and released his brother into his consciousness. He knew what to do now. He tensed.

"You're right. I won't catch you."

Hugo lunged, and Xi barely parried. Hugo faked a move right but went left and pretended to stumble. Xi cried out, threw himself forward, and thrust his knife at Hugo. Hugo turned at the last second, and the knife landed in his shoulder. Xi shouted triumphantly.

Hugo didn't feel the pain. Instead, he opened his hand and let his knife fall, but before it hit the floor, he caught it with the other hand.

In a single sweeping motion, Hugo arced the knife upward and plunged it into Xi's chest. Xi stopped cold and staggered backward. A bubbling sound left his lips, and while Hugo watched, his eyes rolled back and he fell.

For a full minute, Hugo stared at the motionless body.

Finally.

Xi was dead. Hugo had gotten his revenge. He had avenged his brother. He looked through the broken window beside him and didn't even notice the icy blizzard outside.

Epilogue

The aircraft rocked in the turbulence, but Hugo wasn't paying attention. A hand touched his shoulder. It was Mikko.

"Hey, buddy. How you doing?"

"Okay. A little tired, and my shoulder hurts constantly. Other than that, I'm okay. Can't wait to get home, though."

"I hear that."

Hugo leaned back. It was over. The whole thing was over. The police had taken care of Klaus, who was at this very moment in an interrogation room with a couple of police inspectors to sort out this whole mess. Mikko leaned forward.

"I think Sussie has something for you."

"What?"

"A surprise."

Hugo turned his head to look at Mikko and saw Sussie approaching him. She handed him a phone.

"Here."

He took it, eyeing her warily. "Hello?" he said into the phone.

"Hey, Hugo. It's me."

Hugo froze at the sound of his brother's voice. A wave of relief broke over him, and tears began streaming down his cheeks.

"Felix! You're alive!"

Felix chuckled and said, "You're a real Einstein. Of course I'm alive—you didn't really think I was dead, did you?"

Hugo sniffed. "The thought had crossed my mind."

"But you didn't have to worry. The doctors took good care of me, and Madeleine will come by later. I'll tell her we talked."

"Good. I'm so glad to hear your voice."

"All right, enough about me. Tell me what you've been up to for the past twenty-four hours."

Hugo grinned. "Not so much, you know," he said. "The usual."

Felix chuckled. "Come on."

So Hugo told his brother about the twenty-four hours he'd just lived through. He told him about the mission to Russia and the trip to Helsinki and how they'd crashed. He told Felix about London and how close they'd all come to dying.

Felix whistled. "Sounds like you had a full schedule."

"You can only imagine," Hugo said, "but I had invaluable help from your team. They're truly amazing."

"Yeah, they're the best. But wait, I have someone else here who wants to talk to you."

"Who?"

Another voice came on the line. A woman's. "Hugo?"

A wave of heat rolled through him. "Lita."

"How are you?"

"I'm okay. I'm in the air now, on my way home."

"Thank goodness for that."

They chatted for a few minutes, and Hugo was overwhelmed by his good fortune. His brother had survived, and he was on his way home to the most beautiful woman he had ever seen. Life was good. No, it wasn't good.

It was great.

About the author

Filip Forsberg is a Swedish author living in Malmoe. He's the creator of the science-fiction thriller series featuring Jonathan Jarl and the Amber group and the techno thriller series featuring Hugo Xavier and the Novus group. He and his wife Tina have four children.

Thank you.

Thank you for reading REVENGE, if you have time to spare, a short review on Amazon would be greatly appreciated. I hope you enjoyed reading about Hugo as much as I had writing about him.

Why do reviews matter?

As an indie publisher, I publish my books using Amazon Kindle Direct Publishing and my books are thus available on Amazon. And reviews on Amazon is the lifeblood that sells books, and I will be eternally grateful for your support.

Link Amazon

If you want to receive my monthly newsletter, you can sign up here: Sign up

To follow me on Bookbub:
https://www.bookbub.com/authors/filip-forsberg

Website: https://filipforsbergbooks.com/

Facebook:
https://www.facebook.com/filipforsbergauthor/

Twitter: https://twitter.com/FilipForsberg8

Best regards,

/Filip

Made in the USA
Las Vegas, NV
27 July 2021